Ghosts and the after life

by
Gil Jackman

authorHOUSE®

AuthorHouse™ UK Ltd.
500 Avebury Boulevard
Central Milton Keynes, MK9 2BE
www.authorhouse.co.uk
Phone: 08001974150

First published by AuthorHouse   02/24/2011

ISBN: 978-1-4567-7619-0 (sc)

PROLOGUE

These are true tales of long forgotten ghostly appearances and spiritualism, some well documented at the time, others merely existing in myth and legend. If there is truly a God then it follows that there must be a Devil, for evil must be present to counterbalance good.

What then is spiritualism, and of course the related medium-ship - its companion and means of communicating from another world to our own? We are not being too critical to say that most mediums and their séances are fraudulent; hoaxes fostered on the newly-bereaved to cruelly make them believe they have been in touch with their loved ones.

Yet every now and then there is a sighting of a ghost, an experience of unnatural phenomena, or an amazing demonstration of spiritualist powers, that cannot be put down to simple causes of imposture or subterfuge. These as seen or heard by people who are far too reliable, incorruptible, righteous and honourable to forsake the truth for deceit, or to countenance anything that smacks of trickery or falsehood in their reporting afterwards.

The lengthiest story in these pages has already been the subject of several works on the subject of Spiritualism, and we make no apology for the use of the capital letter when we write of this subjective science. And yet nothing has been produced on Daniel Dunglas Home for many years, nor has his name been brought forward in a respectful light for these several decades. Here indeed is one of the most remarkable human beings ever to grace the earth with his presence, and the accounts of his exploits are backed by the written testimony of worthy men of the period.

What follows are true accounts inasmuch as they have been well documented by reliable sources, and these sources are named in the text for the benefit of readers who wish to pursue further studies.

You might find that the writing style is somewhat pedantic, and you would of course be right, but no apologies are offered for this either. The writer completed this somewhat rambling collection in the 1950s, so please bear this in mind when the text uses expressions like "not long ago", "ninety years since" and "at the present time". Having spent most of his long life with a fascination not for the bloodcurdling and highly publicised Gothic tales of the macabre, the author showed more interest in the lesser, often more mundane, yet always more believable, stories.

His name is not important for he was, after all, merely a collector, a compiler of other people's sightings and reports. That his studies have at last seen the light of the publishing day will be enough, for if his writings are any indication that he sincerely believed in these writings, and then he will be among us now, and will surely know.

CHAPTER ONE

Introduction - Ghosts

To our forefathers the word conjured up scenes of horrific happenings: usually misty appearances of wraiths - of people that were long since dead. Nearly always these ghosts or earth bound spirits appeared at nighttime and in some remote place, such as a quiet lane or ancient house.

These spectres of tradition were sometimes headless and some of them would appear in letters. In early times these apparitions were thought to be not unconnected with witchcraft. The belief in these phenomena is almost as old as human existence on this earth. It certainly dates back to very early times but in more recent times we have somewhat different explanations for these mystic appearances or apparitions.

It is known that the cult or belief known in modern times as Spiritualism is the explanation of many of the accounts of haunting by people that are dead.

Furthermore, knowledge of Spiritualism clears up many of the deep-rooted accounts of ghostly haunting of two or three hundred years ago. We now know that a spirit medium could have been, and most probably was, responsible for many of the rapping's and misty appearances. Nevertheless many people hold that ghosts, wraiths or spirits have no existence outside our own fancy and emotion, that common-sense tells us – or should tell us – that all ghostly appearances and even spiritualistic séances are either palpable frauds, the object being to extract money from the credulous, or sheer nonsense.

Such doubters would find it extremely difficult to explain messages received through a medium telling, for instance, of the whereabouts of hidden documents, wills, deeds or other valuables. During the past hundred years or so there have been a number of noteworthy spirit mediums that have been well known to be perfectly genuine.

Perhaps the most marvellous was Daniel Dunglas Home, 1833-1886. In his day and generation this man was responsible for some astounding happenings. On many occasions, and in the presence of reliable witnesses, Home would rise from the ground – sometimes indoors, sometimes outdoors – and float in mid-air and even have burning coal placed on his head. Yet he was never detected of any form of trickery.

Of course there have been other famous mediums and between them they have baffled, and at times even convinced, some of our most clear-thinking scientists. The dawn of modern Spiritualism and the scientific study of psychic phenomena has greatly changed the opinions and beliefs formerly held by the majority of people in England and America regarding mystic signs and omens and communicating with the dead.

Needless to say, Home in common with other mediums had many fraudulent imitators, those men and women who "performed" exclusively for cash payment. These mountebanks or pretenders were sooner or later confounded, for Daniel Home never received payment for any of his marvellous séances. He was called the "master of the mediums", for the phenomena, which he produced or was responsible for marked the zenith of nineteenth century Spiritualism and a large book might be filled, with accounts of the mysterious doings of Home. In one case a large table, on which stood a man of twelve stone weight rose from the floor, and an eyewitness, a doctor, felt under the castors with his hands to make sure they were in fact off the floor.

Concerning psychic phenomena the writer and editor, Andrew Lang, wrote:

"Taking invitation, haunting, disturbances, and apparitions, and leaving "telepathy" or second sight out of the list, he who compares psychical research in the seventeenth and nineteenth centuries finds himself confronted by the problem which everywhere meets the student of institutions and of mythology. The anthropologist knows that if he takes up a new book of travels in the remotest lands, he will find mention of strange customs perfectly familiar to him in other parts of the ancient and modern world.

"The mythologist would be surprised if he encountered in Papua, or Central Africa, or Sakhalin, a perfectly new myth. This uniformity of myth and custom is explained by the identical workings of the uncivilised intelligence on the same materials, and, in some cases, by borrowing, transmission, and invitation."

To put it bluntly, anything unexplained by mortal means, such as the appearance of hosts or wraiths, or visions of people, and sometimes animals that are dead, are termed ghosts. Or in more modern times, earth-bound spirits: these are usually phenomena of sight or sound, or both. The sounds are footsteps, rustling of dresses, knocks, raps, heavy bangs or bumps, noises of slamming of doors, clanking of chains or fetters or dragging heavy weight or at times moving heavy furniture.

As to the phenomena of sight, figures of men or women or even a child are beheld. These are at times seen just for a moment and then vanish, but often are seen for longer periods, as when a figure is passing along a corridor or entering a room that is afterwards discovered to be empty or standing beside or sitting on a bed. In the open, figures are seen in a lane or crossing a field.

So vivid are some of these apparitions that they are taken for real people, particularly if the beholders are unaware that the house or field has the reputation of being haunted or if a former occupant had died a violent death. Some of these phantasms are recognised as such because they appear in a semi-transparent state or because they seem to glide rather than walk. They are usually accompanied by a blast of cold air. It is significant that these knockings, footsteps, appearances etc are produced or occur, or are SAID to have occurred, over a very long period. And in all parts of the Civilised and the Uncivilised world - from the days of the Witch of Endor to our own times, and from the Antarctic regions to Australia.

One writer has maintained, "There could be no ghosts without ancestors". This would seem to be a light-hearted way of treating the subject. There were of course what may be termed "family ghosts" that were said to haunt the manor house or its precincts, particularly if the occupation by one family had been of long duration. Only a few years ago and even now to a large extent, to have a family ghost was a proud boast and a sure sign of respectability. It was at least a sign of ancient lineage almost as proud a boast as having come over with the Conqueror – a decided move up the social scale.

Dr Margaret Murray, once President of the Folklore Society, stated on the highest authority that there were fewer ghosts about in Britain now than formerly. Dr Murray should have known much about ancient legend and mystery, for she said this many years ago when she was 85. She declared that ghosts were not so widely reported nowadays and there was a good practical reason – the introduction of electric light into most homes.

"If you think there is something in the room," she famously stated, "all you have to do is put on the bedside light".

Which should be most comforting to nervous people.

During the past 90 years or so the whole subject of haunting by apparitions of what are now termed earth-bound spirits, or by similar phenomena, has formed the subject of serious investigation by various societies both Scientific and Psychical.

In particular this is so with regard to what bearing these manifestations have on the cult of Spiritualism.

So far back as 1895 the Psychical Society collected some 400 cases of haunted houses in Britain and it was further reported that a new house seemed just as likely to have the reputation of being haunted as an old one.

This of course is true today.

There were investigations of the subject long before the above date. Various books also were written and although these things were little understood, notwithstanding they found Royal favour. It was distinctly dangerous before the Restoration to openly ridicule witchcraft, ghosts omens, spells and hauntings, seeing that beliefs in these things found Royal support and were seriously discussed at Court. Open ridicule would have had very serious consequences.

However, with the coming of Charles II there also came the scoffers, who we may be sure gave full vent to their long pent up feelings. Less by argument than by ridicule, says Andrew Lang, by inveigling against the horror, too, of the hideous witch prosecutions, and the laughers gradually brought hauntings and apparitions into contempt. Few educated people dared to admit that their philosophy might not be wholly exhaustive.

Even ladies sneered at Doctor Johnson because he, having no thread of common sense before his eyes, was inclined to hold that there might be some element of truth in a world-old and worldwide belief. And the romantic Alma Seward told, without accepting it, Scott's tale of "The Tapestried Chamber". That a hundred years after the heyday and triumph of common sense, people of education should be found gravely investigating all that common sense had exploded, is a comfortable thought to the believer in Progress.

The world does not stand still.

There have always been scoffers just as there have always been impostors. There were scoffers before the Restoration and there are certainly scoffers today. Scoffers at ghostly apparitions and scoffers at Spiritualism, but some of the activities of Daniel Home would take a lot of explaining away. However, scoffers were not so harmful to the public at large as were the impostors. The very nature of the subject opened wide the gates for pretenders and impostors, particularly those seeking financial gain.

This should not detract from the genuine mediums, although it has a great tendency so to do. If all had been impostors then at least they all seem to follow the same general rule and all imitate the same phenomena said to occur in haunted houses or places or at séances.

Today there are still a large number of people who will read ghost stories, albeit with mixed feelings. Very few people will admit they believe in ghosts yet in most cases they will not resist a ghost story. It has been said that the loudest scoffers are generally the most ardent listeners. On the other hand it is not unknown for educated and reliable people to admit they have seen an apparition – that is the form of someone that they know to be dead – and still declare they do not believe in ghosts. W. MacQueen Pope said, "I am not a spiritualist: indeed I am dubious of many of those forms of manifestation but I don't dismiss their case. I believe in what I see".

The ghost stories that follow are, so far as it is possible to check, "authentic".

That is to say that they have been seen – even if it is many years ago – by reliable witnesses who would have no interest in inventing such accounts and whose word would be implicitly believed in concerning matters of everyday life. I am a great believer in the adage that there is no smoke without fire. And that there cannot have been at all ages and times and places such a wealth of talk about the possibility of earth bound spirits or ghosts, without some of it at least – however small a part – being true.

Because if nothing of the kind had ever occurred then it would not be possible to invent it.

A number of people say they are willing to believe in ghosts when they see one. To all such folk I would say. "You may never see one, so you are unlikely to be convinced. The ability or the faculty to see ghosts is not given to all, only to a few, although that few is rather more numerous than may be supposed."

In the 1930s a more subtle form of witchcraft was practised in a large old private house not a thousand miles from Denmark Hill in South London. It was done in the form of a séance but was really an involvement with the Black Arts, and part of one ritual took the form of drinking the blood of a black cat. It was suggested in extenuation that some of the practices were merely methods of persuading a client who thought he was bewitched – there were still such people – that his misfortunes or ill luck had been neutralised.

In this connection there was at Castletown, in the Isle of Man, a witchcraft consultant. People who were seriously convinced that they had had a spell cast upon them called upon him frequently to defeat a curse. There was also a museum there wherein was a "Witches Kitchen", and a monument for "the nine million human beings known to have been burnt at the stake as a sacrifice to superstition".

There are other places up and down England where the Black Art was practised at that time, notably Liverpool, parts of Cumberland, north and south east London – the Old Kent road district above all other places – and a number of places along the south coast. The belief in witchcraft, like the belief in ghostly hauntings, goes back to very early times, not only in England but also in all parts of the world, particularly in Africa, where there are still Witch Doctors.

CHAPTER TWO

The Depths of Africa

It was said many years ago "There is always something new out of Africa". To many of the half-savaged peoples in various parts of the world Christianity is still a new belief and connected loosely with the centuries-old belief, ancestor-worship, the witch-doctor and the Taboo. Even today the Kikuyu have a tradition of people turning into animals, lycanthropy or werewolfism, trances and levitation. All these strange beliefs are age-old and are to be found in many of the primitive people of the world, including Europe.

Of course the credulity of the people has at all times been taken advantage of and impostors, pretenders who for financial gain pretend they have supernatural powers, have made large sums of money out of them.

According to the belief expressed by Pennethome Hughes at the time, Mau Mau was a form of witchcraft. The term itself meant a violent and virulent reaction against European settlement in Africa. Some at least of the disturbances was merely organised hooliganism cashing in on disturbed conditions. Mau Mau was explained as due to all sorts of factors – racial, cultural, economic and of course political - then the term witchcraft was added. His opinions were based on direct evidence in the form of the oaths that were taken by those pledging themselves to the cult.

Civilised people were horrified at the stories of the sacrificed rams, with unpleasant things done with their entrails, the eyeballs skewered on twigs, the smearing of initiates with blood and so on; all parts of age-old practices well known all over the world, even in England at one time.

The Kikuyu have always been a tribe with a strong magical tradition and even today they have a certain number of rites. Many are particularly connected with the sacrifice of rams – about which they are said to hold very sincere beliefs and which connect them with the Semitic tribes described in the Old Testament. Certain families are believed to be gifted with second sight. There are also various ceremonies in connection with the sacrifice of goats and within living memory when the tribes went to war they always first sacrificed a he-goat, skewering its dismembered parts on to pieces of sacred wood.

All such customs are of course centuries old and had long been practised by the heathens in Africa in the remoter parts that lay beyond the mission stations and the coming of the white civilisation. It is a form of witchcraft and is of course anti-Christian. The "witch" districts in Europe in the Middle Ages were always those where the old pre-Christian peasant beliefs fought out against the new faith.

Of course all forms of witchcraft and black magic and such like ceremonies are anti-Christian and have in past ages frequently been made use of by the political opposition to a new and feared regime. It happened in the Roman Empire, in Scotland at the time of the Renaissance and in France in the 17th century. There would always be a certain class eager to join a witch movement, if only because it was against the Government or the new religion or new culture. There would be those who for some reason cannot come to terms with those innovations for some failing peculiar to themselves, or there may be martyrs or some misguided, and of course many ill adjusted and evil, people. Witchcraft in Europe was a struggle between real forces – the old pre-Christian faith in a degenerate form and Christianity, the age-old fight between Good and Evil.

Also it was a very real fight between modern medicine and the old faith cures of the witches and between rational thought and irrational fear. To a large extent this fight still goes on in Africa. Usually the fight is against apathy and the ignorance of centuries. On the side of Christianity we have the best elements of African opinion, which is something to be thankful for. At least we get rational thought against what can only be termed irrational fear.

Doctor Grantly, Dick Read and other recent writers declare that the witch doctor still holds sway in the remote parts of Africa today. There seems little doubt that faith plays a great part in some of the cures. Cases are reported from Bechuanaland or general or partial paralysis being completely cured by the witch doctor without medicines. On the other hand many of the witch doctors have considerable medical knowledge so are highly skilled in the use of herbs.

European experts have investigated their ceremony for the reincarnation of the dead and authorities have accepted the transference of thought from far distances.

Dr Read reports cases that have come to his knowledge of African women who had not been pregnant for seven or eight years taking herbal medicines which enabled them to produce milk and feed a grandchild whose mother had died in childbirth. Also the witch doctors have a wonderful knowledge of poisons. A missionary told Dr Read, "There is no doubt that the African has many medicines which he uses for various diseases and though I could not get accurate information about them I was given varieties of certain roots which did this and herbs which cleared that. But it would necessitate a lot of investigation to discover the active principle of these concoctions".

Dr Read has to admit that the witch doctors are crafty and have powers of which we know nothing. "Weird and strange are the happenings in Africa. Inexplicable to Western minds are the forces harnessed from nature." The witch doctors are said to exorcise evil spirits. We learn that even today in the Congo there are a number of people both male and female who are believed to be witches or warlocks some of them are reputed werewolves with the power to turn themselves into animals. These people are greatly feared by the natives and implicit trust is placed in the witch doctors as being the only people who can protect them from the evil of reputed witches.

Father Andrew Dupeyrat the French explorer missionary writes an account of his adventures among Papuan and New Guinea cannibals. He encountered a young man, Isidoro by name, a member of the Ilide tribe who lived near the sources of the Dilava. This young man was intelligent and was of the Christian Faith but he was said by the natives to have the power to change himself into a cassowary; this is a large bird rather like the ostrich, and they are able to run very swiftly. In swimming the cassowary beats its sides with its strong wings! This produces a sound rather like a railway engine and can be heard at a great distance.

It appears that Isidoro had broken from the Christian Faith and had disappeared into the forest where he was said to have been guided by some heiropliant and at length became known as a sorcerer. Father Dupeyrat was anxious to meet Isidoro again and said as much to the natives one night.

One of the old men present said: "Father, we tell you this is the truth. Isidoro Ain'u'Ku has the power to change himself into a cassowary".

Father Dupeyrat says, "We could not help laughing when our other guests earnestly seconded the old man's story. We had heard all those ancient legends about men who turned into beasts before. Suddenly one of them made a sign and we all fell silent.

"From far away we could hear the sound of a cassowary swimming. We were talking about Isidoro and someone murmured in a strangely altered voice, "He must have heard us. He is coming". Now the interesting thing was this: cassowaries do not travel by night. Nor, for that matter, do the Papuans. There are too many dangers lurking on the rough mountain trails as they wind along the precipices. The notion that someone might be playing a trick on us was thus ruled out. Besides, the practised ears of our guests, and even our own heaving, could not have deceived us. It was, without doubt, a cassowary.

"It should be mentioned that Isidoro's village, Ilide, was beyond the main range of mountains, on the opposite side to its western slopes on which was perched the little mission station of Inondo. Thus the journey from Ilide to Inondo, even for a Papuan, entailed a good five hours of steep climbs and almost vertical descents over a series of razor-backed rides, plunging ravines and narrow gorges. The whole way lying through dense virgin forest at altitudes varying from three thousand to nearly eight thousand feet.

We shrugged our shoulders. No one could possibly make such a journey by night, unless he took pains to light his way with resinous torches and advanced with great caution – a process that would stretch the travelling time to at least ten hours, instead of five. Meanwhile the sounds of the cassowary drew rapidly nearer. Soon we heard clearly the drumming of its massive feet on the clay floor of our small courtyard. Then, abruptly, it ceased. A few seconds later our door was pushed open and someone entered. It was Isidoro.

"I heard that you were here. I have come to see you".

We began to talk of one thing and another. Our Inondo friends, grey with fear, said nothing. Isidoro, who appeared quite fresh and at ease, stayed nearly an hour. We did not, at any point, make any mention of the cassowary, nor did he.

"I am paying a visit to Inondo", he said finally getting up. "I am going back there to sleep. I'll see you tomorrow."

We shook hands and he departed. Scarcely had the door closed behind him when we heard once more the thudding of the cassowary's feet and wings.

I leaped outside. The night was black as ink. I could see nothing and my shout received no answer. But beneath the black sky with its sparse spangling of winking stars, under the loud rustling of the wakeful forest, could be heard, unmistakable and baleful, the dying thunder of the cassowary's swimming feet."

The whole incident was a complete mystery. At a later interview with Isidoro Ain'u'Ku, Father Dupeyrat attempted to discover the truth of the remarkable happening. The only explanation he was able to get from Isidoro was this.

"You, a priest, have powers to do extraordinary things. I wanted to show you that I, too, have such powers". Isidoro appeared to be greatly annoyed at being asked for any explanation.

Africa, of course, is not the only country that has its tales of werewolves and other lycanthropic monsters. There have been many similar accounts for centuries past in Europe.

Like one that on a lonesome road
Doth walk in fear and dread,
And having once turned round, walks on
And turns no more his head:
Because he knows a frightful fiend
Doth close behind him tread.

Coleridge

CHAPTER THREE

A Remarkable Passage of an Apparition

Considering the age of this account it is certainly one of the best-authenticated statements of its kind, also one of the most striking. This ghost story was published in the "Cornish Magazine" and was then prefaced by the following editorial note:

'The following narrative is not only remarkable in itself, it has a remarkable history. In April 1720 Daniel Defoe published his, "History of the life and adventures of Mr Duncan Campbell, a gentleman who, though deaf and dumb, writes down any strangers name at first sight: now living in Exeter Court, over against the Savoy in the Strand". In August a second edition was called for, of which some copies included a "pamflet, which had been printed in June", "Mr Campbell's Pacquet, for the Entertainment of Gentlemen & Ladies."

This "pamflet" or "pacquet" contained the ghost story that is to follow.

At one time it was commonly supposed that Defoe wrote the account himself, but Defoe asserted it was actually written by the Rev Doctor John Ruddle of Launceston, Cornwall, in the year 1665. The story was published in the antiquarian column of the "Evesham Journal" in 1921.

John Ruddle wrote:

'In the beginning of this year, a disease happened in this town of Launceston and some of my scholars died of it. Among others who fell under the malignity there triumphing, was John Elliiot of Treherre, Esq. A stripling of about 16 years of age, but of more than common parts and ingenuity. At his own particular request, I preached at the funeral, which happened on 26 day of June 1665. In my discourse I spoke some words in commendation of the young gentleman: such as might endear his memory to those that knew him, and withal, tended to preserve his example to the fry which went to school with him, and were to continue there after him. An ancient gentleman, who was then in the church, was much affected with the discourse.

'The reason why this grave gentleman was so concerned at the character was a reflection he made upon a son of his own, being about the same age. He, but a few months before, had been not unworthy of the like character I gave to the young Mr Elliiot, yet was now, by a strange accident, quite lost as to all his parents hopes and all expectation of any further comfort by him.

'The funeral rites being over, I was no sooner come out of the church but I found myself most courteously accosted by this old gentleman: and with an unusual importunity, almost forced against my humour to see his house that night. Nor could I have rescued myself from his kindness, had not Mr Elliiot interposed and pleaded title to me for the whole of the day, which as he said, he would resign to no man. Hereupon I got loose for that time, but was constrained to leave a promise behind me to wait upon him at his own house the Monday following.

'This then seemed to satisfy, but before midday came I had a new message to request me that, if it were possible, I would be there on the Sunday. The second attempt I resisted, by answering that it was against my convenience, and the duty that mine own people expected from me. Yet was not the gentleman at rest, for he sent me another letter on the Sunday, by no means to fail on the Monday, and so to order my business as to speak with him two or three days at least. I was indeed startled at so much eagerness and began to suspect that there must needs be some design in the bottom of all the excess of courtesy, for I had no familiarity, scarce common acquaintance with the gentleman or his family.

'On the Monday I went and paid my promised devoir, and met with entertainment as free and plentiful as the invitation was importunate. There also I found a neighbouring minister who pretended to call in accidentally, but by the sequel I suppose it was otherwise. After dinner this brother of the coat undertook to show me the gardens, where as we were walking, he gave the first discovery of what was mainly intended in all this trial and complishment. First he began to tell the unfortunity of the family in general and then gave an instance in the youngest son. He related what a hopeful, sprightly lad he lately was, and how melancholic and sottish he was now grown.

'Then did he with much passion lament that this ill humour should so incredibly subdue his season: for says he, the poor boy believes himself to be haunted by ghosts. And is confidant that he meets with an evil spirit in a certain field about half-a-mile from this place, as often as he goes that way to school. In the midst of our twaddle, the old gentleman and his lady (as observing their cue exactly) came up to us. Upon their approach, and pointing me to the arbour, the parson renews the relation to me: and they (the parents of the young) confirmed what he said, and added many minute circumstances, in a long narrative of the whole. In fine, they all three desired my thoughts and advice in the affair.

'I was not able to collect thoughts enough on the sudden to frame a judgement upon what they had said. Only I answered that the thing that the young reported to them was strange, yet not incredible, and that I knew not then what to think or say of it. But, if the lad would be free to me in talk, and trust me with his counsels, I had hopes to give them a better account of my opinion the next day.

'I had no sooner spoken so much, but I perceived myself in the spring their courtship had laid to me: for the old lady was not able to hide her impatience, but her son must be called immediately. This I was forced to comply with and consent to, so that drawing off from the company to an orchard near by, she went herself and brought him to me, and left him with me. It was the main drift of all these three to persuade me that either the boy was lazy, and glad of any excuse to keep from the school, or that he was in love with some wench and ashamed to confess it. Or, even, that he had a fetch upon his father to get money and new clothes that he might range to London after a brother he had there. They therefore egged of me to discover the root of the matter, and accordingly to dissuade, advise or reprove him, but chiefly, by all means, to undeceive him as to the fancy of ghosts and spirits.

'I soon entered into a close conference with the young man, and at first was very cautious not to displease him, but by smooth words to ingratiate myself and get within him, for I doubted if he would be too distrustful or too reserved. But we had scarcely passed the first situation and begin to speak to the business, before I found that there needed no policy to screw myself into his breast. For he must openly and with all obliging candour did over, that he loved his book, and desired nothing more than to be bred a scholar: that he had not the least respect for any of womankind, as his mother gave out. That the only request he would make to his parents was that they would but believe his constant assertions concerning the women he was disturbed with, in the field called Higher-Broom Inartils. He told me with all naked freedom, and a flood of tears, that his friends were unkind and unjust to him, neither to believe or pity him; and that if any man (making a bow to me) would but go with him to the place, he might be convinced that the things were real, etc., etc.,

'By this time he found me apt to compassionate his condition, and to be attentive to his relation of it, and therefore he went on in this way:

"This woman, who appears to me," saith he, "lived a neighbour here to my father, and died about eight years since; her name Dorothy Dingley, of such a stature, such age, and such complexion. She never speaks to me, but passeth by hastily, and always leaves the footpath to me, and she commonly meets me twice or three times in the breadth of the field. It was about two months before I took any notice of it, and though the shape of the face was in my memory, yet I did not recall the name of the person, but without more thoughtfulness, I did suppose it was some woman who lived thereabout, and had frequently occasion that way. Nor did I imagine anything to the contrary before she began to meet me constantly, morning and evening, and always in the same field, and sometimes twice or thrice in the breadth of it.

"The first time I took notice of her was about a year since, and when I first begin to suspect and believe it to be a ghost, I had courage enough not to be afraid, but kept it to myself a good while, and only wondered very much about it. I did not often speak to it, but never had a word in answer. Then I changed my way, and went to school the Under Horse road and then she always met me in the narrow lane, between the Quarry Park and the Nursery, which was worse. At length I began to be terrified at it, and prayed continually that God would either free me from it or let me know the meaning of it.

"Night and day, sleeping and waking, the shape was ever running in my mind, and I often did reflect these places of Scripture", with that he takes a small Bible out of his pocket, and recites. "JOB.VII.14: "Thou scarest me with dreams and terrifiest me through visions". DEUTERONOMY XXVIII.67. "In the morning shalt thou say, Would God it were even: and at even though shalt say: Would God it were morning: for the fear of thine heart, wherewith thou shalt fear, and for the sight of thine eyes, which thou shalt see".

I was very much pleased with the lad's ingenuity in the application of these pertinent Scriptures to his condition, and desired him to proceed.

"When," says he, "by degrees I grew very pensive, inasmuch that it was taken notice of by all our family: whereupon being urged to it, I told my brother William of it, and he privately acquainted my Father and Mother, and they kept it to themselves for some time.

"The success of the discovery was only this: they did sometimes laugh at me, sometimes chide me, but still commanded me to keep to my school and put such fopperies out of my head. I did accordingly go to school often, but always met the women in the way".

'This and much more to the same purpose, yea as much as held a dialogue of near two hours, was our conference in this orchard, which ended with my proffer to him, that without making any privy to our intends I would next morning walk with him to the place, about six o'clock.

'He was even transported with joy at the mention of it, and replied, "But will you sure, sir? Will you sure, sir? Thank God. Now I hope I shall be relieved."

'From this conclusion we retired into the house. The gentleman, his wife and Mr Sam were impatient to know the event insomuch that they came out of the parlour into the hall to meet us. Seeing the lad look cheerfully, the first compliment from the old man was, "Come Mr RUDDLE: you have talked with him: I hope now he will have more wit. An idle boy! An idle boy!"

'At these words the lad ran upstairs to his own chamber, without replying, and I soon stopped the curiosity of the three expectants by telling them what I had promised, and was resolved to be as good as my word: but when things were safer they might know all. At present I desired them to rest in my faithful promise that I would do my uttermost in their service and for the good of their son. With this they were silenced, though I cannot say satisfied.

'The next morning before five o'clock, the lad was in my chamber, and very brisk. I arose and went with him. The field he led me to I guessed to be twenty acres, in an open country, and about three furlongs from any house. We went into the field, and had not gone about a third past before the spectrum in the shape of a woman, with all the circumstances he had described her to me in the orchard the day before (as much as the suddenness of its appearance and emanation would permit me to discover) met us and passed by. I was a little surprised at it, and though I had taken up a firm resolution to speak to it, yet I had not the power, nor indeed to look back. Yet

I took good care not to show any fear to my pupil and guide, and therefore only telling him that I was satisfied with the truth of his complaint.

'We walked to the end of the field and returned, nor did the ghost meet us that time above once. I perceived in the young man a kind of boldness, mixed with astonishment; the first caused by my presence and the proof he had given of his own relation, and the other by the sight of his persecutor.

'In short, we went home, with I somewhat puzzled, and he much animated. At our return the gentlewoman, who inquisitiveness had missed us, watched to speak with me. I gave her a convenience, and told her that my opinion was that her son's complaint was not to be slighted, nor altogether discredited: yet that my judgement in his case was not settled. I gave her caution, moreover, that the thing might not take rid, less the whole country should ring with what we had yet no assurance of.

'In this juncture of time I had business that would admit no delay: wherefore I went to Launceston that evening, but promised to see them again next week. Yet I was prevented by an occasion that pleaded a sufficient excuse: for my wife was that week brought home from a neighbour's house very ill. However my mind was upon the adventure. I studied the case, and about three weeks after went again, resolving by the help of God to see the utmost.

'The next morning being the 27th day of July 1665, I went to the haunted field by myself, and walked the breadth of the field without any encounter. I returned and took then to her walk, and then the spectrum appeared to me, much about the same place where I saw it before, when the young gentleman was with me. In my thoughts it moved swifter than the time before, and about ten feet distance from me on my right hand, insomuch that I had not time to speak, as I had determined with myself beforehand.

'The evening of this day the parents, the son, and myself, being in the chamber where I lay, I propounded to them our going all together to the place next morning, and after some assertion that there was no danger in it, we all resolved upon it.

'The morning being come, lest we should alarm the family of servants, they went under the pretence of seeing a field of wheat, and I took my horse and fetched a compass another way, and so met at the still we had appointed. Thence we all four walked leisurely into the Inartils, and had passed above half the field before the ghost made appearance. It then came over the stile just before us, and moved with that swiftness that by the time we had gone six or seven steps it passed by. I immediately turned head and ran after it, with the young man at my side: we saw it pass over the stile by which we entered, but no further. I stepped upon the hedge at one place, he at another, but could discern nothing: whereas I dare over, that the swiftest horse in England could not have conveyed himself out of sight in that short space of time.

'Two things I observed in this day's appearance. One: that a spaniel dog, who followed the company unregarded, did bark and run away as the spectrum passed by: whence it is easy to conclude that it was not our fear or fancy which made the apparition. Two: That the motion of the spectrum was not gradation, or by steps, and the moving of feet, but a kind of gliding, as children upon the ice, or a boat down a swift river.

'But to proceed, this ocular evidence clearly convinced, but withal strangely frightened the old gentleman and his wife, who knew this Dorothy Dingley in her lifetime, were at her burial, and now plainly saw her features in this present apparition. I encouraged them as well as I could, but after this they went no more. However, I was resolved to proceed, and use such lawful means as God hath discovered, and learned men have successfully practised in these irregular cases.

'The next morning being Thursday, I went out very early by myself, and walked for about an hour's space in meditation and prayer in the field next adjoining the Inartils.

'Soon after five I stepped over the stile into the disturbed field, and had not gone above thirty or forty paces before the ghost appeared at the farther stile. I spoke to it with a loud voice, in some such sentences as the way of these dealings directed me: whereupon it approached but slowly, and when I came near it moved not. I spoke again and it answered, in a voice neither very audible nor intelligible. I was not in the least terrified, and therefore persisted until it spoke again, and gave me satisfaction. But the work could not be finished at this time: wherefore the same evening an hour after sunset it met me again near the same place, and after a few words on each side, it quietly vanished, and neither doth appear since, nor ever will more to any mans disturbance. The discourse in the morning lasted about a quarter of an hour.

'These things are true, and I know them to be so with as much certainty as eyes and ears can give me: and until I can be persuaded that my senses do deceive me about their proper object, and by that persuasion deprive myself of the strongest inducement to believe the Christian religion, I must and will assert that these things in this paper are true.

CHAPTER FOUR

Theatrical Ghosts

I should have headed this "Ghosts of the Theatre" because I do not refer to the artificial sheet-covered ghosts that appear on the stage in connection with a performance but rather with apparitions that appear or are said to appear at odd times not observing any cue or speaking liens. And I may add not always in costume and not always actually on the stage.

On the subject of theatrical ghosts Mr W. MacQueen Pope, famous theatrical historian, says.

"The ghost I know best is my old friend the Ghost of Theatre Royal, Drury Lane. The world of the theatre is a topsy-turvy one. Its people work when others play and make reality out of make-believe. They live in illusion - and they create illusion. So it is not surprising to find that this ghost who haunts that world famous old theatre does not behave in a manner generally accepted as conventional for spooks and spectres.

Midnight hour, when churchyards yawn and graves give up their dead has not attractions for him. He walks only by day. He has been seen only between the hours of 9am and 6pm. He makes no noise; he utters no eldritch shrieks, ghastly groans or blood-curdling yells. There is no clanking of chains. There is not even a chill in the air when he is around, although one man said he felt that phenomenon. He even eschews the pleasant little touch of horror of carrying his head underneath his arm or of decorating himself with gory smears. He troubles nobody. He just walks his round like the gentleman he appears to be. He is purely a "local" ghost.

He is seen in only one part of the house and always moves in the same direction in his walk – anti-clockwise.

He comes quietly out of the wall of a room on the upper circle level – now used as a bar – walks across it, through a glass door and turns left into the upper circle. There he ascends the stairs, walks right round the back down the stairs on the other side, through another door and through the wall again in the room – also a bar – which is on the opposite side of the theatre to that from which he appears.

That is all there is to it.

So far as can be ascertained he has neither regular days, nor regular hours, beyond his limitation of 9am to 6pm. Sometimes he is seen frequently.; sometimes months elapse. There is no sort of warning. He just walks. Nor does he dislike company. Members of the audience have seen him when a matinee has been in progress, and he has been seen by cleaners busy with their jobs of scrubbing and sweeping, he has been seen by all sorts of people.

The story goes back for at least two hundred years, during which period Drury Lane has been rebuilt and burned down. Nothing shifts him however, not even the big H.E. bomb, which dropped right in the middle of his walk during the last war. It is little use hanging about on the off chance of seeing him. That has been tried. Cameramen have lain in wait, and the late Harry Price spent hours with me in an endeavour to meet him. With true contrariness he appeared the next day.

Their majesties the King & Queen evinced the liveliest interest in him when I was privileged to tell them the story. But the ghost showed no loyalty and had not the courtesy to appear for them. One thing however is apparent. He is a good judge of a play and is seen most frequently during the run of a success. He does not patronise the "flops". And if we see him just before a production we are filled with hope. There was no sign of him when the "Lane" opened, after its long wartime closing, with "Pacific 1860". But two days before "Oklahoma" was produced he was there sure enough. Although the majority of the people who saw him for the first time had no knowledge of our "haunt", the description is always the same.

He is known as the "Man in Grey". He wears his three cornered hat on his powdered hair or wig, his long riding cloak is draped about him, the end of his sword can be seen and his riding boots too. It is even possible to glimpse his features – a strong well-cut face with a good chin and clear-cut nose. The general impression is the same as when you see figures on a stage through gauze.

The ghost is not a thing of mist and shadow but there is the effect of something in between. Nobody has ever gotten nearer than forty feet – if you do he is gone. But if you stand still, you will see him again – further off. He is best seen at a distance. And although he comes from back stage and returns back stage through the proscenium Wall, he is never seen there. Now most haunts occur as the result of a sudden or violent death.

There is seldom a manifestation – or continued appearance – after a peaceful end. As there is absolutely no trace as to who he is or why he walks in Drury Lane, one is compelled to associate him with that skeleton discovered just over a century ago in a tiny bricked-up room in the thickness of the Wren walls with a dagger in its ribs. It was never identified. Someone was murdered in Drury Lane and quietly bricked in.

The skeleton is as anonymous as the ghost – just two of Drury Lane's many mysteries and strange happenings, which include other ghostly manifestations, for which I will not vouch personally. An attempt at regicide in a brawl between a monarch and his son, and a clean-cut case in the Green Room. Yet that murder, which was dealt with as manslaughter, left no ghost – unless our man in grey is the result of it. But he never goes near the Green Room. He does, however appear from the wall adjacent to where that skeleton was found. No doubt the majority of those who read this will smile cynically when I say I have seen our ghost scores of times over the years. They will probably make the usual gag concerning the taking of more water with it.

However, it does not apply, for I am a teetotaller.

But there is one thing about the disbelievers'. They are never quite sure. Not long ago when I was taking a party round Drury Lane, which I frequently do, and telling them the story on the spot where the ghost appears, I was undergoing the usual fire of chaff and the disbelieving grins. Suddenly – and with no connivance on my part – a workman in grey overalls came silently through a doorway, which is just by the spot. You should have seen that gang of disbelieving scoffers run for their lives. They did not believe in ghosts – oh no – but they were taking no chances.

Drury Lane Theatre has other and more modern ghosts. Soon after the death of Sir Augustus Harris in 1896 it was said that his ghost was occasionally to be seen in one of the private boxes. A number of people testified to having seen it. However, the same box is said to have been haunted previously. It is know as the Haunted Box. A vision was seen there even in the lifetime of Harris.

Some years later, after the death of the world famous Dan Leno rumours spread that the dressing room of that great little comedian was haunted and it is said that his spirit pervades the room even to this day. The late Stanley Lupino, at a time when he was playing in pantomime at the Lane, declared that Dan Leno appeared to him in his dressing room, for he was at the time occupying the identical dressing room formerly used by Dan for many years.

Later still, during the run of Oklahoma, Betty Jo declares she was actually assisted in a difficult part of a comedy scene by unseen hands that guided her to the correct "setting of the stage" and that after this when she had got the hang of the situation the scene went smoothly. This took several nights to accomplish but when she had conquered she swears she felt a kindly pat on the back.

Joe Grimaldi – the originator of the Pantomime clown – was at one time said to haunt the stage of Drury lane and also the old Sadlers Wells, where he was seen in a box with all his clowns' make-up on. It has not been reported so far that he has haunted the rebuilt Sadlers Wells theatre.

It is small wonder that Grimaldi haunted the Lane. He experienced some troublous times there during his lifetime, and he also had a wayward son. They lived at one time at Garmault Place quite near Sadlers Wells. The house is still standing. While playing at Drury Lane, Joe one evening received a visit from a sailor brother, John. He had just arrived from some distance land and had brought his savings with him amounting to £600.

Unwisely and unfortunately for him he insisted upon showing this money to all and sundry in the Green Room. Joe warned his brother of the danger of carrying this money about with him. It was arranged that brother John should wait in the Green Room until Joe should be free after the performance. They were both to visit their mother later in the evening. Alas, when Joe had finished and changed, brother John had vanished. Nor was he seen or heard of afterwards. What became of him was forever a mystery.

Other London theatres as well as some provincial theatres have the reputation of being haunted. The Haymarket Theatre in London is said to be haunted by ghosts of former actors and managers – J.B. Buckstone and Mr Morris. At irregular intervals Buckstone is seen to wander along the passages and is to be seen occasionally on the stage. There are also tales of mysterious opening and closing of doors. This is attributed to Morris and Buckstone.

I am no theatrical historian but it has been said that the Theatre Royal at Bristol is the oldest in the country. Personally I should have said that Drury Lane is much order but then it has been rebuilt on several occasions. It may be the Bristol theatre has never been rebuilt. There appear to be conflicting tales as regards the haunting of this old theatre. Macready is said to walk the stage at midnight "speaking lines that no one can hear", so said a stagehand some years ago. But a member of the orchestra said "It is not Macready, but Mr Powell, the first manager of the theatre, who walks about the stage gesticulating as though uttering once again the thirty-six lines of execrable verse that David Garrick wrote for the opening of the theatre on May 30, 1766".

A third opinion is that of Mr Douglas Millar a former manager who resigned 1931. He says. "I understood it was neither my first predecessor, Mr Powell, nor Macready but some actress who had forgotten her lines and one night I stayed in the theatre all night to "lay" her. To be quite frank, I did not see a thing".

Yet, says D J Buchanan, the theatre is undoubtedly haunted, not perhaps by grisly ghosts, "but by the ghosts that walk in memory's garden". You feel it immediately you get into the little auditorium, with its narrow passage and oaken panels and sounding board above the proscenium, "the whole decorated with carving, painting and gilding executed with much taste".

Garrick called it the "most complete theatre in Europe" and at its 165th birthday some of the newspapers called it the oldest theatre in Europe. This of course, is not true. Without searching the records one may safely quote Milan, for example, as possessing an older theatre, but in this country the Royal building is the oldest of its kind – old not to be thronged by ghosts. One need not be psychic to feel them.

And perhaps, after all, the wraiths of all those who were associated with the theatre's old fame return visibly to the scene sometimes, when the audience and the players and the orchestra, and even the ghost-hunting managers have gone home to bed.

Mrs Siddons and Edmund Kean would be there, and Dodd, Baddeley, Quick, Bannister, Bensley, Elizabeth Iuchbald, Grimaldi, Foote, Dimond, Elliston, John Philip Kemble, Stephen Kemble, Mr & Mrs Charles Kemble, Fanny Kemble, Mrs Jordan, Charles Mathews, Charles Keau, Liston, the Incledons, Munden, Cooke, Macready, Ellen Tree, Jenny Lind, Mr & Mrs Sunis Reeves, George Riguold, Arthur Stirling, Marie Wilton, the Sisters Terry, Madge Robertson (Mrs Kendle) and Henry Irving.

What a romantic assembly of shadows.

Mr Powell would rise from his grave at the cathedral in order to see the show. You would probably find him in the company of his co-directors, Messrs Arthur & Clarke, laughing at the manner in which they evaded a prosecution for staging the first performance in an unlicensed house. They advertised it in aid of charity and as "A Concert of Music and a specimen of Rhetoric". The "Specimen of Rhetoric" was Steels "The Conscious Lovers".

If Mr Powell's ghost were not to be found in the auditorium, you might look for him on the stage, for he was a leading actor, and took a leading part in "The Conscious Lovers". Or you might find him complimenting James Paty, the architect, and Gilbert Davis, the builder, on the excellence of their work: or behind the scenes telling Edward Shuter, the comedian, what he thought of him. Shuter behaved in very bad taste at Powell's funeral. Dressed in scarlet and gold with a gold-laced hat, he marched up to the closed doors of the Cathedral outside which a great crowd had assembled, gave a tat-tat-tat with his cane, and quoted in mock heroics the speech that Romeo makes when breaking open the Capulet's tomb.

What sort of shadow show would be staged by our theatrical company of celebrated ghosts? A variety entertainment or tit-bits from the respective successes of each would be apt. Sarah Siddons might appear as Portia, Behidera, Mrs Candour, Lady Macbeth, or even as Hamlet, a part in which she anticipated Sarah Bernhardt by nearly fifty years. Or she might re-enact the part of Countess of Salisbury, for which in 1779 she received the munificent salary of £3 a week. She and Kean would be top-liners and probably Dodd would be put on first while the audience was settling down to wait for them.

Elizabeth Iuchbald might follow, and recollecting her "first appearance on any stage" she might quote a few of Cordelia's lines in King Lear. Maria Wilton might be seen dressed in pale blue silk and spangles as No-Wun-No-Zoo, a pantomime character, descending from the stage clouds, or Madge Robertson as Cinderella or Little Eva.

William Charles Macready, the re-enactment of Iago, Virginius, Lear or Henry IV, would lead to the reiteration of his farewell speech in January 1850. "Let me therefore at once and for all, tender you my warmest thanks, joined with my regretful adieu, as in my profession of an actor, I most gratefully and respectfully bid you a last farewell."

And presently Ellen Terry would "come back", not as a gracious lady, but as the girl who played on this stage long ago. "A girl of about 14, of tall figure, with a round, dimpled, laughing, mischievous face, a pair of saucy grey eyes, and an aureole of golden hair, which hung down her back". And there would be many, many recalls for her before the daylight came to ring down the curtain.

Despite the addition of a new wing of dressing rooms the ghost of Mrs Siddons haunts various parts of the theatre to this day, she has even been seen in the wardrobe room situate in the flies. But mostly she is seen in her old star dressing room, the closed door of which forms no hindrance.

Although there are many accounts of headless horsemen, and even one account at least of a coach and six headless horses, (the ghost of Francis Drake is said to have been seen in various parts of Devonshire & Cornwall but particularly at Plymouth driving a hearse drawn by six headless horses) I have only been able to trace one tale of a haunted circus.

This perhaps may be classed under Theatrical Ghosts. Circus people are known to lead such a roving life that it would be difficult for a ghost to haunt in the same place twice, unless of course the portable big-top tent could by some miraculous means conceal in its folds a phantom horseman but the ghost of which I refer appeared in a brick built circus, the well known Saugers Circus in Westminster Bridge Road London. I remember being taken there as a very small boy in 1887. This was certainly a substantial building although somewhat primitive. I well remember that after the Ring show there was a performance on the stage, and for this oil footlights were lowered from the flier and set in position in front of the proscenium. A man lit the footlights and also oil lamps on the wall at the side of the proscenium with a taper. I have been contradicted about this but I am sure of my facts.

The ghost here was said to haunt one of the dressing rooms. It was of a young boy that was apprenticed to a troupe of acrobats and the tale was that he was so badly treated in the course of learning tumbling that he died of his injuries and his wraith was seen afterwards in the dressing room wringing its hands. True or not, those who related it to me all those years ago implicitly believed the story.

For the following ghost of the theatre I shall have to again draw upon an account of Mr W. MacQueen-Pope, as it happens to be a ghost I had not heard of before. This concerns a dressing room at the St James's Theatre, London SW. There is a true ghost in that playhouse, who takes his place with the ghosts less material, if such a word can be used of such things – ghost memories as it were – with which this story is concerned.

If you go into one of the dressing rooms – the number withheld out of respect for nervous players – to see a friend, and happen to take off your overcoat whilst there, when you assume it again you will feel unseen hands giving you a lift with it, expertly and gently, and you will feel the whisk of a ghostly brush over the shoulders, a pat here and there to get the garment into proper position. Some old dresser lingers yet, unable to tear himself away from the place where he was so happy. He is never seen, he is discreet and does not wish to scare or frighten, he takes no liberties, and he only wants to give service in the true St James's fashion.

CHAPTER FIVE

Warwickshire Happenings – And a few from Worcestershire

The county of Warwick is particularly rich in ghost stories. This is perhaps not to be wondered at when we remember how steeped it is in history and romance. There is certainly more history and romance to the square mile to be found in this greenwood of what is left of the ancient Forest of Arden & the Shakespeare Country than in any other county in England.

Michael Drayton, author of the "Polyolbion", "The Wars of the Barons" and other important works, was born at Hartshill in the north of the county in 1563 – one year before Shakespeare called Warwickshire "This Heart of England". He might have added that it is also the heart of romance. Warwickshire is indeed the heart of the physical conformation of England. As might be expected the neighbourhood of Kenilworth, Warwick and Stratford is so saturated in history as to be most susceptible to superstition, ghostlore, witchcraft etc.

Mention of the Forest of Arden reminds one that it has been said more than once in the past that the most noteworthy survivals of ghost tales and witchcraft in Warwickshire have occurred in the country south of the Avon. This is known as Feldon or "open country".

The country to the north of the Avon known as "The Woodland" which embraces the Forest of Arden, does not appear to have had so many curious hauntings, or at any rate not so many have survived as in the south or Feldon country.

The famous Rolbright Stones may be included in the accounts of ghosts, witchcraft etc. The Rolbright Stones have been for many years the scene of séance and rituals appertaining to witchcraft and folklore. Some of these little meetings may be harmless enough but the local authorities have thought fit to erect 8ft railings round these stones in order to preserve them from disfigurement from idle sinister hunters. There are also those that would collect chippings or scrapings to make ingredients for some mystery, or witches potion, or ancient medicines. Originally there were 60 stones, but time and destructiveness have reduced the number to 22.

The Rolbright Stones are situated in a very remote position and are supposed by some to be ancient Druidic tumulus covering the graves of chieftains or pre-historic kings. The local people still relate various traditions regarding these stones and some of these tales may be distorted forms of some original legend.

There is a story that a Danish prince came to invade England. At Dover he was told:

"When Long Compton you shall see,
King of England you shall be!"

Forthwith the prince and his soldiers proceeded to Long Compton. They in due course arrived at the spot where now stand the huge stones. So delighted was the Prince to have come so near Long Compton, their goal, that he stepped forward in advance of his soldiers saying. "It is not meet that I should remain among my subjects, I will go before".

For his conceit, so goes the legend, some unkind spirit turned the whole party into stone and this is the stone circle we see today. The Kings Stone stands apart from the rest – on the other side of the road in fact. The circle is a little over a hundred feet in diameter. A cluster of five great stones in an adjoining field is known locally as the "Whispering Knights". Their secret is supposed to be that they do not intend to budge from their present position.

Many are the tales told of the happenings to farmers that have attempted in the past to move one of these stones. One was carted away on an occasion to make a bridge over a ditch. Such dreadful things happened to the man that ordered the removal of the stone that he speedily repented his folly and was very glad to reinstate it to its original site.

That Druids and other orders and associations do meet here at times is certain, and various ceremonies are performed, usually of course at midnight and at full moon. Some of these resemble ancient Maori rites and oracles. Indeed they may be of foreign origin. Eusebius and other authors of the fourth century throw a little light on the late Greek thaumaturgy. Papyrus verso CXXV (about the fifth century) contains elaborate instructions for a magical process, the effect of which is to evoke a goddess, to transform her into the appearance of an old woman, and to bid to her the service of the person using the spell. Some of these strange superstitions are of Roman origin and are mentioned by Pliny, Plutarch, Suetonius and others, as also are Greek and Roman hauntings.

CHAPTER SIX

The Meeting at Ragley Hall

At Ragley Hall, near Alcester, in February 1665 was assembled what can only be described as the nucleus of an unofficial but by all accounts sincerely active Society for Psychical Research. Ragley Hall was then in the possession of the Conway family and Lady Ann Conway convened the meeting for two distinct reasons. First, because all her life she had suffered from violent, chronic and never-ceasing headaches and this party were invited to meet her medical attendants.

These included Mr Valentine Greatorex, Dr Henry Stubbe, physician of Stratford-on-Avon, and Dr William Harvey, discoverer of the circulation of the blood and who at the battle of Edgehill Dr Joseph Glanville, who wrote "Sadducisius Triumphatis" in which he relates something of what took place at Tagley, Mrs Foxcroft, Lady Roydon and Lord Orrey, who wrote a play called "The Black Prince", in which the famous (infamous) Nell Gwynne appeared.

The other reason for calling this meeting was that Lady Conway was most anxious to discuss witchcraft, a subject that was of the greatest interest to her and also to most of her invited illustrious friends gathered there. Lady Anne Conway was the wife of Edward Conway, and she was by all accounts a most energetic woman with interests in many subjects. She is said to have been a ceaseless letter writer.

The above-mentioned Mr Greatorex was than an unlicensed practitioner, and his admirers knew him as the Irish Stroker, and also as the Miraculous Conformist. Greatorex claimed that he possessed the powers of miracle. After the Restoration Greatorex felt a strong impulse to essay the sort of healing by touching or stroking. Greatorex seems to have been successful with some cases but only partially successful with others. Dr Stubbe declared that The Irish Stroker was most successful with hysterical and hypochondriac patients.

Reading between the lines it would seem that Lady Conway was the most interested in the conversation of Greatorex and his account of his experiences of "second sight". He had been present at a witch trial and had also been an eyewitness at levitation séances during which a man had floated seemingly unsupported in mid air. Greatorex was able to give Lady Anne and her assembled party the fullest information regarding this seeming miracle, although he did not claim that he was personally responsible for the phenomenon.

He related that two bishops were also present when the man – a butler to Lord Orrey – was seen to rise from the ground. Whereupon Greatorex and another put their hands on the man's shoulders, one before with the other behind, and endeavoured to press the man down with all their strength. In spite of this the butler continued to rise and was forcibly taken from them. He floated in mid air for a considerable time to and fro over their heads. This levitation is said to have happened in Ireland.

At the close of the meeting at Ragley Orrey assured Lady Roydon that the tale was true. At this period this levitation was regarded as being due to witchcraft. In the light of more modern times we know that the butler was either knowingly or unknowingly a spirit medium. Quite similar levitations have occurred at spiritualist séances upon more than one occasion in much more recent times. Mr Valentine Greatorex next gave an account of the trial of a witch at Cork on September 11, 1661. This concerned the mysterious falling or throwing of stones in a haunted house at, or onto, a person said to be bewitched. The victims, that is the people at whom the stones were thrown or upon whom the stones fell, were a servant girl and a Mr Moses. It was sought to prove they were bewitched.

The girl had been much troubled having little stones thrown at her wherever she went and that after hitting her they would fall to the ground and then vanish. Also Bibles and articles would "fly from her". It was claimed the girl was bewitched. Today we should say the girl was psychic, and quite possibly unknown to herself was indeed a spirit medium. The cult of spiritualism was of course quite unknown at that period.

Dr Joseph Glanville had much to relate at Ragley of strange experiences and happenings. The outstanding investigation and one that held his listeners spellbound was of a phantom drummer. This account is rather lengthy but it is interesting and mysterious and is well worth relating.

Dr Glanville had first hand knowledge of this adventure and gives a full account of it in his book "Sadducisius Triumphatis". It does not directly concern Warwickshire but actually started in that city of mysteries - Gloucester. A magistrate there was a Mr Phillip Mompesson, who was not a native of Gloucester but lived at Tidworth in Wiltshire, and who also had business interests in London.

On March 9, 1661 a tramp was arrested and duly brought before Mr Mompesson. The tramp, as we should term him today, was a half wild shrivelled up man in a filthy condition, and he used vile oaths as he was brought into court by the troopers. He seemed to possess enormous strength and struggled violently, in fact it was with great difficulty that he was restrained. He was charged as a "vagrant and a disturber of the peace, who had been wandering the city beating a drum and demanding alms. His name is unknown and he refuses to tell it". The man was still struggling, and at last broke away from his captors and leaning against the bars of the dock he shouted: "What my name is matters not, but all men know my high office. I am the Devils Drummer!"

The man seemed so sincere and impish that this declaration seemed to hold the court spellbound for the moment, for all the local people present, including lawyers and civic officers, knew well the age old Gloucestershire tradition of the drummer sent by the Evil One to "beat the way to Hell" for a dying sinner. They believed implicitly in the legend that the beat of a drum heard near a house at night foretold the death of one of the occupants ere dawn.

Further the beat of a drum was considered a sure sign that the unfortunate one would die without confessing his sins. All this the audience at Ragley understood quite well. It is not possible to say if they were all believers. At this period the existence of ghosts, spells, witches, curses etc was the accepted belief of all classes of society, particularly in small provincial towns. There were, of course, exceptions and it seems the presiding magistrate at Gloucester was one of them. Phillip Mompesson was of a practical turn of mind and he refused to believe in or to be impressed by any such supernatural stories of Devils Drummers and the like.

The ragged and deformed creature in the dock was obviously mad. However, he had to be given a trial and so the case proceeded. While the accused man was held firmly by the troopers the only exhibit in the case was brought in. This was a large black drum, which had the appearance of being at one time a military drum, but had long since been discarded and was now battered as to the shell, and very dirty in appearance and resembled the type of drum used by showmen at country fairs.

A number of witnesses were produced and proceeded to relate how the prisoner had marched round their homes, playing his drum and asking for money and food. To all who refused his request for money he had made vile threats, and then proceeded to predict misfortunes for the household and even to pronounce curses and spells. He had been given money in many cases out of fear. It would seem his real offence was the curses he uttered. The prisoner refused to speak for himself and was sentenced to two years imprisonment in Gloucester jail. At this the prisoner pointed at the drum, he shouted, "Give me my drum. It must stay with me, it is in my charge".

This request was of course refused and the drum was taken from the court. To the prisoner then the magistrate said: "You have done mischief enough with this thing. It shall be taken from you and you shall not have it back".

The person was then taken by the arms by the troopers and an attempt was made to take him out of the court. The demented creature struggled again from their grasp back into the dock, and he screamed, "Give me my drum. He who takes it from me shall suffer the torments of Hell. It must stay with me".

The magistrate ordered the men to remove the prisoner. Once more there were violent struggles as the man endeavoured to break away, and he seemed to possess almost superhuman strength. All the time he was shouting threats and abuse. Eventually he was overpowered and removed from court. It was observed that all this excitement and uproar had greatly upset the magistrate.

They had at various times to deal with troublesome prisoners at Gloucester, some of whom had been even more violent than his half wild creature, but never before had Phillip Mompesson been threatened with personal violence and curses. This seemed to have a very bad effect upon him. He was trembling all over and beads of perspiration stood on his forehead. This was very unusual; normally Mompesson was a strong-minded practical man, but it was clear that he was now in a very agitated state. He called for an adjournment and retired to his usual inn for some stimulants and a meal.

He was somewhat revived after a little while, but could not entirely drive away the haunting sounds of the threats of that loathsome prisoner. Indeed, the experiences of that morning were to have a far-reaching effect upon Phillip Mompesson.

In a few days he was called to London. He had personal business to conduct and the change of scene acted as a tonic, for in due course he seemed to forget all about his unpleasant adventure at Gloucester. He stayed three weeks in London and then returned to his home at Tidworth, Wiltshire. At home he received an unpleasant reminder of the case he had tried at Gloucester. For some unknown reason the old drum he had confiscated had been sent to his house, for he saw it on a table so soon as he arrived. There was a note from one of the officials at Gloucester but no actual reason was stated for sending the battered old drum to him; he had certainly not asked for it. This seemed to indicate that even the prison staff regarded the drum with superstitions, awe. At once Mompesson ordered one of his servants to remove the drum to the attic where was stored an assortment of other useless rubbish.

The drum was thus certainly out of sight but no longer out of mind. The wild shock of seeing the drum at his house again upset his serves. Alas his nerves were to be still more upset as a result of housing this ill-fated drum.

That same evening Mompesson observed that his wife was in a very agitated state of mind, something was obviously amiss and later on she told of hearing mysterious noises about the house in the night. These were extraordinary loud rattling noises. The children had heard them and the servants also. After hearing a description of the strange noises from the servants Mompesson decided to have the whole house searched in an endeavour to discover the cause of the disturbance. We are able to gather from Mompesson's writings some details of this strange occurrence and of his anxiety.

Before the search could commence there came from one of the upper rooms a strange sinister rattle, this sound increased until it became an actual roar that the doors and windows shook and the vibration caused objects to fall from shelves and tables. Clearly this could have been no idle imagination. Mompesson says there were "great knockings at the doors at the outside of the walls, changing to a thumping and drumming on the top of the house and then by degrees going off into the air".

During this phenomenon Mompesson says he rushed upstairs and "ran from room to room". However, he failed to discover anything that could account for the disturbances. Eventually all the noises ceased abruptly and it was then that the magistrate marshalled all the children and his servants outside the house. They then commenced an organised search of the garden and the outside of the house, and also the roadway for a distance of 60 yards or so in either direction.

Alas, the search was fruitless: Nothing whatever was discovered that could have caused the rattling and vibrations. Everyone was ordered back into the house and next Mompesson questioned every member of the household. All held the same opinion that the cause of the disturbance was "some sort of ghost or spirit, quite invisible". The magistrate would not permit himself to agree to this explanation but for the next seven weeks, according to his writings, the thumping and knocking continued throughout the house.

The cause was quite unknown but the magistrate would not believe that there could be any supernatural agency responsible for the mysterious disturbances. The footman, John, had ventured the opinion that the old black drum in the attic might be the cause of all the trouble. At least the servant was listened to and the result was that the whole family and the staff of servants were assembled in the attic and were ordered to watch the drum while the noises were actually in progress. It is recorded that the drum did not move or emit any sounds or even vibrate during the disturbances. This was of course considered proof that the drum had no connection with or could be responsible for the unearthly sounds.

The very next night the noises were louder than ever and even more pronounced, so that there could be no mistaking the beats of a drum. From now on for four or five nights a week over three months the noises continued "from bedtime until early morning". It was thought that even if the drum was not responsible for the unseemly disturbance, that if the drum were destroyed it may have the effect of "laying" the ghost to speak and perhaps the noises would cease. In any case the drum was not wanted so it would not be a loss.

Therefore the magistrate's wife suggested to her husband that the drum might be destroyed or at any rate returned to Gloucester prison. However Mompesson was still firm in his belief that the drum could not be responsible for the disturbances and he refused to make such order. Now the trouble increased. The noises now invaded the children's bedrooms and "beat upon the bedsteads with such violence that everyone feared they would fall in pieces".

At Ragley the Rev. Joseph Glanville assured Lady Conway that he had actually been a witness of some of these occurrences. He said he saw "little modest girls of between seven and eight years old, as I guessed, in the bed. He saw their hands outside the bedclothes, and heard the scratching above their heads, and felt the room and windows shake very sensibly". Further when he tapped or scratched a certain number of times, the noise answered, and stopped at the same number. Glanville continues with must more. To add to the chaos visual phenomena now became part of the performances.

Bedclothes were crumpled up by unseen hands and small articles of furniture and ornaments would float in the air and at times fall to the floor. These increased horrors of course frightened the children almost to distraction. However, worse was to follow.

After about three months of these mysterious and frightful happenings the children were one night lifted out of their beds and violently shaken and let fall on the floor. Shrieks of terror would follow of course. The children had with the rest of the household become hardened to the sounds of drumming after so many months but to be lifted from bed and roughly treated and then to drop them on the floor was devastating to the sensitive nerves of the children. At long last the father was forced to admit that the invisible presence whatever it was could in some way be connected with the evil drum in the attic. It had now become necessary for some of the servants to sleep in the children's bedrooms to somewhat assuage the terrors of the little ones. Still Mompesson would not get rid of the drum. This was strange seeing that he was apparently satisfied that it was, or at least may have been, responsible for all the disturbances.

Quoting from Mompesson's account, "On November 5 'the invisible haunting' made a mighty noise. The footman, John, observing the boards in the children's room seeming to move, he bade it give him one of them. Upon which a board came, nothing moving that he saw within a yard of him".

"Nay let me have it in my hand", upon which the spirit, devil or drummer pushed it towards him so close that he could touch it. This occurred in the daytime and was seen by a room full of people, including visitors from other houses in the neighbourhood. Afterwards the room had "an offensive sulphurous smell".

At this stage the magistrate was advised by his wife to seek the advice of the vicar, a Mr Cragg. This he accordingly did, and in due course the vicar with neighbours came to the house with the object of holding a meeting "which they hoped would exorcise the spirit". When Mr Cragg was kneeling in prayer at the foot of one of the beds in the children's room the unseen drummer broke out into violence and this seems to be within a few inches of the vicar's head. This scared him that he fell over and as he was getting upon his feet the others in the room saw a bed staff rise from its place at the wall, flying through the air and strike him on the leg. At the same time chairs and ornaments were seen to float in mid-air. This proved too much for the ghost layers and they ran from the room and down the stairs. A shower of shoes and ornaments followed them as a parting gift.

It is on record that Mr Cragg wrote to his ecclesiastical superiors asking for advice. But he would not enter the house again. News soon spread that there were mysterious happenings at the house of the magistrate Mompesson. Thus it came about that few people would venture near the house after dark. Some of the more nervous folk even in daytime would make long detours rather than pass in sight of the "dwelling where the Devils Drummer has lodged himself".

One man only in the village of Tidworth, George Todds the blacksmith, dared to brave the ban. He had been heard to say at the local inn, "I fear neither ghost nor devil".

This brave boast came to the ears of Mompesson's footman John, who invited the blacksmith to spend the night in the house. Todds agreed and the magistrate gave permission for the blacksmith to sleep one night in the footman's room. Alas for the brave boast of George Todds. Two or three hours in the haunted house were enough to send him running through the village street only half dressed, his eyes staring and making straight for home. This was just after midnight and Todds afterwards made a sworn statement of his adventure.

He states, "There came a noise in the room as if one had been shoeing a horse. And someone came as it were with a pair of pincers, snipping and snapping at my noise."

No one it seems ever doubted the truth of this statement. There is a lot more telling of the horrors of that house wherein was said to lodge the Devils Drummer.

The disturbances now took on a much more formidable activity. One day soon after the blacksmiths adventure one of the maids working in one of the bedrooms heard a loud panting sound: "such as a dog will make when out of breath". The maid started to back away, grabbing a bed staff as she did so to defend herself against this unknown evil. One end of the staff was pulled from her grasp and then began to rise slowly in the air above her head. The maid was too horrified for the moment to move but soon she screamed out and other members of the household came in all haste to her rescue.

They watched for several minutes utterly dumb-founded as the staff floated about the room. According to the Mompesson's account after this incident the bedroom was "filled with a noisome smell and the atmosphere very hot and that without a fire, on a very sharp and severe winters day". By this time the fame of the haunted house at Tidworth had spread to all parts of the country and of course lost nothing in the telling. Embellished versions of the evil events eventually reached the court of Charles II. The account fell upon fertile ground because the king was always a firm believer in the supernatural and further he was at all times suspicious of rebel tricks. He therefore appointed a Royal Commission to make a full enquiry into the alleged haunting of the house at Tidworth by the Devils Drummer.

Now comes the most remarkable part of the occurrence. Immediately the Commissioners arrived at the magistrate's house with the object of making a full investigation the disturbance ceased. However, they only stayed one night but not a single drumbeat was heard or in fact any other curious noise or happening. No articles of clothing or furniture floated about in mid-air. All was calm and serene. The same quiet prevailed at the time of the birth of one of the children, so it seemed that the drummer or whoever or whatever was responsible for the disturbances was chiefly concerned in tormenting his oppressor.

Now all this of course points to one significant fact or at least a grave suspicion. This is that there was some kind of local conspiracy that would have been responsible for all the strange phenomena. In fact some years later towards the end of his life, several Wiltshire dignitaries openly accused Mompesson of having engineered the whole affair. Of course there could be more than one opinion about this but today these unseen ghosts or spirits that throw heavy objects about and commit other violence are termed poltergeists and many investigators into the psychic are now of the opinion that poltergeists are not psychic manifestations.

However at the time of the appointment of the Royal Commission the local people and members of the household so impressed the enquirers that although they did not actually see or hear anything out of the ordinary they nevertheless expressed their opinion in the report to Charles, "that Mr Mompesson's residence was plagued by some demon or spirit". It is now undiscoverable if the King took any further action. It is unlikely that he did.

Now so soon as the commissioners had departed all the evil manifestations started up all over again. This again is that might have been expected – but added to the drumming and the floating of objects in mid-air were now acts of personal violence and a number of strange sounds unheard before. Scratching noises were heard in the bedrooms and sounds as of a cat purring and on one occasion the children's legs were beaten until they were black and blue. The family Bible was found torn and mutilated in the grate. An iron spike was discovered in Mompesson's bed with the point upwards. The spike was wedged in position beside the pillow. At long last after eighteen months of these manifestations and annoyance, Mompesson became less stubborn and in fact so far did he unbend that he agreed to his wife's oft-repeated suggestion that the convicted drummer in Gloucester prison should be approached.

This seemed to be the most practical method yet suggested all things considered of attempting to solve the mysterious evil. Of course the right man to approach the imprisoned drummer would have been Mompesson himself but for reasons best known to himself he decided to appoint Mr Greene to visit the prison and interview the convict.

Greene thinking to do the right thing did not question the old man when he was admitted to the cell. The object was to hold a general conversation. However the convict was as stubborn and sullen as he had been at the trial. He just refused to speak. After several attempts Green had to give up and prepared to depart. The drummer may have had a very good idea as to the object of this visit but he at last spoke, and he asked: "What might be the news in Wiltshire, sir? Tell me – do the people talk much about a drumming in a gentleman's house there"?

It was not altogether an unexpected question but it seems Greene was incapable of handling the situation properly for he replied, "I have heard of nothing else these last months".

This had the effect of greatly exciting the prisoner for he laughed a shrill wild laugh. It sounded like the laugh of a maniac – it may have been that the old man was far more intelligent than he appeared to be and all the seeming wild behaviour a mere pretence. However, he shouted: "I have done it, I have plagued him, and I shall never be quiet until he hath made me satisfaction for taking away my drum".

This statement was made the excuse for charging the man a few weeks later at Salisbury with practising witchcraft and sorcery.

At the trial he repeated many times. "I am the Devils Drummer. Give me my drum." He also repeated what he had said to Greene in the cell at Gloucester Prison. "I have plagued him. I shall never be quiet until he heath made me satisfaction for taking away my drum".

This was shouted several times during the proceedings, and the old man was found guilty. He could have been sentenced to death for the crime, but it almost seems that the judge felt as nervous of the prisoner as Mompesson had felt at the Gloucester trial nearly two years before. The drummer was sentenced to be transported for life. At this he again screamed curse and threats and as he was dragged away again demanded the return of his drum, "the drum that has been given into my charge".

According to Mompesson's account, and in fact the statements of other reliable people including the chief witnesses in the case, all disturbances at the house at Tidworth ceased so soon as the drummer had left the country. In due course the old black drum in the attic was given to the magistrates children for a plaything.

The people at the Ragley meeting were much impressed by Dr Joseph Glanville's account of the mysterious happenings at Tidworth. There was a feeling that the drummer must have been a magician or a warlock who had by some means bewitched not only the drum but also in revenge for the drum having been taken from him, the house and family of Philip Mompesson. If the account were true there could be no other explanation. At later periods and even down to the present time there have been many controversies concerning the true identify of the evil looking man who pretended that he had been responsible for all the disturbances in the magistrates house at Tidworth.

On the other hand, as I have stated above, there existed at the time very strong feeling that Mompesson was alone responsible for all the disturbances. It is however difficult to believe that he could have been responsible for some of the levitations, the floating of objects in mid-air. At this period such apparatus as used by the more modern pretenders and professional conjurers were quite unknown; also it is most unlikely that Mompesson would have caused his children to be beaten and to be taken from their beds and dropped on the floor.

It would be more difficult still to define his object for so doing. However his habits, good or evil, would be known to his neighbours and to his personal friends and it would seem they had reasonable grounds for accusing him of bringing about the manifestations at his home.

Joseph Glanville gave it as his personal opinion that the evil drummer in Gloucester jail revenged himself in Mompesson by witchcraft.

In considering this case it should be remembered that at this period as I have before stated, witchcraft was implicitly believed in throughout England by all classes of the community, with few exceptions. This belief in witchcraft continued over a very long period and in a modified from, almost to within living memory, particularly in rural districts where indeed there are remnants of it today in places. The popular belief was that a witch or a warlock had power to cast a spell over an enemy and so cause disturbances in the house or elsewhere – even at a distance such as the movements or objects without human contact.

It was the practice, over a long period, when building a new house to bury a small bottle or vial containing potions or herbs under the step of the front door in order to mollify the curses or evil spells of witches. These witch bottles as they were called are frequently discovered when demolishing old houses. Not only cottages were thus "protected" but also larger houses also thus indicating that these real or so-called witches were held in awe by a large portion of the community and their vile practices feared. It was sincerely believed that no harm could befall the occupants of a house the threshold of which was so protected.

In 1950, when demolishing part of the Royal mews at Hampton Court, a number of tobacco pipes were found built into some of the walls, some of these pipes contained tobacco that had not been used. Although these pipes may have been put there to mollify a curse, experts regarded this as another instance of workmen building in such objects merely for luck. There have been several contemporary instances. The mews were built during the Napoleonic Wars – between 1797 and 1800. They were probably first intended as barracks, hence the "good wishes". The present writer examined some of the pipes and the walls, and the oak beams were 15inches thick.

Joseph Glanville was born at Plymouth in 1636 and died in 1680. He held the rectory of Wimbish in Essex in 1660. He wrote various books, among them "The Vanity of Dogmatising", "Lux Orentalis", "Scepsis Scentifica", "Philosopical considerations touching Witches & Witchcraft". He was generally looked upon as a learned man and held in high esteem wherever he went. From the style of his writings he was considered to be sincere in all his various studies and beliefs. Subsequent writers would quote from him - a sure proof of his sincerity

In the light of modern science and modern beliefs and discoveries it is highly probably the old drummer was psychic and what would now be termed a spirit medium. It seems possible, even probable that he and

Mompesson had met before. Mompesson also was most likely psychic, though it is not possible to be sure at this distance of time. To the doubters Mompesson wrote late in life: "if the world does not believe it, it shall be indifferent to me, paying God to keep me from the same, or the like affliction".

It has been said that Phillip Mompesson was descended from Sir Giles Mompesson. 1584-1651. This Sir Giles was the son of Thomas Mompesson of Bathampton, Wiltshire.

In 1614 Giles was elected to parliament for Great Bedwin, Wits. In 1616 he suggested to Sir George Villiers, the powerful favourite of James I and subsequently Duke of Buckingham, the creation of a special commission for the purpose of granting licences to keepers of inns and alehouses. Thus the pockets of the special commissioner and the king's impoverished exchequer might benefit. Villiers adopted the suggestion, and accordingly in Oct 1616 Sir Giles Mompesson and two others were nominated commissioners for the licensing of inns. They were invested with the fullest powers.

Mompesson performed his duties with reckless audacity. This at once brought him an evil reputation and in consequence public feeling was against his re-election as MP for Great Bedwin and an investigation was held into his procedure of granting licences. Witnesses came forward to give convincing evidence of the infamous tyranny with which Mompesson or his agents had performed the duties of his office. It transpired he had prosecuted no less than 3,320 innkeepers for technical breaches of obsolete statutes and to grant licences in Hampshire alone to 16 inns that had been previously closed by the justices as disorderly houses. In due course Mompesson was committed to the case of the sergeant-at-arms. New charges were brought against him daily. On Mar 3 he managed to elude the vigilance of his jailers and was soon on his way to France.

A proclamation was issued for his apprehension and he was expelled from parliament. He was to be degraded from the order of knighthood, and then to be conducted along the Strand with his face to the horses tail, pay a fine of £10,000 and forever be held an infamous person. He was to be imprisoned for life. It is thought that the character of Sir Giles Overreach in Massenger's, "New Way to Pay Old Debts" was intended to portray Giles Mompesson.

In his old age Mompesson had become less stubborn and less sure of himself, yet as a younger man he had been a magistrate at Gloucester for ten years. It is safe to assume he never encountered a prisoner that impressed him so much or whose behaviour affected his life, as did the Devils Drummer.

Most of the ghosts of the seventeenth century or earlier seem to have had a set purpose or an object for their haunting. If spoken to in the approved fashion – which is if the orthodox words were used – the ghost would reveal the spot where money or jewels or other valuables were hidden. Other spirits urged the removal of some article formerly the property of the spirit when on earth to an appointed place or site or in some cases demanding that its body be exhumed and re-interred elsewhere, or even, the payment of a debt to an appointed person.

Now in her turn Lady Conway had tales to tell at Ragley of mysterious happenings of this nature, most of which was to be attributed at that time to witchcraft. According to the account of Glanville a ghost vouched for by Lady Conway was agitated about the sum of 28 shillings. This spirit of an elderly woman persecuted by her visits one David Hunter, a near-herd at the house of the Bishop Down and Conor at Portmore in1663. Mr Hunter did not even know the woman when she was alive, but she made herself so much at home in his dwelling that his little dog would follow her as well as he would his master.

This spirit however was invisible to Mrs Hunter. When Hunter had at last executed her commission she asked him to lift her up in his arms. He said afterwards "She was not substantial but felt just like a bag of feathers". She then vanished and he heard most delicate music as she went over his head.

Lady Conway cross-examined Hunter on the spot and expressed her belief in his narrative in a letter dated April 29, 1663. It is true that contemporary sceptics attributed the phenomena to potsheen, the local homemade brew, but as Lady Conway asks, how could potsheen tell Hunter about the ghosts debt and reveal that the money to discharge it was hidden under the hearthstone?

The motives and methods of the circle at Ragley resemble the modern Society for Psychical Research. They were interesting reports of abnormal phenomena, and the evidence of eyewitnesses. The S.P.R. however are rather keener in introducing tests and proof of the reports.

Now what of the headaches of Lady Ann Conway? None of the famous doctors did her any good and to the end of her life she maintained she got most relief from a teaspoon full of small beer. It is on record that this was the only nourishment she had in the last days of her final illness. Much history is attached to Ragley Hall. Horace Walpole was at one time a frequent visitor and it has received Royal visits within living memory. It is now in the possession of the Seymour family. Ragley is not within its ghosts even today. The Evesham-Alcester road skirts the park for a considerable distance and at one point the trees meet overhead, rendering the road almost dark even in daytime.

It is a lonely spot and when the park contained deer – only a few years ago – the noise made by their antlers mingled with the hooting of owls rendered this road eerie on a dark winter's night. At a bend in the road and still under the trees is a water trough, not much used now although full of water in the days of the motorcar. The trough is fed from a spring in the park and this spot, this bend in the road is known locally as the "Haunted Water-trough". Here is said to appear a White Lady and at times a coach and four.

Some years ago I met several people who declared they had seen the coach and four, and it was seen at times to leave the road and career across the fields at terrific speed. This would seem to indicate that it followed the course of an old and now disused road. Within sight of Ragley but in the parish of Salford Priors stood Pophills House the home at one time of the Rawlins family. This large old house was demolished in 1848 because it was said to be haunted by the ghost of a girl who had committed suicide. All that remains now is the barn – Pophills Barn, and at one time no one would venture near it at night.

CHAPTER SEVEN

Chadshunt House and Coughton Court

In the Edgehill district and one and a half miles from Kineton is Chadshunt House. This ancient manor house has an ornamental lake in front. There is a pretty little island in the middle of the lake. Altogether a picturesque and romantic spot, yet for many years and even to the present day there has been a ghost story attached to this house.

Chadshunt House was for a long period the seat of the Newsham family. The most notorious of which was Old Squire Newsham, who died in 1836. He had been a noted character locally during his lifetime, much given to sport and strong drink. He is said to have "handled the ribbons" in expert style. Be that as it may, there is a tradition that since his death, and even to the present day, the restless spirit of Old Squire Newsham drives a ghostly coach and four down the avenue in the park. Reliable people have many times testified to having heard sounds resembling those of invisible horses' hoofs and invisible wheels grating on the gravel drive.

Other parts of Warwickshire have their ghostly "Night Coach", notably Meridan and Mickleton near the Gloucestershire border but still in the area known as Shakespeare's Country. Also at Ilmington there is a table of a spectral pack of Night Hounds.

About 10 miles from Stratford-on-Avon, and on the ancient Rickwield Street, is Coughton Court. This is a large old manor house standing well back from the road and in a small park. At one corner of the park and surrounded by an iron railing is the base of an ancient stone cross, which is said to mark the SW entrance to the great forest of Arden. This is, or was, in the Woodland country and forms the highlands of the county north of the Avon as distinguished from the Feldon – the open country south of the Avon. It is said that at this cross in ancient times travellers entering the Forest, or having successfully emerged, were want to offer up a prayer or thanksgiving for protection from the robbers who were known to frequent the forest.

At one time the manor house was surrounded by a moat. For many years Coughton Court has been in the seat of the Throckmorton family and was originally built by Sir George Throckmorton in the reign of Henry VIII. From Oct 29 to Nov 3, 1605 the house was occupied, first by Sir Everard Digby and his wife, and later joined by the Jesuit Fathers Garnet and Greenway, with Miss Brooksby and Ann Vaux daughters of Lord Vaux of Harrowden. The use of Coughton Court from Thomas Throckmorton was obtained on the pretext that these people wanted to attend a hunting match in the neighbourhood. They had brought with them swift horses. Thomas Throckmorton was at the time residing at Weston Underhill in Bucks. In actual fact the party were awaiting news of the result of the Gunpowder Plot – hence the swift horses. Eventually Thomas Bates, Catesby's, servant, brought the news of the failure of the Plot.

Many romantic tales are told of the old mansion and it is small wonder that it gained the reputation of being haunted. At times ghostly footsteps are heard ascending the main staircase, these footsteps have been heard by responsible people but have never been accounted for. They occur mostly at night, but have also been heard in the daytime. From the top of the stairs the footsteps can be heard proceeding round the drawing room to the Southwest turret, where they cease. In 1780 Sir Robert Throckmorton had the floor of this turret taken up and an old short sword was discovered beneath the boards. This sword is now at Buckland, Bucks. It is said that with this sword Sir Frank Smith of Ashby Folville rescued the King's standard at the Battle of Edgehill.

The footsteps persist to this day. The room in the turret mentioned above is said to have been used as a chapel, and during the sojourn of Sir Everard Digby and his party Mass was said and special prayers for the success of the plot. The prosecution at the subsequent trial alleged this much, though this was denied by Garnet.

The windows of this turret command a view of the countryside in all directions. Thus intruders could have been observed from afar. The turret in the Northwest corner was opened in 1860 and found to be hollow from top to bottom and without a staircase. There were however two ladders tied together and these still remain. 30 feet below is a priests hiding place complete with a portable alter-stone 6ins x 4ins. A subterranean passage is said to lead from the priests hiding place under the field in front of the house to the road. Coughton Court is now a showplace and is open on certain days in the week.

Ghostly footsteps are sometimes heard along a lonely footpath across fields between the village of Bidford and the hamlet of Barton – this is the "drunken Bidford" of the Shakespeare epigram. It may be remembered that Shakespeare is said to have composed the epigram after a drinking match at the Falcon Inn at Bidford. These footsteps are mostly heard in the daytime but have been heard at night. The present writer has a least one possible explanation of this seeming phenomenon. The path runs for some distance almost parallel to a road and is bordered on the other side by the river Avon. When the river is in flood both the footpath and the road are under water. For this reason a causeway has been constructed at the side of the road and by this means it is possible to walk dry-shod for about a quarter of a mile until higher ground is reached.

Culverts are constructed at intervals to drain the water off the road into the ditch. These culverts are covered with limestone slabs. The field that is said to be haunted by footsteps is about 250 to 300 yards distant from the road. Anyone walking along the causeway is not heard from the field-walk but when they walk over the stone slabs the sound of their footsteps are heard across the field and this most probably accounts for at least some of the supposed hauntings. Sound travels far along this unfrequented road. In these days of motorbuses both the road and the path are only occasionally used.

The road too had a ghost legend. At the first and only bend this road joins the ancient way known as the Rickwield Street, an Early British or Roman road. At the bend are, or were, a series of white painted posts. This spot is known locally as the White Posts. It is here that a coach and four are said to be seen, indeed a number of people declare they have seen it. At this bend the road is exactly parallel with the field in which footsteps are said to be head. The present writer can vouch for it that at one time – 60 years or more ago – when the field was pasture, cattle and particularly horses were reluctant to be turned up in this field for the night. Carters had the greatest difficulty getting the animals to enter the field. However eventually they would be driven in.

Next morning the horses would be exhausted as if they had been running about all night and they were bathed in sweat. It was said witches had ridden them. There are of course quite similar accounts in plenty of haunted fields in various parts of England and of horses taking violent dislikes to certain fields. The writer knows of some in Herefordshire.

The hamlet of Barton too has its ghost legend. Fear of legal proceedings for slander of title, by spreading a rumour that a certain house is haunted, prevents my indicating any particular house but an ancient stone built house in Barton contains a sealed room, and the house has a ghost. It is of a man in a 17th Century square-cut suit, and he is seen in a bedroom occasionally and always at night. He was seen upon one occasion by a farmer's daughter, a well-educated woman who declared even after she had seen the apparition that she did not believe in ghosts. This is by no means a singular instance of people seeing what they know must be a ghost and yet they do not believe in them.

There was another old stone house in Barton that contained a sealed room. The present writer has slept in the adjoining room. The owner of the house declared he had sealed up the room because "he had no use for it".

The Avon flows quite near the footpath as it ends Barton hamlet. It was here, well within living memory, that a servant maid committed suicide by walking backwards into the river after being accused by her mistress of stealing some money. The mistress afterwards discovered the money where she herself had put it.

About a mile up stream on the opposite bank of the Avon stands an ancient manor house, Hillborough. It is the "Haunted Hillborough" of the epigram, attributed to Shakespeare. According to the recent discoveries of Mr W J Fraser Hutcheson, Hillborough was at one time the home of Anne Whateley. She was Shakespeare's "other Anne". It will be recalled that in the Episcopal Register at Worcester, there was discovered some years ago a record of a grant of a licence for a marriage between "Wm. Shaxpere and Anna Whateley of Temple Grafton". The date is November 27, 1582, and Hillborough is in the parish of Temple Grafton.

The manor house was built in the reign of King Stephen. It may be one of the defensive manor houses that the monarch permitted the Norman barons to erect on their estates. In a corner of an oak panelled room is an "aschchain" – a locker for the reception of bows and arrows. The present owner tells me that some of the deeds are very ancient. In the yard is a medieval token of manorial rights – a dovecote. This is a particularly fine specimen of a Norman dovecote, and in a good state of preservation. It is now quite undiscoverable why this manor house was termed "haunted" but the house to this day contains a bricked-up room so there may have been some doughty doings here in the long ago. Hillborough Manor House is in a very remote position even today, so this and its great antiquity are indeed highly favourable to the supposition of its being haunted.

There is a tradition I give here for what it is worth, and it is this. That after the battle of Worcester Charles II sought refuge here, but there are so many tales of the escape of the King on this occasion that it is difficult to select those most worthy of credence. Various houses and oak trees claims to have harboured the merry monarch during his flight. However the Hillborough tradition is more credible than some of the others. Here indeed was what seemed to be safe refuge tucked away as it is in a quiet valley and far from any large town. It was of course more remote then than now.

The story goes that the King was hotly pursued and had brought with him to Hillborough his treasure chest, his object being to leave it in the safe keeping of his friends while he hurried on to the village of Marston on the other side of the river. Here he was sheltered by one of his supporters named Tomes and was put into the kitchen disguised as a serving man. The house at Marston is still standing and is shown together with the meat jack used on this memorial occasion. Charles here successfully evaded his pursuers but according to the tradition, the followers at Hillborough, after burying the chest left in their charge, were all overtaken and killed.

The chest is said to have contained money and other valuables. However, the chest could not have contained the famous and valuable diamond George or Charles II because this was concealed at Market Drayton in Shropshire. The gallant Colonel Blague, who had charge of this treasure, was captured and thrown into the Tower. Blague eventually escaped and the George found it way to the King in France.

It would be strange indeed if the rural districts of Warwickshire were not subject to superstitious beliefs in witchcraft and ghost-lore, such as it is in historic manor houses and ancient country sects. In a number of cases these old buildings may be said to have their own familiar ghost. In fact it is usual to look for such romantic hauntings if the house is known to have been the scene of some exciting episodes in former days.

Not many yards from Hillborough is Cranhill Corner, where three roads meet. This is the Evesham – Stratford road, and a branch connects Temple Grafton. At the junction of the roads at one time stood a gibbet. In 1802 Thomas Palmer was gibbeted here for wife murder. Palmer's body hung for a considerable time, and it is recorded that the finger bones were used by local men as pipe stoppers. In due course the gibbet was removed and part of the post now forms a beam over the kitchen fireplace of the cottage nearby. The other part was made into gateposts.

The present writer remembers many years ago hearing an old carrier woman at Bidford relate how as a small child she had ridden past this gibbet at night and had heard Palmer's bones rattle in the wind. She was small enough at this time to ride under the cart in the horse's nosebag. Her father was the carrier at that time. His name was Dance. She afterwards married a carrier named Cox.

Ragley is not the only place in Warwickshire to have a ghost of a White Lady. There is another at Chesford Bridge. To anyone familiar with the bridge and its immediate surroundings this haunting is not surprising. It is not quite clear who the White Lady is supposed to represent. It has been suggested that it may be the restless spirit of Ann Hawtrey, who in 1820 was employed as a domestic servant at Dial House Farm. One night she cruelly murdered her mistress Mrs Dormer, whose descendants still occupy the house. It is reported that the murderess was a very handsome woman, but this did not save her. She was arrested and charged with murder, and eventually hanged at Warwick April 20, 1820. The White Lady may be the earthbound spirit of Ann Hawtrey revisiting the scene in remorse for her crime.

In November 1820 at Littleham Bridge, between Stratford-on-Avon and the village of Hampton Lucy a farmer, William Hirons of Alveston, was waylaid, robbed and murdered by four men. His body was discovered next morning in the greensward by the roadside with his head resting in a hole. It is said that it was afterwards impossible to fill this hole in. No matter how many times the whole was filled with earth it was sure to be empty again next morning.

In due course the four men were arrested and charged with murder. Eventually they were all hanged at Warwick on April 1821, and it is worthy of note that one of these men was Thomas Hawtrey; the brother of Ann Hawtrey who had been hanged exactly a year earlier for the murder of her mistress.

There are numerous accounts up and down England of holes in the ground that cannot be filled in because a man has been murdered at that spot or of gaps in hedges or walls that cannot be filled because a murdered body has been dragged through it.

From Naunton in Worcestershire comes an account of two farm labourers that were in love with the same girl. The girl was employed at the farmhouse, Naunton Court, Naunton Beauchamp. The girl herself seems to have been indifferent but in any case her opinion was not asked as to her choice but arguments among her two suitors extended over several years as to who should marry the girl.

All this happened in the thirties of the nineteenth century.

With the mentality of farm labourers of that period the two men at length decided that as they could not both marry the girl neither should anyone else. Therefore they would kill her. This drastic action was put into effect one night. They murdered the girl and dragged the body across a field and through a hedge to another field where they buried it. They were soon discovered and arrested and charged with murder. Both men confessed to the crime and both were hanged at Worcester.

To this day the field across which the body was dragged is known as the Red Trail and the gap made in the hedge remains still a gap in spite of all efforts extending over many years to set hedge plants in it. Men still living and known to the present writer have repeatedly planted hazel and hawthorn and other plants there but nothing will grow in that gap.

CHAPTER EIGHT

Whaley Bridge

There are many stories of ground being rendered barren because some crime had been committed on it.

On July 16th, 1823, William Wood, a manufacturer, was returning from Manchester to his home in Eyam. Between Disley and Whaley Bridge he was stopped by three footpads, who attacked him fiercely when he refused to give them his money. In the course of the fight he was thrown down, and one of the thieves battered his head with a rock as he lay on the ground. The skull was crushed and forced into the soft ground of the bank with such violence that it made a hole there. The three men then robbed the lifeless corpse and made off.

Later in the day the body was discovered by a passing carrier and taken to the Joddrell Arms at Whaley Bridge. One of the murderers, Joseph Dale, was executed at Chester on April 21st, 1824, although the others seem to have escaped arrest, though long afterwards one is said to have confessed to the crime on his deathbed.

William Wood was duly buried and in 1874 a stone monument was put up by the roadside to commemorate the murder. But William Wood had his memorial long before that. The hole that his battered head had made in the bank remained empty and barren. No grass would grow in it, and all attempts to fill it up with earth or stones were fruitless.

In 1859 Alfred Fryer, author of *Wilmslow Graves,* visited the spot, and tried the experiment of putting stones into the hole. He always found them removed shortly afterwards and scattered about the surrounding grass. He describes the cavity as being only four inches in diameter, completely free from vegetation and with nothing in its surroundings or position to protect it from being silted up after the first heavy shower. On two occasions only he saw a few stones in it, at all other times it was completely empty.

Several people in the district told him of unsuccessful attempts to fill it up. John Fox stated that he once packed it full with stones and carefully sodded it over, only to find stones and sods lying on the bank next morning and the hole empty as before. He added that it had been like that for thirty years to his knowledge.

Fryer was unable to find any explanation for this curious phenomenon, and he was obliged to fall back on, "some physical reason hitherto unexplained", and leave it at that.

The Clattering Glat

A similar but less well-authenticated story used to be told of a spot on the road from Wenlock Edge to Church Stretton.

A long time ago a man murdered his own father there, and dragged the body through the hedge into a little wood beyond. He carefully mended the hole in the hedge with thorns and branches, and left it looking much as it had been before.

But the next morning the space was open again and through it the corpse was seen by some passers-by. The murderer was caught and hanged, and the hole in the hedge could never be kept closed afterwards. No matter how many times it was mended, it was always found open again shortly afterwards. It was known locally as the Clattering Glat.

The Field of the Forty Footsteps

Not far from where the British Museum now stands there was formerly a field known as the Field of the Forty Footsteps. Here two brothers fought a duel and killed each other, on account of a worthless woman according to the *Arminian Magazine* for 1781. Another tradition has it that the duel was fought because they took opposite sides in the Duke of Monmouth's rebellion.

Whatever the true cause of the duel, they left traces of the fratricide on the soil, for wherever their feet pressed during the fight the prints remained and no grass would grown on them.

A letter written by Thomas Smith on July 17th, 1778, and published in the *Gentleman's Magazine,* says:

"*The print of their feet is near three inches in depth, and remains totally barren; so much so that nothing will grow to disfigure them. Their number I did not reckon, but suppose they may be about ninety. A bank on which the first fell, and who was mortally wounded and died on the spot, retains the form of his agonising posture by the curse of barrenness while the grass grows round it.*

"*A friend of mine showed me these steps in the year 1760, when he could trace them back by old people to the year 1686; but it was generally supposed to have happened in the early part of the reign of Charles II.*

"*There are people now living who well remember their being ploughed up, and barley sown to deface them; but all was labour in vain - for the prints returned in a short time to their original form. There is one thing I nearly forgot to mention; that a place on the bank is still to be seen where, tradition says, the wretched woman sat to see the combat.*

"*I am sorry I can throw no more light on the subject; but am convinced in my own opinion that the Almighty has ordered it as a standing monument of His just displeasure of the horrid sin of duelling.*"

The Field of the Forty Footsteps is built over now, so we shall never know whether the footprints finally faded away, or whether they remained in mute evidence of bygone wickedness until the day when the builder hid them from human sight forever.

The Man from Staffordshire

In the early years of the nineteenth century, a Mrs Morris lived at Chirbury with her daughter Jane. She was a widow who had been left badly off, and it was locally thought that she would have to part with her estate in order to make ends meet.

If this happened, a local man named Thomas Pearce hoped to acquire it, as it had formerly belonged to his ancestors. It seemed more than probable that he would have his wish until her brother introduced a Staffordshire man, John Newton, (whose real name was Davies but called himself Newton whilst in Montgomeryshire), who was to act as his bailiff.

For after that things took a different turn.

Newton was evidently an excellent bailiff, for in a little over two years he restored her income to its old level. Perhaps because of this, or merely because he was a stranger and somewhat taciturn, he was rather unpopular in the district, and he made two powerful enemies for himself.

One was Pearce, whose hopes he'd dashed; the other was a young farmer named Robert Parker who was in love with Jane Morris. The girl preferred Newton and the disappointed lover decided to revenge himself on his rival. He and Pearce met and devised a scheme for getting rid of the interloper.

One dark November evening, about six o'clock, they set upon Newton when he was returning from Welshpool and overpowered him. They brought him back to the town where they accused him of highway robbery with violence. They were well known and respected local men, whereas Newton was a stranger, and an unpopular one at that.

The evidence was enough to hang him, and he was duly executed in 1821 during a thunderstorm.

At his trial he asserted his innocence and said that the grass would not cover his grave for a generation, in proof of it.

Nor did it.

The place where he lies in Montgomery churchyard was clearly marked for many years as a sterile patch about the size and shape of a coffin. The Rev. R. Mostyn Price published an account of the matter in 1852 in which he says, "Thirty years have passed away and the grass has not covered his grave."

Several attempts were made to break the curse by bringing new seeds and fresh soil, but they were all unsuccessful. In 1852 turf was laid down, and this did grow for a short time except over Newton's head, where it withered at once. A few months afterwards all the turf died, leaving the grave in the same state as before.

By 1886, considerably more than a generation after the execution, the bare patch was smaller, but still there. Today it can be seen in the form of a distinct cross of sterile ground with the grass growing strongly around it.

The "proof" of poor Newton's innocence has persisted for more than a hundred years - and is still there for all to see.

CHAPTER NINE

Mrs Webb of Barly

Of ghosts that may be said to serve a useful purpose there was a well-known one in the village of Barly near Rugby.

Here a tall old lady named Webb, a native of the place, died on March 3, 1851. Her age was 67. She had married rather late in life – a wealthy man older than herself. The husband pre-deceased her and left her all his money and property, so she thus was in comfortable circumstances. Mrs Webb had one characteristic, in that she was miserly in her habits; though this is not always to be considered a bad policy in life. In due course she became ill and was nursed by two neighbours, Mrs Griffin and Mrs Holding. A nephew Mr Hart, who was a local farmer, visited her every day. Mrs Webb had made her will in favour of this nephew, wherein she left him her entire estate. The illness proved to be her last, and in spite of careful nursing she died as stated above.

After the funeral the house was shut up for a month or more. The neighbour, Mrs Holding, lived next door with her uncle and one night they were alarmed to hear loud and heavy knockings and thumps against the partition wall of the house next door. They knew that no one had been there since Mrs Webb died and that the house was empty; the furniture having been removed by the nephew. However, there was a small built-in cupboard in the partition wall and much of the thumping seemed to come from this cupboard. There were other strange sounds also like the dragging of furniture about the rooms. The time was two o'clock in the morning.

Soon after this, Mrs Webbs house was taken over by a family named Accleton. This family was badly in need of a house and Mrs Webbs was the only vacant one in the village. The husband and wife occupied the bedroom in which Mrs Webb had died while their daughter, a girl of about 10, slept in a small bed in the corner of the same room.

About 2 o'clock in the morning loud knockings and thumps were heard in the house. There were tremendous crashes as if a pile of furniture had been dropped on the floor. This of course greatly alarmed the inmates, the child particularly. The noises were quite unaccountable. Mrs Accleton felt apprehensive because her husband's business took him from home quite a lot and she feared being left in the house at nights. However, nothing could be done at the moment, and the noises did not occur every night.

One night, again at two am, the parents were awakened by the violent screams of the child, "Mother, Mother, there's a tall woman standing by my bed shaking her head at me".

The parents at once arose but could see nothing and did their best to pacify the little girl. At four o'clock they were again awakened by the child's screams, for she had seen the tall old woman again. In fact she appeared to her no less than seven times on seven subsequent nights.

After this, and during her husband's absence, Mrs Accleton had her mother to sleep with her, and one night at 2am the usual hour, the spirit of Mrs Webb appeared quite plainly. It seemed to move towards her with a gentle appealing manner. This same spectre appeared afterwards to Mrs Griffin and Mrs Holding, and it also appeared to another neighbour, a Mrs Radbourne. Mrs Accleton asserted that luminous balls of light hovered about the room during the presence of the spirit, and that on one occasion the spectre of Mrs Webb pointed to a trapdoor in the ceiling, leading to the loft of the house.

Each person who saw the spirit testified likewise to hearing a low unearthly moaning noise – "strange and unnatural-like" but somewhat similar in character to the moan of the old woman in her death - agony.

The whole subject of the strange hauntings was discussed in the village and Mrs Accleton suggested that the appearance of the ghost of Mrs. Webb might possibly be connected with a hidden hoard of money in the roof. This suggestion was passed on to the nephew, Mr Hart the farmer, who favoured the idea and he at once proceeded to the house, and with the assistance of Mrs Accleton searched the loft with the aid of a candle. A bundle of papers, writings, deeds, and such like were first brought to light and afterwards a large bag of gold and bank notes. The farmer exhibited a handful of the sovereigns to Mrs Accleton.

It is strange that the knockings and thumpings and the moans did not cease upon the discovery of the old woman's hoard. It was found that there were certain debts owing by the deceased woman and Mr Hart proceeded to pay them, after which all disturbances ceased.

Sir Charles Isham, Bart, and others, most carefully investigated the circumstances of this haunted house at Barly, says the Rev F.G. Lee, D.C.L., Vicar of All Saints, Lambeth. The upshot of which was that the above facts were, to the complete satisfaction of numerous enquirers, completely verified.

Two carpenters employed to refloor a room discovered money hidden under the oaken floorboards of an old house. The money was in gold and there was too much of it to be taken away by the men at that particular time. They agreed to come for it in the morning before the other men on the job of restoring the house arrived. They were to share the money equally. One of the carpenters was there an hour before the appointed time.

He took the lot. He afterwards disappeared for a time and eventually set himself up in business as a builder. He prospered for a while but afterwards fell upon evil times. He married and had four sons all of whom were doomed never to prosper; each son suffered from some deformity and none of them lived to old age. Each son went into business on his own account but they seemed cursed. They could not succeed. Of course local people, who knew of the finding of the hoard of money and its disposal, said this was clearly a case of the sins of the father falling upon the children and the ill luck was even extended to the grandchildren and the great grandchildren.

This is a Warwickshire happening: I will not disclose names or even the name of the town but I can personally vouch for the truth of all the facts as stated.

Clopton House

Clopton house is an historic mansion about a mile and a half from Stratford-on-Avon. The house dates from the time of Henry the Seventh. Only the porch entrance however remains of the original building. It has been stated that Shakespeare and his friends were visitors here upon more than one occasion and must therefore have passed through this porch way. The house was the scene of the tragic story of Charlotte Clopton, who is said to have died of the Black Plague that raged in the town in 1564.

At least she appeared to be dead.

As is usual in such cases she was buried in great haste in the vault of the Clopton Chapel attached to Stratford church. A few days later another member of the Clopton family died and he too was carried to the ancestral vault. As the bearers descended the stone steps into the tomb they saw by the light of their torches – burials took place at night – Charlotte Clopton in her burial shroud leaning against the wall. She was dead now. It was discovered that in the agonies of hunger she had bitten a piece of flesh from her arm.

That is the legend. True or untrue it is said her ghost haunts Clopton House to this day. It might well haunt the church. "Perhaps," says George Morley, "in all the traditions, superstitions and legends of the Warwickshire greenwood there is not one more fearsome and touching than this one. Recounting the melancholy fate of beautiful Charlotte Clopton, whose story is said to have been made use of by Shakespeare in the vault scene of "Romeo and Juliet", though of course he has added the glamour of romance to the picture and laid the scene in Mantua."

Clopton House is said to have another ghost in a room at the top of the house, once used as an oratory in ancient times, when the Cloptons were Roman Catholics. It is said that upon one occasion – no date is given – a monk was murdered near the top of the staircase. The body was dragged along the corridor to a window and dropped out on to the courtyard below. A dark stain said to be the blood of this monk can be traced from the door of the bedroom to the staircase. It is said that all attempts to wash out or even to plane out this stain have been in vain. There are of course similar stories in plenty in other parts of England of indelible bloodstains. Small wonder then that the room at Clopton, now a bedroom, is said to be haunted by the figure of the monk. There are reliable reports of people having heard terrifying sounds and groans at night while occupying this bedroom.

The One-armed Knight

Warwickshire possesses one spectral Coach and six. This is said to be in connection with the ghost of a famous Elizabethan Knight, one handed or one-armed Boughton of Lawford Hall, near Rugby. The coach driven by Boughton is said to appear only at midnight and travels at terrific speed. Upon one occasion several Warwickshire gentlemen and a number of clergymen met together one night with the object of "laying" the ghost of one-handed Boughton and his coach and six. They are said to have captured the perturbed spirit and enclosed it in a phial, which they threw into a gravel-pit filled with water. It is recorded that Sir Theodosius Boughton in 1780 firmly believed in this legend of the "laying" of the ghost of his ancestor. When Sir Francis Skipworth asked permission to drain the pit in order to discover if it contained fish, permission was refused by Sir Theodosius who declared that his "ancestor One-Handed Boughton rested there and should not be disturbed".

However at some subsequent date the pond was drained and the phial recovered and given into the keeping of Mr. Boughton Leigh of Brownswer Hall.

Over the years many people have declared they have seen the ghost of One-Handed Boughton, and when eventually it was decided to pull down Lawford Hall because it was considered to be cursed, the belief in the ghost was so strong in the minds of the local people that it was difficult to obtain workmen to demolish the building. An old man named Wolfe of Long Lawford in 1871 related that as a boy living at Kings Newnham, a nearby village, with his parents he remembered a man rushing into their cottage out of breath and in a great state of agitation saying:

"I've just seen One-handed Boughton. I saw him coming and opened the gate for him, but he flew over it with a carriage and six."

This man was quite convinced he had indeed seen Boughton and this in broad daylight.

Some Diverse Cases

Kings Newnham above mentioned has the remains of a derelict church. The site has at one time been used as a rick-yard. In 1852 Lord John Scott had the place cleared and during excavations of the site of the body of the church it was evident that the entire ground had been used as a burial place over a long period. Human bones were discovered almost at the surface. Deeper down was found a leaden coffin enclosing one of wood. This contained the body of a man carefully embalmed. It was discovered the man had been beheaded. There was no indication as to the name of the man beyond the letters T.B. worked in black silk upon the breast of his shirt.

Also unearthed were the coffins of the Earl of Chichester 1653, and Audrey Countess of Chichester 1652. Also Lady Audrey Leigh, the daughter of the above 1640, Sir John Anderson and also Lady Marie, daughter of Lord Chancellor Brackley. The coffin of Lady Audrey Leigh was opened. The lady lay in a perfect state of preservation, a handsome girl of sixteen or seventeen years of age, with long eyelashes.

In the very heart of Warwickshire, which as we have seen is situated in the heart of England, is the picturesque village of Long Compton. It is in a gentle hollow near the southern border of the county, not far from the famous Rollright Stones. It is probable that the environments of this village may in some way account for the survival of a belief there in witchcraft.

Here in comparative recent times – September 1875 – a native, one James Heywood, declared there were no less than sixteen witches in the village. The extraordinary thing is that many other people in the village shared his opinion. In particular was cited an old woman, a native of the village, aged 80. Her name was Ann Tennant. It is not possible to say at the present time in what way this old woman incurred the hatred of the villagers, but she surely drew upon herself the unwelcome attentions of a superstitious section of the village. So incensed did witch-hunter James Heywood become that he was determined to kill poor old Ann Tennant.

He said she was a "proper witch". He followed her to a wood one day where she was want to gather sticks and stabbed her with a pitchfork. So severely did he stab her that she died almost immediately of her wounds. Heywood then declared he "would kill all the damned witches in Long Compton". Of course Heywood was immediately arrested and charged with murder. When water was brought to him in the police cell he refused to touch it declaring there were witches in it. At his trial he said, "If you knew the number of people who lies in our churchyard who, if it had not been for them – the witches - would be alive now, you would be surprised. Her was a proper witch".

Of course today he would be termed mental, but back then he was sentenced to death and executed at Warwick. Thus the ignorant took the law into their own hands and this as recently as 1875. The Jacobean Statute of witch trials was repeated in1736. After this date no one could be lawfully sentenced to death for witchcraft. It is safe to conclude that many perfectly harmless old women died at the hands of any half-witted clod that cared to accuse them of being witches.

These old women were not always sentenced to death on the gallows but at times to the ducking stool – this often proved a death sentence as the old women expired from shock during the ducking. Even after the law was repealed public ducking of so-called witches took place. The last one on record was in April 1751, when Ruth Osborne and her husband were taken out of the workhouse and ducked at Tring. Ruth Osborne died as a result of the ducking.

In 1875 one woman at Tysoe, quite near to Long Compton, was accused of possessing the "evil eye". This woman was likewise reputed to be a witch by the local people. On one occasion some people from Brailes, another local village, in revenge for some imaginary evil she was said to have committed, scored her hand with a corking-pin, which was supposed to mollify the effects of the evil eye.

It would seem that the correct method in dealing with witches was to draw their blood. Shakespeare alludes to this in Henry VI First part, where Talbot says to La Purcell "Blood will I draw on thee, thou art a witch". However I will not agree with W.H. Penfold, writing in 1939, that Warwickshire is and has at all times been a hotbed of ghostlore and witchcraft. I believe Montague Summers also said very much the same thing, except that he was writing of witchcraft only, and upon which he was an authority.

Certain it is that superstition seems to have lingered here longer than in most other parts of England. It still lingers in the remote districts in spite of the march of modern science and education, and other civilising influences. In this connection the introduction of broadcasting must have given such superstitions a nasty jolt. However the fear of witches must have been very real to the villagers in the past. It was mostly love of money that induced these old women to play on their neighbours' credulity, and there are recorded instances of these old women scaring even themselves into a belief of their own evil influences. The villagers, of course, hated them as we have seen. Anyone – man or woman – that was cursed by one of these real or so-called witches were considered doomed. It was believed that witches sent storms and barrenness, drowned children, made horses throw their riders, brought the ague, could kill with the evil eye, slay with lightning, dry up springs and prevent butter forming in the churn.

King James in his book on witchcraft confutes the possibility of its being mere melancholy that induced poor old women to believe they were witches, in as much as witches were often fat, rich and happy. However, we may be persuaded they had their uses, for it was often known for physicians to set the blame onto these old women in some cases of a doubtful disease. This was usually to cover their own inability to cure.

It is highly probable that many cases in the past of the alleged practice of witchcraft, particularly in remote places and among ignorant people, can be attributed to the activities of a spiritualist medium. Also it may be added that these old women may not always have been aware that they were mediums. It was a common belief in rural Warwickshire 50 years ago that the seventh son of the seventh son, or of course the seventh daughter of the seventh daughter, was gifted with the power or ability to "charm". That is to cure various ills and complaints including warts and whitlows

Ghosts and the after life

by touching the affected part and at the same time muttering incantations over them. That cures have been effected is actual fact.

At Pebworth, just over the Gloucestershire border – it is a "Piping Pebworth" of the Shakespeare epigram – was said, on the authority of the vicar, to have resided or to have harboured a witch as recently as 70 years ago. She had the reputation of being able to cure various ailments by "charming". She is said to have completely cured a young woman of St Vitas Dance with which she had been afflicted since childhood. Also it is claimed she cured a very bad whitlow, which disappeared directly after some muttered words and the application of a little saliva. In the old woman's cottage it is said articles of furniture would travel from one room to another without anyone touching them and on one occasion a pot of broth deliberately removed itself from the fire and emptied itself into a basin in the next room. Such phenomena are, in the light of more modern times, quite well known to be attributed to the agency of a spiritualist medium. I have met people who could remember this woman.

Just over the borderline in Worcestershire, although still in the district of Shakespeare Country, is the village of Cleeve Prior. This is situated on a hill above the Avon and is much beloved by visitors who favour a quiet holiday, and by artists for the same reason. Cleeve Prior has many historical associations. A monastery was founded here somewhere about the year AD 571, and it was annexed to the church at Worcester.

There are remains of a Roman military camp here and a number of minor Roman roads can be traced in the vicinity. These smaller roads were for the purpose of conveying stone and timber to the greater Roman station at Alcester, 7 miles away. In 1811 near the stone quarries two earthenware jars were found beneath sixteen inches of soil. One jar contained over 100 Roman coins closely packed. The other jar contained 600 silver coins, all of which were in an excellent state of preservation. They were of the reigns of Gratian, Valentinian and Theodosius. This was considered to be the greatest hoard of Roman coins ever found in England. It is significant that a few of the gold coins were found upon examination to be spurious, thus indicating that there were coiners of counterfeit money even under Roman rule.

The manor house at Cleeve is very picturesque. It is a stone building and is approached by a remarkable avenue of yews. The house contains a priest's hiding place measuring 5 feet x 2 feet. In this village about the year 1840, a young farmer in a quarrel with a neighbouring farmer's son dealt a fatal blow. This was before the days of telephones and at a period when Cleeve Prior was just a sleepy little village, (the Banns book in the church dates from 1825 only 187 marriages are recorded up to 1925). The local police were not too vigilant, therefore it was not a difficult a matter to spread the tale in the village that the murderer had also died of his injuries received in the fight. A mock funeral was duly arranged and a coffin filled with stones was interred in the village churchyard.

So far so good, for the young murderer was actually in hiding at his father's spacious farmhouse. This lasted very well for a time, nearly a twelvemonth in fact, but eventually the confinement became too irksome, to say the least, for a healthy young man. So it came to pass that he would venture out on dark nights and take long walks using the unfrequented footpaths he knew so well. This went on for a couple of years or more, but as may have been expected he was eventually seen and recognised by some of the villagers who had met him on these lonely walks. This gave rise to a scare that the ghost of farmer so-and-so had been seen. Most people in the village really thought this was a ghost of the murderer, but gradually it became obvious that this was indeed he in the flesh, and afterwards the man went abroad. The present writer was acquainted, years ago, with a man, or native of the village – born 1840 – that had as a boy met the "ghost" upon more than one occasion. Doubtless there have been quite similar cases in bygone times in other parts of England.

At Abbots Salford, also near the Worcestershire border though actually in Warwickshire – it is on the opposite bank of the Avon to Cleeve Prior – is a very ancient manor house known as Salford Hall. It is known locally as Salford Nunnery. Originally it belonged to the Abbot at Evesham – 4 miles away – and was built in 1471 by the monks. It was intended as a place of rest and study. The oldest part of the house is on the right as one faces it. It is altogether a very interesting old house and remains an unspoilt and picturesque specimen of a stone manor house. It was enlarged by the Alderfords in 1602; the date over the porch being incorrect.

The original building had been confiscated in 1543 by Henry VIII and given to Sir Philip Hoby, who later passed it to Anthony Littleton from whom it went to the Alderfords as mentioned above. Their enlarged portion was constructed in the form of the letter E in honour of the first Elizabeth. The last Alderford left two co-heiresses who inherited the property. One was the wife of Sir Simon Clarke, the other of Mr Charles Stanford. Eventually one of the Stanford's left it to Robert Berkeley for his life and then to this second son and then in default of a second son to the family of Eyston of Hendred, Berks, to descend in the same way.

When the house passed to the Stanford family it returned to Catholic hands and has remained in Catholic hands ever since. It is probably that mass continued in secret here for the persecuted Catholics of the time. In the attic is a priest's hiding place, the entrance to which is through a cupboard having a false backing and shelves. This is thought to have been constructed by Nicholas Owen the Jesuit lay brother, for he is known to have constructed many such hiding places in the district, and the chapel attached to the house was served by Benedictine Monks between 1727 and 1808.

In that year Mrs Stanford offered the house as a shelter to a community of English Benedictine nuns who had escaped from France at the French Revolution. The society consisted of an Abbess, sixteen professed nuns and a school for young ladies, noviciates. In 1856 the inhabitants were removed to their permanent home, the present Stanbrook Abbey near Worcester. From 1856 the house has been used as a farmhouse. The chapel was in use as such until 1948 when a new chapel was erected nearby.

The house contains many rooms, some of which are rather small; all have low ceilings. There are some very handsome fireplaces with richly carved overmantles. At the top of the house is a fine gallery seventy-five feet long, with four-light transomed windows at each end. There is also some good heraldic glass in the house and mullioned windows. On the roof is an alarm bell-cot. A subterranean passage leads from the house to the church at Salford Priors. When this passage was opened some years ago it was found to contain among other things the skeleton of a donkey.

What I am about to relate may not suit all tastes but it is perfectly true. The present writer had the facts first hand many years ago. At Bidford – before mentioned - 2½ miles away lived a midwife. I will mention no names. One night this midwife received a visit from a man on horseback, and who was leading another horse with an empty saddle. He was a messenger from an unknown destination and the services of the midwife were required. She would be paid double fees but she must agree to ride blindfold. The man would accompany her and she would be brought back to her cottage afterwards.

All this sounds very romantic and maybe theatrical but it should be remembered that this took place many years ago when such incidents were not unknown. There were no street lamps at this time and the roads were unfrequented after dark. The midwife agreed and was graciously assisted into the saddle. She was now led by devious ways for some miles to a large house. It was of course perfectly obvious that a circuitous route was chosen in order that the midwife should not know to which village she was taken.

However, being a native she knew every village and hamlet and the roads to them for many miles around. Also, she fortunately had a very good sense of direction. In spite of the elaborate detour she knew perfectly well she had arrived at Salford Nunnery. She had not been inside the building before so was unable to recognise articles of furniture, and also the patient was a stranger as were the few other women she saw in the house.

Upon leaving the house, her duties over, the midwife was taken through a room that had an enormous fire burning in the fireplace. She came to the obvious conclusion that here the body of the child would be destroyed. She was duly taken back to her home by the same circuitous route and paid the promised double fee. She was not sworn to secrecy for the reason that they had fondly believed she had not known whence she had been taken. This was related to the present writer many years ago by the midwife – then a very old woman, she had no reason to invent such an account, even had she been capable of so doing. The date of this adventure would be about 1850.

CHAPTER TEN

The Edgehill Visions

Since the battle of Edgehill in 1642 to the present day there has always been astonishing tales of ghostly armies fighting the Battle of Edgehill over again. This is surely a most long standing legend, and is the more remarkable that it is not a select few that have seen and heard these phantom skirmishes, but almost the entire villages of Kineton and Radway. The story goes back to the Christmas Eve following the Battle when the shepherds of Radway and Kineton heard sounds resembling the beating of drums, the clattering of armies, and the shouts of the soldiers as if a terrible battle were in progress. The noise of cannon fire was also heard. Following the sounds ghostly armies appeared in view; visions of course, but it is said they continued for some hours.

At the finish the shepherds hurried to the village of Kineton and aroused Mr William Wood and the Rev. Samuel Marshall. Little could be done just then but the next night these gentlemen and some others watched near the battlefield and had a similar experience to that of the shepherds. These visions have appeared on many occasions since and nearly always at about the same season.

Eventually the remarkable story came to the ears of King Charles, who sent Colonel Kirke, Captain Dudley and some other officers to investigate. It is reported that all these men experienced the same phenomenon, as did the shepherds and the Rev Marshall. In fact the vision was so clear on this particular occasion that the officers were able to recognise many of the participants in the battle. Mr Wood and Mr Marshall first recorded this account of a very remarkable happening.

It has been repeated in detail upon many occasions since. It is claimed to this day that the vision of the troops of King Charles and Cromwell steal from their graves at midnight at Marlborough Farm and engage in a fierce battle. Prince Rupert is seen on his charger crashing through hedges and down the main street. The spectre of Captain Henry Kingsmill on a white horse is also said to be seen here. He was killed in the battle and an effigy and a tablet in Radway church commemorate him.

This vision of phantom armies is not to be lightly set aside, for it is of long standing and has earned for the villages of Kineton and Radway the reputation of being the most haunted villages in England. So alarming indeed have these phantom armies become that the aid of the Birmingham Psychic Society has been sought. They came well prepared with infrared photographic equipment, spiritualist medium and shorthand writers. Alas the vision or apparitions do not appear to order and the Society drew a blank. The population of Kineton – 950 – is as far from the solution as ever they were. Mr Bernard Payne of the Psychic society is of the opinion that the apparitions are linked with graves inside Marlborough Farm.

At Warmington, a village near Kineton, there are reports of ghostly voices sometimes heard singing in the parish church. This is also a long standing haunting. The voices are usually heard at midnight and always at a time when the church is known to be locked and in darkness.

Just over the Warwickshire border at Cropthorne, near Evesham, and said to be the prettiest village in England, stands a fine substantial house. For many years it has been haunted by heavy footsteps, which appear from the sound to enter the front door and ascend the stairs, and then proceed to the attic. It is assumed that the "something" then sits down and removes first one and then the other of the heavy boots. They are each hard to fall with a thud. It has been known for people to stand on the stairs and hear the footsteps pass between them – this in quite recent years. At all times when dogs have been present – on one occasion it was a mastiff – they have remained paralysed with terror, their hair literally standing on end.

The present writer can well remember as a very small boy in a hamlet near Evesham having an old woman pointed out to him that had the reputation of being a witch. The local people believed implicitly that this old woman was indeed in touch with the Evil One. Her husband was also regarded with awe. Between them they ran a small market garden holding. They had grown up children. I remember being told how scared the villagers were of arousing this old woman's displeasure, and they would go to considerable lengths to avoid doing so. She was said to be able to change herself into a cat or a rabbit, and upon one occasion a local farmer discovered a cat worrying his horses in a field one night. He struck at the cat with his stock, and the tale went that the next morning the old women had her arm in a sling.

This is lycanthropy, and the people were known as werewolves. According to the recent writings of Doctor Grantly Dick Read, a former Harley Street obstetrician, the belief in lycanthropy still exists in many parts of Africa. Dr Read states:

"Europeans have been persuaded without the slightest doubt that they have witnessed this turning of human beings into animals. There seems to be no question that capable observers, men who are endeavouring to get to the bottom of the truth of these things have seen the reincarnation of people who have recently died. If intelligent men with nothing whatever to fear can tell you sincerely that certain things have happened and they have witnessed them, then there must be something in it."

It was said this old woman would ride across fields on a hurdle, and she would do this even in daytime and during ploughing operations. I find it was a quite a common belief at one time in the villages of Warwickshire and Worcestershire that witches could ride hurdles. The witches of our fairy tale books usually rode besom brooms. Perhaps we may assume that a besom broom would be a more commonplace article in a town than a hurdle. There were many other tales about this old woman, including an account of a man that made an appointment to meet her at some distant spot in order to nullify a curse or spell.

The man was late and hurried towards the appointed place – he said afterwards that he seemed to be urged onward and dragged through hedges and over open land to keep the appointment. All such accounts may of course be remnants of old wives tales, but the present writer can answer for the fact that a young man living with his parents at a nearby cottage – still standing although condemned – refused to do some hoeing for this old women. Whereupon she became so annoyed that she declared the young man should never do another day's work.

It so happened that he never did. Various hindrances occurred, unlooked for obstacles cropped up to prevent this young man working and eventually he fell ill. In time he got a little better but not well enough to work again. He was ill on and off for a period of two years, and although he rallied from time to time he was never able to work again. Eventually he died after two years of inactivity. Of course, all this may have been coincidence but I can answer for it that the man never worked again.

Some years before the above event, a neighbour's daughter who had travelled abroad a great deal had from time to time made small presents of clothing to people in nearby cottages. The old woman was not included among these. The story goes that this evil old woman became so incensed that she put a curse upon this young woman and all her female offspring. Curse or no curse, spell or no spell, certain it is that this unfortunate young woman lived a most unhappy life and some years later was confined to her bed for twelve years with chronic rheumatism. She was quite helpless and had to be lifted about, and eventually she died a miserable death. So also later did her only daughter and granddaughter. The local people believed that this old woman was capable of casting evil spells upon them and that such was her power that any curse uttered by her would surely be followed by terrible happenings to who ever had been unfortunate enough to incur her displeasure.

When this old woman died her married daughter burnt all the books on witchcraft and the like that she found in her mother's cottage. Some of these books were so old that they were in manuscript.

The cottage is still standing in the hamlet of Moor.

A miserly old lawyer became possessed, late in life, of an ancient manor house, complete with ghost, in Warwickshire about 8 miles from Stratford. The old lawyer thus became a full-blown Lord of the Manor when the manor and the estate came into his possession. It is recorded that a former owner had also been noteworthy on account of his miserly habits.

The lawyer had not been in possession a week when the ghost of the miserly former owner put in an appearance. The lawyer was accosted one night in the drive and was not a little surprised when the spectre said: "Follow me."

The lawyer followed and was led to a lonely hollow in the adjacent wood. "Dig and you will find", and the spectre pointed to a huge moss-covered stone. *"There you will see the accumulated hoard of Roger R – the miser. I am he. In life I sent the poor and needy penniless from my door and damned them for their impertinent supplications. For this I am doomed to experience the pangs of starvation throughout endless eternity, unless the hidden treasure be wisely dispensed".*

The next moment the bewildered lawyer found himself alone. Needless to say before many days had passed the whole of that buried wealth had been transferred by him to his own private coffers, and in a short time was being expended regardless of the ghost's warning, in the wildest extravagance.

Gallants more famed for their profanity than their wit, accompanied by powdered and painted beauties, now held high revel in those ancestral halls.

More especially on one Christmas Eve, when as the clock struck midnight, the lights grew dim and blue and the miser's ghost in phosphorescence all its own, appeared slowly descending the broad oaken staircase. It was cursing, as it did so, the founder of the feast, who, squandering in debauchery his easily acquired gold, condemned by doing so, the perturbed soul of Roger R – to walk the earth to all eternity.

Another form of tormenting spirit is reported from a vicarage near Malvern, Worcestershire. In this case nothing unusual is ever seen, but the noises created or brought about by this spirit are loud enough to keep the vicar awake and are quite unaccountable. The noises are howling, screaming, door slamming and throwing things about - and always at nighttime.

Fortunately for himself the vicar, a middle-aged bachelor, has very strong nerves, but the disturbances have proved very distressing and a local committee have been formed to endeavour to drive out the "evil spirit". The committee consists of a surgeon, a bishop, a Church Army sister and three other women. They have been praying daily for over a year – so far with little success – for the disturbances to cease. Certainly the noises seem to have quietened down a little but have by no means ceased according to the reports of Mr Cyril Martin-Doyle the surgeon.

The committee has been reinforced, and it now consists of Mr Martin-Doyle above mentioned, his wife, a bishop, a curate, an anaesthetist, a stockbroker, a wine merchant, a teacher, a law student and the Church Army sister. The vicarage has been searched again and again, and all windows and doors have been shut every night when the committee is in attendance. They also make sure that the house has no other occupants. Between midnight and 1am the listeners have heard an uncanny owl-like sound, a door slams and a faint scream and a whistle follow this.

The committee has promised the vicar that some of them will pray daily that God will cast out the spirit or cause the phenomena to cease. Yet still the disturbances have been going on for several years.

The manor house at Little Woolford near Shipston-on-Stowe was formerly the seat of the Ingram family. The house was afterwards used as a school. Like Ragley it is said to be haunted by a certain "White Lady". Fortunately for the scholars the ghost does not appear until midnight. Also the last of the Ingrams is said to haunt the house and the adjacent fields where he is seen tearing about on horseback. On the left hand side of the entrance gateway is a projection in the masonry. This is the back of a large oven. The front opens at the rear of a wide fireplace. Some years ago a number of IOUs were found in this oven dating from the seventeenth century. These were for money lost at play while some Cavaliers were concealed here in the time of the Civil Wars. The tale goes that some Cromwellian soldiers halted at the house one night and lighted a tremendous fire. This gave the Cavaliers a roasting they did not forget. Tradition has it that King Charles himself was one of the unfortunate men.

One of the few manor houses in Warwickshire so far untouched by restorations is Baddesley Clinton. The interior as well as the exterior is quite unspoilt in that there have been no structural alterations. The house is exactly as it has stood for centuries. There is a find Jacobean fireplace in the hall. On the first floor adjoining the banqueting room is a room known as "Lord Charles" room. This room is reputed to be haunted by the ghost of a handsome youth with raven hair. Some years ago two aunts of the then owner Mr Marmion Ferrers saw this spirit. They were children at the time and they remembered the handsome face for the rest of their lives. Occasionally a lady in rich black brocade is seen in one of the corridors – this ghost always appears in daytime. Marmion Ferrers above mentioned died 1884. He was the eighth in decent from father and son from Henry Ferrers of Elizabeth's time. Both men were learned antiquarians.

Well within the memory of the present writer the inhabitants of the remote parts of Warwickshire regarded the wych elm with awe. They were very reluctant to cut down such a tree or even a branch for fear of invoking the evil attentions of a witch.

Needless to say the wych elm is merely a species of the elm. The tree is rather smaller than the common elm, the leaves are however much larger and the branches generally have a tendency to droop hence it is sometimes termed the Weeping Elm.

It has nothing whatever to do with witchcraft but it is on record that a gentleman from Sussex coming to reside near Warwick was desirous of making a few alterations to his estate. He engaged men from Northamptonshire to cut down a wych elm and afterwards told some of the local men they could have the branches of the tree for firewood. A week or more passed and none of the wood had been removed. When the gentleman asked, the reason he was told was, *"Why, mister we do not want the old woman amongst us to be sure".* It was found to be a general belief locally that to burn wych elm would bring the evil powers of a witch upon them and their households.

Some years before that, a storm had blown some boughs from a large wych elm in Off Church Park near Leamington, the seat thereof the Dowager Countess of Aylesford. These boughs were left just where they fell. No one would move or even touch them for fear of the evil tidings that may befall them. They were left to rot.

One Avon-side village was inhabited during the present writers young days by a most extraordinary character, a very mysterious man whom we will call Ted. He was in fact not a native of the village but of a small town four miles away. I will not mention his real name because relatives of his are still living in the neighbourhood. This man was not very tall but was wiry and industrious. Altogether a keen intelligent man and a good tradesman – a blacksmith- but he was also extremely handy at other trades. He was usually looked upon as a man not to be tampered with or annoyed, for the very simple reason that he was sure to get even with the offender and any evil done to this man was always repaid one hundred fold. He was generally regarded with a certain amount of awe and by some looked upon almost as a warlock. However he was very capable at the kind of jobs that few of the villagers understood and for this reason he was at all times fully employed.

Ted was careful with his money and a life long abstainer and non-smoker. As a young man he had been fond of all kinds of practical jokes and would delight in playing strange and annoying tricks on the villagers. Nothing was safe from him. He could lock people out of their homes in such a way that the rightful keys would not unlock the doors yet it was the work of a few seconds only for him to unlock the doors when called upon.

At the time, 1875, that ubiquitous being, or phantom, known as Spring Heel Jack was scaring people in the Midland counties, where he had graduated from the south and east of England. Ted upon several occasions would initiate the jumps and leaps of this mysterious person or spirit, and in quiet lanes has been known to frighten people, usually women, almost to distraction. Everyone knew that Ted was responsible for these and other annoyances but he was never at any time discovered in the act. He was said to be a cross between W.W. Jacobs, Bob Pretty and Uriah Heep.

Upon one occasion a local stonemason asked Ted to help him move some fallen willow trees from a riverside meadow to the stonemasons yard.

Ted was promised half the trees to repay him for his services. The job took the two men nearly a day to move the trees but when they were safely in the yard the mason would not keep to the bargain and only offered a small portion of the timber to Ted.

Next morning when the mason looked out of his window into his yard the trees had entirely vanished. Neither were they ever seen again. The mystery was, and still is, how Ted moved the trees and where he took them.

CHAPTER ELEVEN

The Bridge at Pershore

An old man Mr Alfred Denmick aged 84 in 1954 and then living at Pershore related his experience when a farm boy. He declared that he had met a ghost upon two occasions; the first was while he was at a farm at Camberton and had to walk to his work from Pershore. He was returning home one night, and when he had rounded the bottom of Pensham Hill and was approaching the bridge at Pershore, he met a man coming over the bridge towards him. Mr Denmick said afterwards, "I heard the crunch of his footsteps on the gravel and distinctly saw him walk right up till he was level with me. Then I turned and said 'Good night, Sir', but the man had vanished. I ran the rest of the way home."

Some years later Mr Denmick was walking home from the railway station at Pershore, which is situated quite a distance from the town. It was about 6pm one winter's night and he had two friends with him. As they approached a house a woman let herself out of a garden gate and walked across the road and straight through a brick wall, which then stood surrounding a coppice on the way to Mount Pleasant. This woman appeared to be only two or three yards in front of the party. Mr Denmick declares that he not only saw the woman quite clearly but also heard the rustle of her dress as she walked.

"I never heard such a rustle of silks and satins in my life, and a fine figure of a woman she was too."

Some time later one of the two men who were with Mr Denmick at the time claimed to have seen the same apparition. The other man of the party neither saw nor heard anything unusual.

Footsteps at Wick Rissington

The account that follows is of mysterious footsteps, heard at the rectory at Wick Rissington. As this is near Cheltenham it is neither in Warwickshire or Worcestershire, although very near the borders of both.

I quote from the "Evesham Journal", May 27, 1960.

"A true ghost story was related at the fortnightly meeting of Evesham branch of the international Friendship League by the Rev. H. Cheals of Wick Rissington. He told the members of the haunting of his rectory. Mysterious footsteps were heard soon after the birth of one of his daughters. Nightly at 2am, heavy footfalls were heard on the stairs and across the landing, but disappointingly, nothing was seen.

"The speaker discovered by discreet inquiry that former servants sleeping in a particular room at the Rectory had been frightened on seeing an old man with a white beard who visited their room in the early morning. Later when one of his own children asked who that "someone" was on the landing, the vicar and his wife decided that the thing would have to go.

"However, after special prayers had been said, the thing did not go and took offence at being considered an unwelcome intruder. Consequently the activities increased. Violent explosions throughout the house, and even under their bed, startled them so much that further advice was sought.

"It was thought that as there seemed no evil intent and no one had been harmed, acceptance of the intruder would possibly ease the shattered calm. The noise of crashing china and glass had been frequent and on a certain date each year, the loud smashing of an attic window, together with the sound of tinkling glass, had been clearly audible, but nothing had been found broken.

"Some members of the family felt a cat affectionately rub itself against their legs, and although the speaker had not seen it, the feeling had been unmistakable. Others actually saw the animal. In one room during all the seasons, the perfume of roses could be smelt, but this, together with the other strange happenings, vanished with the birth of another child."

A member who lived in an old house near All Saints Church Evesham, recounted experiences with her own ghost, who she thought to be a monk, as the smell of incense was strong when he was about. Locked doors had been seen to open and a chair in which she was sitting was moved forward by a shove from behind. Unfortunately, her ghost had gone, probably as she had laughed at him and had never been afraid.

Milner Field and the Salt Family

Saltaire was a small factory community built by one Titus Salt between 1851 and 1876. He was a teetotaller, self-righteous, God-fearing industrialist of the type that the nineteenth century seemed to breed in great amounts. He did not want to simply employ his workers but to own them. His workers were expected to live in his houses, worship in his church, and follow his precepts to the letter. He would not allow a public house in the village. They were compelled to be sober, industrious and quiet.

On the other hand, Titus Salt showed a rare degree of enlightenment in terms of social welfare, and there is no question that his employees enjoyed cleaner, healthier, more comfortable living conditions than almost any other industrial workers in the world at that time.

Though it has since been swallowed up by the great sprawl that is the Leeds-Bradford conurbation, when it was built Saltaire stood in clean, open countryside. A vast change from the unhealthy stew of central Bradford at that time, where in the 1850s there were more brothels than churches and no covered sewers.

On a sloping site overlooking the River Aire and the Leeds to Liverpool Canal, Salt built a massive textile mill known as the Palace of Industry, the largest factory in Europe, spreading over 9 acres. Nearby, in 1870, Titus Salt Junior built an ornate palace of stone and called it Milner Field. In 1870 the fortunes of the Salt family appeared excellent and perpetually secure.

But in 1893 the textile trade suffered a sudden and disastrous slump, leaving the Salt family dangerously over-extended. The family abruptly lost control of the company, and in much consternation and shame they had to sell the house, mill and associated holdings.

Then began a strange and sinister series of events.

Without apparent exception all the subsequent owners of Milner Field suffered odd and devastating setbacks. One whacked himself on the foot with a golf club and died when the wound turned gangrenous. Another came home and found his young bride naked in the arms of a business associate. He killed them both and in doing so made his appointment with the hangman.

Before long the house developed a reputation as a place where you could reliably expect to come to a nasty end. People moved in, and just as abruptly moved out again, with ashen faces and terrible wounds. By 1930, when the house went on the market for one last time, no buyer could be found for it.

Milner Field stayed empty for twenty years, and finally in 1950 it was pulled down. Now the site is overgrown and weedy, and you could walk past it without realising that one of the finest houses in the North of England had once stood there. It seems remarkable to think that a century ago Titus Salt Junior would have stood on this spot, in a splendid house looking down the Aire valley to the distant but formidable Salt's Mill. It would have been clanging away and filling the air with steamy smoke, and beyond it was the sprawl of the richest centre of woollen trade in the world.

And now it was all gone.

The Woodshed in Fleet

The following account was related to the present writer many years ago by an old man, a retired baker at Fleet near Aldershot. I have every reason to believe the man was sincere. I knew him over a number of years and he had no reason to invent or to magnify the details of this occurrence.

I first became acquainted with him in about 1908 and when he had just retired. When he first started in business on his own account Fleet was a very small place, little more than a village and he had of course customers in the remove outlying villages going his rounds with a pony and van. He came interested in antiques particularly clocks and had was fortunate in those days to pick up many bargains in the course of years from cottagers' and other customers. It was a deal in clocks that first brought me in contact with him. At various times I purchased from him the movements of old Grandfather clocks with fine quality brass dials, also Lantern Clocks and on one occasion a fine English Chiming Bracket Clock. His name was Shaw and I will not reveal his other names.

During the apprentice days of Shaw in Fleet, a boy was required by the baker to deliver bread with a pony and van. This boy would not of course be an apprentice but a good reliable lad was required. A boy was found in Aldershot. He had just left school and had been brought up by an aunt, for his parents were dead. The aunt impressed upon the baker that the boy would have to live in, as Aldershot was too far away for him to go home every night, and anyway she felt she was too old to look after him any longer. She had brought him up and now he must look after himself.

The boy seemed suitable and he was duly engaged by the baker, but was unable to board and sleep him so he found an old lady in Fleet that lived in a cottage alone and she could put the boy up. This of course meant that board and lodging had to be paid by the baker so he was unable at first to pay the boy a large wage. It was impressed upon the old lady that the boy must be at the bakery at 5 every morning to load the van and deliver the bread in time for some of the customers breakfast.

Things went smoothly for some time, but as the boy grew older he made friends with other boys and became rather lax and stayed out later at night. He had joined a boys club and was not so punctual as formerly. He was late getting to work several mornings and was reported by the baker accordingly without much improvement. Eventually the baker went to the old lady and asked her to use some influence to get the boy up early so that he could start to load the van at 5.

There was some improvement for a time after this but the boy again became lax, so the old lady told him she would bolt the door every night at 9. If he could not be in by 9 he would have to sleep in the woodshed in the garden all night. After this, things went very well for a time and then came Christmas week, and one bitter cold night the boy stayed longer at the Mechanics Institute where there had been a singsong and party. When he reached the cottage all was in darkness, so he knocked long and loud and at last the old lady put her head out of the upstairs window. She told the boy he would have to sleep in the woodshed in accordance with her former threat. It should be mentioned that the front door of the cottage faced the garden, and the side of the house abutted onto the road. The boy went to the woodshed, but it was so cold that although he tried he could not sleep, so he went again to the cottage door and plied the knocker. This time the old lady did not get out of bed but shouted to the boy that she would not open the door.

The boy said, "If you do not open the door I shall throw myself down the well".

The old lady did not reply, and neither did she open the door. The boy went to the well, which was covered by a large stone, and twisted the stone round so that it fell into the well with a great splash. The boy then hid in the garden near the cottage door. Presently the old lady came down and walked up the garden, clad only in an old skirt and her nightdress.

The boy ran from his hiding place and into the cottage, shutting the door and bolting it.

He said, "Now you go and sleep in the woodshed the same as you told me".

He then sat in a chair by the remains of the kitchen fire, intending to open the door after a few minutes. Alas he fell asleep and did not wake until 5 o'clock. He opened the door and rushed up the garden to the woodshed.

The old lady was there – but she was dead.

For a long time thereafter the woodshed became the site for unnatural happenings. Local people passing by often heard noises and saw strange lights at night. They said it was the restless spirit of the old lady, still angry at her senseless death. The boy returned to live with his aunt, filled with remorse and terror at what he had done. He sank into a long melancholy and was unable to carry out any work for any period more than a few days.

One night he returned to the cottage, and was seen entering the woodshed, obviously determined to appeal to the old lady's ghost to forgive him and give him peace. However, it seems that the old lady was not so forgiving, and in the cold light of dawn two farmhands on their way to work found the boy.

He was still there – but he was dead.

No noises were ever heard nor lights were ever seen again in the place, and soon after there was a new owner in the cottage, who tore down the woodshed.

CHAPTER TWELVE

Some Short Tales

At a period when the district of Nine Elms – now part of Battersea – was a proud residential neighbourhood, and before Vauxhall Gardens had degenerated into a cheap pleasure ground in, 1768 to be exact, there lived at Nine Elms a Captain Hollymore. This gentleman, then in perfect health, had told his friends that his mother had frequently told him that he would die on the 10th of November 1769. It is not possible now to state by what means the mother was able to predict the death of her, son or why he should given credence to such a prophesy.

Certain it is that on Friday the 10th November 1769 Captain Hollymore, while still apparently in good health, sent for his lawyer and made his will and he also gave orders about his funeral. He then called his friends about him and assured them that he should die that night. Sure enough next morning he was found dead in bed without the least signs of his not having died a natural death.

A tormenting ghost, whose object seems to be to tease and mystify all people who come to live in the house, haunts a house in Silvester Road, East Dulwich, in the South London district. Before the housing shortage this house remained vacant for years. No one would stay longer than a few weeks – just long enough to seek other accommodation.

An old man sat one night waiting for his daughter – a Salvation Army lass – to return. He sat in an upstairs kitchen, where there was a frosted glass panel to the door, and the door was shut. The man was alone in the house. Presently he heard his daughter coming up the stairs and he saw her shadow pass the frosted glass panel. He concluded she had gone to bed. In a few minutes he went himself to bed and called "Good Night" outside his daughter's room as he passed. There was no reply so he opened the door and peeped in. The room was empty, his daughter had not yet returned. Indeed she came in a few moments later. She declared she had not been home before. This and similar happenings occurred quite frequently.

A house in Forester Road, Peckham Rye in the South London district is haunted by a thump. This does not occur very often but it is loud enough to be very alarming. It always happens at night. The present writer has heard it. One night all was quiet outside and inside the house, which is in a quiet neighbourhood. The owner and myself were chatting. The alarming thud came from the room above a front room.

The owner exclaimed, "Merciful Heavens, one of the children has fallen out of bed".

He rushed upstairs but all the children were asleep. There was no one else in the house. We searched round the house but no one was to be seen back or front. It has since been ascertained that some years ago a former occupant of the house hanged himself in the upstairs room from whence the thump proceeds.

On the estate of Lady Craven at Ashbury, Wiltshire, two workmen's cottages were erected at a lonely part of the estate and on an unfrequented lane. This was 50 years ago and the cottages have never been occupied, for the simple reason that no glass will remain in the windows. As often as glass is fitted to the windows it is out next morning. This act cannot be attributed to mischievous boys, for it is a remote spot and no children live for miles. It is thought that the cottages are built on the site of what was once an ancient tumulus or burial place.

It is intended that the following account will act as a warning to all scoffers; those people that will not bring themselves to believe in the possibility of the appearance of earth-bound spirits. Such people, if they are sincere, should not on any account dabble in spiritualism. Such behaviour may have dire results, as this account will show.

This incident happened in South London in 1936. I will not mention names. An old friend of mine was a solicitor's clerk and taking him all round, he was of more than average intelligence. He held strong views on certain subjects, among them Atheism. In fact he came from an infidel family. His Atheism was not idle talk, for he could, and did, support his belief with quite weighty arguments. Personally I am by no means infidel but also I may add I am no biblical scholar. I was unable to confute all my friend's statements.

When he was 42 years a favourite sister died. This grieved him very much, and I was unable to console him, for he held firmly that death is indeed the end. I could not move him and I felt very sorry for him. Eventually the spiritualists got in touch with him. I cannot say if he approached them or if they were invited by friends to talk to him, as he had a large circle of friends. He did not tell me of this at first in case I might ridicule him and his infidel ideas. However, he was persuaded to attend a séance and eventually it transpired he received messages from the sister that had died.

There seems to be no doubt that he did actually communicate with the sister. There was proof of this when she was able to direct him as to the disposal of some of her belongings and to convey to him the whereabouts of documents and portraits that she had hidden away. More surprising still, it was discovered that he was a medium. It can well be imagined the shock all this would be to a highly sensitive individual. All his atheistic ideas and opinions shattered at one blow. Strong-minded as he undoubtedly was he was quite unable to grasp or to deal with the situation.

Indeed, it may have eased matters greatly had he been less intelligent, and also had he confided in his friends. This he did not do from first to last. He had disclosed these events only to his elder brother. He was promptly scoffed at and reminded that common sense should indicate to him that it was "all humbug". He had no other cares to distract his attention, for he was a bachelor and a total abstainer. As a medium he proceeded to get messages from other relatives, some of whom had been dead for years, particularly an uncle of whom he had been a favourite nephew. This uncle would appear in the bedroom, the locked door proving no hindrance.

It is significant that a collie dog that always slept on an ottoman at the foot of the bed – a most courageous animal normally – would literally quiver with terror and shrink under the bed tail between legs.

All this went on for three months and then my friend lost his reason. He was committed to an asylum and is there yet. There seems little hope that he will ever come out. It would seem that my friend was also gifted with second sight. He was able to see visions. After the funeral of his sister he told me he had seen the whole thing before – the cortege, the sun shining on the coffin, the mourners, everything had appeared to him several days before the funeral.

Second sight is said to be a gift of the Scots, although there are many recorded accounts of other nationalities also possessing this gift or ability. Strictly speaking second sight refers to things or events about to happen but there have been various accounts of visions or happenings that have already occurred.

Sir Walter Scott had a strong faith in second sight. Mrs Mary Howitt, the writer – she wrote "The Forest Minstrel" etc, once had a remarkable experience. She was seated at her desk writing one morning and suddenly everything seemed to fade out and disappear, yet however, she was quietly conscious of a vision forming in her minds eye. She distinctly saw before her a wide tract of country, wild and barren. The scene was quite unknown to her but she knew instinctively that it was Australia, although she had never visited that country.

She saw a large pond or lake and men were approaching. There was anxiety and concern on their faces. They had brought with them ropes and dragging appliances and at once began to drag the lake. In a short time they drew to the side the body of a young man that they lifted out of the water and laid on the bank. As the man turned the body over and the sun shone on the face of the young man, Mary Howitt saw that it was the body of her son. As she watched she saw the men depart from the scene carrying their sad burden.

The vision faded and she found herself once again seated at her desk. Mrs Howitt was so overwhelmed that she was quite unable to continue her work, and she sent for her husband to whom she related all she had seen in the vision. They were now quite convinced that their son was dead. They had not long to wait for the confirmation, and in a few weeks news reached them that their son had indeed been drowned and the circumstances were described exactly as had been seen in the vision. Mary Howitt always regarded the experience as a merciful interposition of Providence to prepare her for what was coming.

Mary Howitt afterwards discussed the phenomena with Mrs Henry Wood the novelist, who expressed the opinion that if indeed second sight really did exist then people of Celtic origin may be more susceptible to such influences, the Celtic temperament seeming more closely allied to the spiritual than the Saxon. Mrs Howitt agreed that this was likely to be the case, partly through the more vivid imagination of the Celts. However, in one of her "Johnny Ludlow" papers, Vol. 1 "Reality or Delusion", Mrs Henry Wood describes a case of second sight, which she declares to be the true. It is also known that some of her novels were founded on fact.

From Redruth in Cornwall comes a remarkable case of second sight. A man named Williams had a dream that he was in the House of Commons and saw one man shoot another dead. Indeed this murder had already actually taken place only a few hours before.

Once, John Bellingham, a merchant, had been wronged or thought he had been wronged by the Russian Government, and had appealed in vain for redress to the then Prime Minster, Spencer Perceval. As a consequence John Bellingham worked himself into such frenzy that he went to the House of Commons and shot Perceval dead. He was hanged for the crime in May 1812.

A nursemaid employed in Weymouth Street, London, had charge of a small boy 3 years of age. He was the only child of wealthy parents and was made much of in consequence, for he was indeed a very beautiful child. The maid had instructions never to leave him alone, not even after he had been put to bed at night and she was expected to remain in an adjoining room. This she accordingly did, and she would be busy with needlework or reading. Altogether the maid had quite a comfortable job at this period. This was in 1875. Of course conditions of employment of domestic servants have changed very much since then.

One evening the girl was most anxious to get out after putting her little charge to bed. The occasion was the farewell meeting with her soldier sweetheart who had been ordered abroad. It seemed difficult to get out on this particular night, although the little boy was sound asleep. At last the girl hit upon a plan as so many nursemaids have done before. She dressed up a long handled broom to represent a sort of scarecrow and tied it to the foot of the bed, thinking that should the little boy wake he would be scared and go off to sleep again.

Altogether a most fantastic idea, because it was much more likely to have the reverse effect. Such was the mentality of some of the nursemaids in 1875. However, having tied the grotesque figure to the foot of the bed the maid departed to keep the appointment with her soldier friend. The little boy did wake up and far from being frightened into going off to sleep again, he was frightened into a fit. It was a large house and his screams were not heard in the rooms below.

When the girl returned the boy was unconscious. It was obvious from the deranged bedclothes that he was in a fit. It was now the maids turn to be frightened, so she hastily got rid of the broom and all sign of the scarecrow and roused the parents. Eventually the boy was nursed back to consciousness, but before he was sufficiently recovered to be able to speak and so tell what had scared him, he had another fit. He was in and out of fits for the remainder of that night.

In the morning he died. Fortunately for the nursemaid the child had not been able to tell his parents the cause of his fright. Had it been otherwise she would without doubt have been charged with manslaughter. A few years before the above event, and at the house Number 50 Berkeley Square, a child was frightened to death in the nursery on the top floor. For many years afterwards the child wearing a Scotch plaid was said to haunt the top rooms of the house sobbing and wringing its hands.

In this case it is not quite clear what exactly scared the child but it must have been something horrific, for it also scared grown up people into suicide upon more than one occasion.

CHAPTER THIRTEEN

No 50 Berkeley Square

Over a long period Number 50 Berkeley Square was in such troublous state that no tenant could be found to occupy the premises for more than a few weeks – usually just long enough to find other accommodation. It is known that George Canning lived in the house some time prior to 1827 but it was some years later than the hauntings began.

At one time the landlords or their agents even offered to pay tenants to remain in occupation of the premises for the first year of the tenancy and the second year was to be rent-free, after that only a nominal rent would be expected. The snag to all this was the stipulation that the tenant must forfeit £1000 if he failed to remain for the full term of his tenancy. Very few people would agree to these terms, but those that did invariably broke the agreement and fled.

Many stories of the hauntings have been related over the years. It appears that only the top rooms were affected by this horrible "something". One man is said to have lost his reason when sleeping in one of the upper rooms through what he saw there. A young girl named Adeline was also said t become so distracted that she jumped from the window of one of the top rooms one night. She was dead when picked up.

No one has ever been able to describe the "Horror" that haunts the rooms although it has been seen upon more than one occasion. Sometime about the year 1850 two sailors, finding themselves stranded in London one cold winter night, wandered into Number 50 intending to sleep the night there. The notice board outside TO BE LET or SOLD assured them that they were unlikely to be disturbed in the empty house. Alas that notice was displayed frequently and no housekeeper could be persuaded to stay there.

The two sailors decided to sleep that night in one of the small top rooms. They accordingly made themselves as comfortable as circumstances would permit, and they lit a fire in the small grate with old wallpaper and some crumbling wainscot, which they tore from the walls. It is recorded they were not the worse for drink but had missed a connection on this cold night and they just required a night's rest.

They were soon asleep, and though it is not possible to say how long they slept, they were both awakened in the night by some strange sound in one of the rooms below. Presently they were both startled by the sound of slow but heavy muffled footsteps, which seemed to be mounting the stairs to the top room. One of the sailors afterwards told the police that the footsteps were not ordinary footsteps but were heavy, ponderous and stealthy, resembling those of some large animal.

The footsteps seemed to stop outside the door of the room occupied by the sailors, and by the light of what remained of the fire they saw the door handle turned and the door began to open slowly. When the door was fully open the men could just discern the shape of the indescribable Horror. Stouthearted men that they were, they became paralysed with fear as the ghastly thing entered the room and moved stealthily and slowly towards the sailors. It seemed to shuffle and to half drag itself across the room towards one of the men.

The other somehow managed to dash past the "thing" and ran down the stairs, but before he had reached the next landing he heard a terrified scream from the room he had just left. He continued his descent, and opening the front door, ran out and collapsed fainting on the pavement. Here the police found him, and later a small party of police and others entered the house. The top rooms, and indeed all the rooms, were empty. The sailor that had remained in the room had been so terrified that he had thrown himself from the window and was discovered in the yard at the back of the house with his neck broken. He had been literally frightened into suicide by the "Nameless Horror".

About a year later a tenant was at long last found for the house. A family from the provinces had leased the house principally for the purpose of the "coming out" of two of their daughters at the London season. One of the daughters was already engaged to an Army officer.

For the first month or so the family were not disturbed in this fateful house. Eventually the fiancé of the elder daughter was invited to stay a few nights. He was reluctant to put the family to any unnecessary trouble and had said he could sleep at his club. However he was told there were plenty of spare bedrooms at the top of the house, indeed some of the rooms had never been in use at all since they had taken the house. The night before the arrival of the officer, and while a housemaid was preparing one of the bedrooms, the whole household was scared by the shrieks of this maid. It was nearly midnight and fearing the house may be on fire the family rushed upstairs and into the room that was being prepared.

They found the maid lying on the floor at the foot of the bed in convulsions. Her features were fixed and her eyes looked in the direction of the corner of the room. She was taken at once in a cab to St George's Hospital where she died the next morning. She did not recover sufficiently to enable her to tell what exactly she had seen in the bedroom. She merely said, "I cannot speak of it, it was far too horrible".

The Army officer duly arrived at Number 50 and another bedroom on the same floor was prepared. The previous adventure was related to him but he was quite unmoved and declared he did not believe in any such ghost nonsense. He ventured the opinion that the housemaid had been merely hysterical. In vain did the family try to dissuade him and the girl to whom he was engaged particularly pleaded with him. He insisted however, and was determined to sleep in that room.

He said, "I'll ring if anything unusual occurs, but do not trouble to come up when I ring the first time because I may be unnecessarily alarmed by something quite trivial and seize the bell on the impulse of the moment. Wait until I ring the second time." In due course the officer retired. The family, however, were determined to stay up for a while – until after midnight at any rate – in order to make sure that all would be well with the occupant of the newly prepared bedroom. We may be sure that the anxiety and apprehension was intense and increased as the time passed. Just after midnight they were alarmed to hear the gentle ringing of the bell. All was excitement at this but they remembered the young man's request to ignore the first ring. They therefore remained where they were in the downstairs room.

The minutes passed and nothing happened; all were agog with intense excitement and then came a frantic and tremendous ringing of the bell that echoed through the house. Everyone seemed paralysed with fear and rooted to the spot. The ringing ceased and was followed by a loud explosion, than all was quiet again. The company rushed upstairs and burst open the door of the bedroom only to discover the young officer dressed in his night gown, lying on the floor at the foot of the bed exactly as they had previously found the housemaid. Also his eyes were fixed on a spot in one corner of the room.

There was however this difference; whereas the servant girl had been in a faint, the officer was dead with a service revolver beside him. He had shot himself. He was yet another victim that was not able to describe the Horror he had undoubtedly seen at Number 50 Berkeley Square. The premises are still standing and no tales of ghostly hauntings have been related of late years, and the lower part of the house is now occupied by Messrs Maggs Brothers, antiquarian booksellers.

CHAPTER FOURTEEN

The Ghost at Ham House

This is yet another account of a ghost frightening a child, a little girl this time, but with no dire results beyond scaring her. In fact the testimony of the child was the means of solving a mystery. The story is well authenticated and was related in 1907 by C. G. Harper. It also carried the authority of several psychical experts.

Ham House is an ancient manor house on the banks of the Thames not far from Richmond. The house was built in the time of James I. It was originally intended as a residence for Henry, Prince of Wales. Later it came into the possession of the Earl of Holderness and afterwards it was owned by Sir Lionel Tollemache, whose widow Lady Elizabeth, Countess of Dysart, received the house as part of her marriage settlement when in 1647 she married John Maitland, second Earl and first Duke of Lauderdale.

At this time the house was magnificently furnished, and at the present time much of the furniture still remains in the house and is of great interest to antiquarians. The house has been much more in the public eye of later years because it has been thrown open to the public, and at least part of its romantic history has been told in the press. It is conveniently situated on the opposite bank to Twickenham, so is more get-at-able than some of the ancient manor houses that are on show.

From all accounts it seems evident that the Duchess was a very handsome woman, for there is a portrait of her painted by Sir Peter Lily to be seen at Ham House. The historian Bishop Burnet described the subject of the painting as, "A woman of great beauty and of greater parts, violent in everything she set about: a violent friend but a much more violent enemy. She was ravenously covetous and would have stuck at nothing by which she may compass her ends".

Writing of an interview he had with her, Sir John Reresby said, "She must have been beautiful and a lady of grace at one time." However, during the lifetime of her first husband Sir Lionel Tollemache, this Lady Elizabeth led a far from blameless life and is said to have had many "affairs". The death of Tollemache under rather suspicious circumstances gave rise to some ugly scandals. Small wonder then that the ghost of the old Duchess is said to haunt Ham House, and she is said to be seen descending the great staircase in rustling silks in the fashion of that period of Charles II.

Tradition has it that she was on her way to meet her lover, the then Duke of Lauderdale, a very wealthy man. It is also said that the Countess saved the life of the Duke by giving herself to Oliver Cromwell, after he had been taken prisoner at the Battle of Worcester. After this the Duke spent 9 years in the Tower. After his release the lovers met again. The gossips were busy and it was said at the time that in order to be at liberty to marry the rich Duke she had brought about the death of her husband.

However, although proof was lacking, certain it is that Sir Lionel Tollemache died suddenly and under grave suspicion in 1670. Also, it is an historical fact that the wife of the Duke of Lauderdale died mysteriously and suddenly in Paris a year later. Thus the two lovers were at liberty to marry, and this they did in 1671. Gossip said, and not without foundation, that the Countess had bribed an agent to poison the wife of the Duke. Nothing however was proved, and after a busy and notorious life the old lady died in 1698. She was in her seventies.

Her bedroom was preserved exactly as she left it and it remained thus for 150 years, when the room was shown as a curiosity. The Duchess's silver mounted ebony stick was also shown, lying on a little table in the bedroom. It was this stick that formed part of another haunting at Ham House. It was said that at times the sound of the stick was heard tapping along the hall and also along the upstairs corridors.

One winter's night about the year 1850, a little girl, the daughter of the butler, was put to sleep in one of the upper bedrooms. It must be assumed that the parents were unaware that the room had the reputation of being haunted. It may even be assumed that this particular room had not been haunted up to this date and that the little girl was psychic. We cannot be sure. According to the testimony of this little girl – related the same night and repeated the next day before reliable witnesses – she was awakened sometime in the early hours of the morning by a strange noise, a scratching or scraping sound.

The child said, "I thought it must be a little mouse or perhaps a bird".

The sound seemed to be on the other side of the room, near the fireplace. The little girl sat up in bed. At the side of the fireplace she saw an old woman kneeling with her back to the bed but the child could see that the old woman was clawing at the panelling in the wainscot near the fireplace. It seemed that the woman was trying to open or remove the panel. The startled child made a noise, a gasp of surprise, and at this the old woman turned round and rose to her feet. She then moved slowly towards the bed and at last clutched the rail at the foot of the bed and stared at the child.

The expression on the old woman's face was so terrifying that the child screamed out, paralysed with fear. This aroused the parents and they of course rushed to the room. They found the little girl sobbing with her face buried in the pillow. The child was calmed and assured she had been dreaming. However the child persisted in her story in the light of day, and even later in the morning and henceforth. She insisted she had actually seen the terrifying woman in the bedroom. The child's account was so convincing that she was asked to point out the panel in the wainscot at which the old woman was clawing. She did so and dream or no dream a carpenter was sent for to remove the panel.

As I stated at the beginning of the story, the account of the haunting is well authenticated but there have been conflicting tales as to what exactly the carpenter discovered behind the wainscot panel. A Mr Hare stated in 1875 that papers were discovered behind the panel, which proved that in that room Lady Elizabeth, Countess of Dysart, had murdered her husband Sir Lionel Tollemache, that she might be at liberty to marry the Duke of Lauderdale. Since the statement of Mr Hare there have been other accounts of what was discovered behind the panel. The most popular, as well as the most apt, is the above account, though there may of course be reasons of a diplomatic nature to cast a doubt on this part of the story.

True or not true the hauntings said to be of the famous, or infamous, Duchess are said to continue to this day.

CHAPTER FIVETEEN

The Sailor's Sweetheart

A handsome girl, the daughter of once wealthy parents, was secretly affianced to a young man much below her station, to wit a sailor. Of course the young lady's father, who forbade the two to meet again, frowned upon this.

The sailor had won the heart of the handsome maiden and there were clandestine meetings. The course of true love destined not to run smooth, for the father one day came upon the lovers unexpectedly, and henceforth the daughter was so closely guarded that further meetings became difficult and rare. So far the story, although true, is commonplace. There have been very many quiet similar cases of wellborn maidens falling in love with men below their standard.

The girl's father quickly arranged a matrimonial alliance for his daughter with a wealthy and cantankerous old miser whom the girl detested. Notwithstanding, in three months the girl was more or less forced into this hateful marriage. As may have been expected the girl was most miserable in her married life, and was moreover shamefully treated by this rich old husband and she soon became little better than his slave, being most cruelly handled.

The evil treatment had the reverse effect of subduing her, for it drove her to vile hatred of this old man who was her husband. Acting upon the advice of an old hag who distilled subtle poisons from herbs - poisons that would leave no trace - the young wife decided to poison her evil old husband. This she did but when the old man died, suspicion fell upon the unhappy wife and ultimately she was discovered and brought before the justices. She was condemned to death. In due course the cold grey morning arrived when she was to suffer execution. She stood on the scaffold. She was granted one last wish, and she requested that her sailor lover should be allowed to accompany her to the scaffold.

This wish was granted and on the scaffold the two embraced for the last time. They kissed and parted, and they were heard to make a half whispered compact, which ended in mutual assurances.

"You will, you promise me, you will?" said the girl.

"I swear it," replied the sailor.

Thus they parted and the execution was carried out. Three years passed, and the sailor was on board a vessel that was being tossed about in the trough of a tempestuous sea. The storm increased in violence and all on board was expecting to be drowned. One huge billow snapped the masts fore and aft as if they were matchsticks. The billow rebounded from the deck and shot upwards like a waterspout till it seemed lost in the clouds above.

Some hours later when the storm had somewhat abated, it was discovered that the young sailor had been spirited away, taken aloft. From that hour the sailor was never heard of again. No, not washed overboard as some people would say. There remains the testimony of the whole of that ship's crew that the devil himself rode the waves on that fearful night surrounded by a posse of friends. They bore in their midst a beautiful girl, who with the magnetism of love drew her sailor sweetheart to her arms, whisking him up from the deck of that shattered vessel into the obscurity beyond.

Phantom Drums

There are numerous accounts of the beating of a drum by a phantom drummer haunting places and even people. A drummer boy apparently haunted Napoleon himself, for during the perilous journey over the Alps the boy had fallen over a precipice and had landed with his drum on a ledge below. Apparently he was unharmed because he picked himself up and began to beat his drum again. There was no time to stop and rescue the boy, and it is said he continued to beat his drum until the army was out of earshot. By all accounts he was left to perish, and the sound of his drum haunted Napoleon at certain periods for some years afterwards.

Another tale of a ghostly drummer comes from Scotland. Whenever a member of the Airlie family is going to die the apparition of a drummer is said to haunt Cortachy Castle, Kirriemuir. According to tradition this haunting is the result of the drummer having so enraged a former Lord Airlie that in the heat of the moment the drummer was threatened with death. At this the drummer threatened to haunt the family ever after if his life were taken. This enraged the master of Cortachy still more and he had the drummer thrust into his own drum and flung from the window of a tower of the castle.

The drummers threat seems to have been carried out, because in 1849 before the decease of the then Lord Airlie, and again in 1884 before the death of Lady Airlie, the beat of the drum was on each occasion distinctly heard by various people; guests of the family. One of these guests was a lady that had never heard of the tradition, and after hearing the drum while dressing for dinner, she innocently asked Lord Airlie at the table who his drummer was. The question had the effect of making the peer turn pale and leave the table. The sound of a drum had preceded the loss of his first wife, and it was only a few months after this interrupted dinner party that the second wife died.

Powys Castle and Cambermere Abbey

The ghost at Powys Castle proved a much more pleasing, almost benevolent, ghost. He was at any rate on a philanthropic errand. This gracious spirit last appeared to a poor needlework woman. During the absence of the family, the Herberts, from Powys Castle, the servants – who did not like her – purposefully put this pious woman to sleep in the haunted bedroom. This room, although seldom occupied, was splendidly furnished. The bed was a large four-poster, and there were too sash windows in the room. A good fire was burning in the old fashioned grate and there were chairs and tables about the room and also a spinning wheel.

This latter the woman had occasionally used. The needlework woman had retired rather late and had just sat down at one of the tables with a candle to read her Bible. She happened to glance up and to her astonishment saw a gentlemen enter the room. He wore clothing of the 17th century, a gold-laced hat and waistcoat and a square-cut coat. He approached one of the sash windows, and putting an elbow on the sill, rested his face on the palm of his hand. He appeared from his attitude to be waiting for the woman to speak, but she was too frightened.

After a time the gentleman walked out of the room. The poor woman rose from her chair and kneeling, she began to pray. While she was thus engaged the apparition appeared again, this time he walked round the room and then stood close behind the terrified woman. Soon he disappeared and again appeared. Then he walked up and stood behind her. At this the poor woman, still kneeling, managed to find courage to speak.

She said, "Pray, sir, who are you, and what do you want?"

The man pointed to the candle and said: "Take up the candle and follow me and I will tell you."

This she did, and he led the way into a very small room, where, tearing up a floor board, he pointed to an iron box underneath, and then to a crevice in the wall where was found a key. The gentleman asked that the box and the key were to be sent to the Earl of Powys, who at that time resided in London. This the woman did, but we are not told what exactly the box contained. What we do know is that the Powys family afterwards provided for this poor Welsh spinning woman liberally until she died in about 1802. The apparition was never seen again.

Cambermere Abbey

At Cambermere Abbey is a family ghost, that of a little girl, a member of the Cotton family. The reason or significance of this ghost seems hard to understand. One of the rooms at the top of this ancient building was at one time used as a nursery but was afterwards converted into a bedroom. In this room has been seen a spirit-figure of a young girl, a child of about 14 years of age, dressed in old fashioned clothing and with a ruff round its neck.

On one occasion this apparition appeared to a niece of the late Lord Cotton who had been put to sleep in this bedroom while on a visit. On this particular evening the young lady was dressing for a late dinner. As she rose from the toilet glass to get an article of dress she saw this oddly dressed child standing near the bed. The bedstead, by the way, was a modern iron one and stood more in the middle of the room away from the wall. As the young lady looked, the child began to run round the bedstead and seemed to be in a state of agitation and to have an agonising look upon its face. Presently the child vanished as mysteriously as it had appeared, leaving the young lady spellbound but still wondering if the figure were real or spirit.

Later the same evening the niece mentioned the incident of this phantom child to her aunt, Lady Cotton. After some consideration it was recalled that some years ago the late Lord Cotton had mentioned the sudden death of a favourite little sister of his. The sister with whom he had been playing in that same room many years ago when he himself was a child, and that the little girl had died only a few hours afterwards.

As I mentioned at the beginning, the purpose of this ghost is difficult to understand, but some years later a second Cotton ghost appeared, although not at Cambermere Abbey.

This second ghost made a unique appearance about 60 years ago at a house on the south coast, once inhabited by the late Lord Cambermere. A young lady visitor took a photograph of the drawing room, though it may be mentioned that she was only an amateur photographer. When the plate was developed the young lady was astounded to see in the photograph the figure of a man sitting in one of the armchairs in this drawing room. The figure was of a tall elderly man with full face and a moustache. The young lady was quite sure this man was not visible in the chair when she exposed the plate, for he was clad in garments that were fashionable 100 years before. It was a photograph of the old peer himself.

Fyvie Castle

Another ghost that appears only when some important event in the family is about to take place is the ghost – or rather there are two ghosts – at Fyvie Castle.

At one time the Gordon family of Fyvie Castle were not only troubled by two ghosts but also by a hereditary curse. This was the curse of one Thomas the Rhymester, a wandering minstrel. It is said a former Gordon, who had the gates closed against minstrels, forbade this man to perform in the castle. This churlish action so enraged Thomas the Rhymester that he there and then declared that the estate should never descend in a direct line until three weeping stones were found. Up to the year 1869 only one weeping stone had been discovered. The curse seems to have been effective, for it is a fact that the Gordons have never inherited in a direct line.

Of the Gordon ghosts of Fyvie Castle, one is said to be a lady in rich apparel of green brocade, seen always at night carrying a candle. She proceeds through one of the tapestried rooms of the castle when an important event is about to happen.

The other Gordon ghost is the figure of a trumpeter, who is seen in one of the corridors and his trumpet is heard when misfortune is about to overtake the ill-fated Gordons. This is said to be the spectre of a trumpeter that during his lifetime was on one occasion seized by the press gang, at the instigation of the Gordon at that time in possession of Fyvie Castle. There seems to have been an ulterior motive for this.

The Gordon was anxious to be rid of a rival to the affections of a pretty daughter of the reeve or bailiff. Unfortunately the girl was not consulted and she remained faithful to the trumpeter. The separation however sent her into a decline and she died of a broken heart.

A pretty romance but tradition has it that it is all true, and Fyvie Castle, like other ancient mansions, has a sealed room. This room has not been opened within living memory. There is a legend that should the door be opened, the master of the house would die and the wife go blind. Faith in this old legend has prevented it being proved.

Fakenham, Norfolk

From the old Hall of the Townshends, near Fakenham in Norfolk, comes the story of the ghost of the "Brown Lady". She is said to haunt several of the bedrooms in the older portion of the house. The purpose or aim of this ghost is quite unknown today but she is said to be a tall and stately lady in rich brown brocade, and she also wears a sort of coif on her head. The features are clearly seen but where the eyes should be are only hollows. She is seen walking about the house occasionally, though not always in the same room, and there is no regular time of her visit.

She has been known to be absent for 50 years and then again appear. There are rumours that her appearance foretells the death of a member of the family, but this is not always the case, because she once appeared to two gentlemen visitors to a house party who were sitting up late. Upon this occasion one of these gentlemen, a Colonel Loftus, afterwards made a sketch of the ghost from memory. At another time a guest asked the late Lord Charles Townsend if he believed in this apparition of the restless Brown Lady.

Lord Charles replied: "I cannot but believe, for she ushered me into my room last night."

CHAPTER SIXTEEN

The Ghost of Glamis Castle

Of all the ghostly hauntings related of manor houses, castles, abbeys or such like in the United Kingdom, the ghost of Glamis Castle is surely the most noteworthy. It is easily the most notorious in Scotland, yet Glamis might also be termed Scotland's most picturesque castle, set in the beautiful vale of Strathmore.

It has been the seat of the Bowes-Lyons, the Queen Mother's family, for six centuries, and Princess Margaret was actually born there. Viewed from almost any angle, the castle resembles the fairy tale castles of the picture books. However, it is a very substantial edifice and some of its walls are 4 feet thick, with the enhancement of the usual conical roofed turrets.

What better setting than Glamis Castle for Shakespeare's Macbeth? One room is known to this day as King Maledus Room, and in it tradition has Duncan being murdered there by Macbeth, "Thane of Glamis". In the great hall one can imagine the ghost of the murdered Duncan calling for vengeance.

However, the real ghost of Glamis is far more frightening and mysterious – so mysterious indeed that the very nature of the hauntings is uncertain. Yet it is of such importance that although it is hinted that there is a sealed chamber, its exact whereabouts and its contents is a closely guarded family secret. The personality of the ghost – some say it is an ancestor – or even the position of the sealed room, is never known to more than three individuals at one time, the three being the Earl of Strathmore, the next heir and for some mysterious reason, the steward or bailiff.

Could anything be more romantic or reminiscent of the fairy tales of our childhood? At various times over a long period the ghost has been written about at some length and discussed endlessly. I cannot say that it has been investigated because the family has always objected to a too close examination of the family ghost or whatever it is.

Among the many investigators of the Glamis mystery was Dr F.G. Lee, a well-known Scottish divine, who about 70 years ago took up the study of ghosts, wraiths and such like. He relates how on one occasion at Glamis he attempted to discover the origin of strange noises that were heard in a certain room, and greatly disturbed the Lord Strathmore of that time. Dr Lee, with the Earl and a party of friends went to the room where Lord Strathmore unlocked the door and fell back in a dead faint at what he saw in the room. He afterwards ordered the door to be bricked up.

He could never be persuaded to tell what he saw in that room. It may be mentioned that upon more than one occasion the heir apparent has promised to tell his intimate friends the secret so soon as he attains his majority and thus becomes entitled to be told.

This promise has never yet been kept.

As each heir apparent is told the secret, the sealed room has to be opened and afterwards a stonemason in the presence of the house steward again seals the entrance.

Of course the gossips have been busy and there are all sorts of wild rumours, none of which seem to have any claim to truth seeing that the secret is so closely guarded. There is a tale of a former Earl, a man of high temper and an ardent gambler.

One Sunday evening about the year 1440 he could find no one to play dice or cards with him. The Earl became desperate and declared he would play with the Devil himself if he could find no one else. The Devil appeared and at the end of the game claimed the soul of the Lord of Glamis. Since then it is said the ill-fated Lord is condemned to play cards in the sealed room every Sunday night until the Day of Judgement.

Another tale or legend is of the days of the clan feuds. A party of Ogilvies fleeing from their enemies the Lindsays came to Glamis to seek shelter and protection. The Lord of the day fled them into a deep chamber under the castle. He then locked them in and left them to starve. It is said their skeletons lie there to this day, as they died; some in the act of gnawing the flesh from their own arms.

It seems there is a secret chamber in the castle, and this rumour is well founded. When Earl Patrick completed the rebuilding of the castle in 1684 he wrote a Book of Record and in it he gives details of the work he had put in hand. He mentions a closet that he had made in the thickness of the walls. This may have been a kind of wall safe, and not necessarily the secret room in question.

At least it is known that the fateful room has a window. Some years ago a house party was in progress and by way of amusement it was suggested by the then Countess, (remember only the Earl is in to the secret of the ghost), that they hunt for the mysterious room. This was during the absence of the Earl of course. Accordingly a towel was hung from each window of the castle. When this had been done there remained one window high up in one of the walls that was without a towel. This then was the window of the sealed room, and forthwith a search was organised to endeavour to find the room.

Unfortunately, the search was brought to an abrupt close when the object was disclosed to the bailiff. It is significant that the house steward always shares the secret. There may of course be a reason for this. It seems probable that he may have an unpleasant duty to perform periodically. Whatever the duty is it is passed to each successive steward. He has always to be present at the re-sealing of those 4 feet thick walls. The gossips say that the house steward is entrusted with the duty of providing food for the imprisoned "something".

It is recorded that in 1537 Janet Douglas widow of the sixth Lord Glamis was executed on Castle Hill, Edinburgh, for witchcraft against Kind James V of Scotland on an indictment afterwards confessed to be entirely false. The gossips say that the noises heard at Glamis are the echoes of the carpenters hammering as they built the scaffold.

The legend of the monster at Glamis is the most horrific of all the tales. It is said that because of a curse on the family, maybe in retribution for that Sunday night gambling, at certain intervals the first born of the family becomes a monster or vampire. Its groans and screams account for the strange noises heard by so many independent witnesses at the castle. The tale goes on that the monster cannot be destroyed or left to die, so it is the responsibility of the head of the family to see that it is fed but kept from public gaze in the closed chamber.

As if the sealed chamber and all it entails is not enough there are reports of other happenings at Glamis Castle. There is a tradition that a bearded soldier in chain armour haunts the old square tower and it is recorded that on one occasion a child was nearly frightened to death some 50 years ago.

The child and its mother were guests at Glamis and the child was asleep in a dressing room of its mother's bedroom. The mother lay awake on this eventful night when she saw a tall figure in armour enter her room, in the vicinity of the dressing room door. At the same instant a cold blast of air extinguished her candle, though it did not extinguish a night light in the child's room, from whence immediately afterwards there proceeded a scream.

The mother rushed into the dressing room and found the child trembling with fear. The tall mailed figure with the black beard had come to the side of the bed and leaned over the child's face. This is said to be the ghost of Duncan.

None of the present buildings at Glamis are older that the 15th Century, yet the hauntings whatever they may be, must have been a perpetual source of anxiety to the masters of Glamis through the ages. In 1877 the Bishop of Brecon during a visit to the castle noticed that Lord Strathmore was very depressed and always sad and gloomy. While discussing the sealed room one day, the Bishop asked if he could be of any assistance in relieving the Earl" state of mind. The Bishop was thanked for his kind enquiry but was told no one could ever help in the matter.

Eagle Street, Ipswich

A house in Eagle Street, Ipswich, was haunted by the ghost of a seaman, dressed in the style of a seaman of 150 years ago. The house is old, dating from the 16th Century, and it has the usual oak beams of houses of that period. It has six rooms, and it has always been the home of seamen. At present it is in the occupation of Mr Cecil Wilson, a merchant seaman and his wife and 10-year-old daughter, Penny.

The ghost is of the aggressive kind and throws articles of all kinds about the place; candlesticks, toys, brushes, shoes, and even a cribbage board – this last being thrown down the stairs after Mr Wilson. An ornamental china boat was also thrown at Mr Wilson on another occasion. The family also complained of thumps and creaks, lights coming and going, weird shadows on the wall; the ghost had even turned out a drawer.

The Wilson's at first complained to the police that a ghost was plaguing them. The police were unable to help. Eventually on December 15th, 1952, Canon Tucker Harvey exorcised the ghost. He prayed "that God Almighty, who has power over all things, will bear away this evil spirit which is terrifying his children.

The ghost was not seen or heard again.

An Attic in Lincoln

Sounds of heavy objects being dragged about in empty attics, slow measured ghostly footsteps over creaking boards of a back attic were heard at the home of Dr Richard Prewer at 3 Greenstone Place, Lincoln. Upon one occasion the doctor's ten-year-old son ran down the stairs, terrified after hearing a noise like the dragging of a big bundle of sticks over the attic floor above the boys room. Dr Prewer ran upstairs immediately and was in time to hear something moving about overhead and then the sound of a door being slammed.

On examination the attic was found to be empty. The dust on the floor showed no trace of disturbance and the only door that could have slammed was jammed open. There are no rats in the house and no trees that could brush against the attic roofs. These mysterious happenings prompted Dr Prewer to write an account of them to a hospital journal in December 1953.

It was discovered that "ghostly noises" were heard in the house long before Dr Prewer went to live there. A patient related to the doctor, without the matter having been mentioned, that on one occasion when she and her mother were looking over the house when it was empty, some years before, the row of servants bells in the kitchen began swinging all together. Yet no one was in the house. Later they both heard sounds identical with those that might have been made by someone walking about one of the upstairs rooms. Yet again the rooms were empty.

At one time during the tenancy of a former owner the servants refused to sleep in the attics because of the ghostly footsteps heard there.

CHAPTER SEVENTEEN

Longevity – Old Parr and Henry Jenkins

It was considered for many years that Thomas Parr – Old Parr – was the oldest man that ever lived, in England at any rate. It may be that India and China could cap this but we have no reliable records for so long ago.

Thomas Parr was born in 1483, at a time before the registration of births and deaths was compulsory, and also at a time when entries in Parish Registers was somewhat erratic. He died in 1635, aged 152, and his great age seems to have been accepted as fact. Dr Harvey, the discoverer of the circulation of the blood, examined the body of Parr, at the request of Charles I and declared there were no signs of decay.

Parr was born at Winmington, Alberbury, near Shrewsbury, the son of a small landowner. He spent most of his life on the land cultivating the small property left to him by his parents. He did not marry until he was 80 and sired a son and a daughter, and later he had another son.

Ten years after his first wife's death, when he was aged 122, he married again. At this time he commenced to tour the country, and continued to do so for the rest of his life. He visited Coventry in 1635, the year of his death. His fame reached the Court, and Charles sent for him upon one occasion. Thomas Parr was received at the Court of St James, and Charles asked, "You have lived longer than other men. What is it that you have done more than other men?"

Old Parr replied simply, "I did penance when I was an hundred years old, sire."

When asked what his religion was, he said, "The King's, always."

When Thomas Parr died in 1635 he was buried in Westminster Abbey, where his epitaph reads:

Thos. Parr of ye county of Salop

Born in AD 1483

He lived in the reigns of ten princes, viz.

King Edward IV,

King Edward V,
King Richard III,
King Henry VII,
King Henry VIII,
King Edward VI,
Queen Mary,
Queen Elizabeth,
King James,

and King Charles.

Aged 152 years, and was buried here November 15th, 1635.

It was said that at the age of 130 years Thomas Parr could still thresh corn. The fame of Thomas Parr is, however, eclipsed by that of Henry Jenkins of Ellerton-on-Swale, Yorkshire.

He died in 1676 aged 169, and there is evidence of his great age.

A lawyer in the course of his business visited the village of Ellerton. He was searching for anyone that could remember the death of a man that had occurred over 100 years ago. He had been informed that only at Ellerton would he be likely to find men old enough to remember the man he was enquiring about, and he was told that Ellerton had several centenarians.

A thatched cottage was pointed out to the lawyer as being a likely place to enquire. Here lived a shrivelled up old man who looked to be well over a hundred years of age. However, he said that his memory was not too good and told the lawyer;

"No, I kens nowt of it, I tell ee. Ask my feyther, and maybe he'll have a mind."

The man of law felt convinced he was being hoaxed and that this was supposed to be part of a huge joke. Surely this aged man could not have a father still alive. However, the man showed the lawyer to the door and pointed to another thatched cottage opposite, and there the lawyer went.

Here he found a much older man crouching over the fire. His advanced age was apparent, and he was also far advanced in senile decay, but he was able to tell his enquirer that his father was in the garden chopping wood and that maybe he could tell the lawyer what he wanted to know.

All this is perfectly true. Out in the garden, in his shirtsleeves, was Henry Jenkins, who had been born in 1500. It was now 1650. Henry was able to give the required information and he spat on the silver given him by the lawyer. He died in 1670 at the age of 169.

There is an obelisk to his memory in the churchyard at Bolton-le-Swale. It has been estimated that if he attended church regularly he must have made 27,000 attendances at this church during his life. There is an entry in the Parish Register that describes him as a very aged and poor man. It is recorded that he gave evidence in a lawsuit in 1667, concerning the tittles of Catterick Church. Here it was stated he was "aged one hundred fifty and seven, or thereabouts."

There is a letter concerning Henry Jenkins written by a lady about the time of Charles II. She says, "Being one day in my sister's kitchen, Henry Jenkins coming in to beg an alms. I had a mind to examine him. He said that to the best of his remembrance he was born about one hundred and sixty-two or sixty-three years ago. I asked him what public event he could longest remember and he said, "Flodden Field" in 1513. 'For I was sent to North Allerton with a horseload of arrows, but they sent a bigger boy from thence to the army with them.' There were also four or five in the same parish that were reputed all of them to be a hundred years old or within two or three year of it, and they all said he was an elderly man ever since they knew him".

Henry Jenkins had one hobby only during his long life, which was fishing in the Swale. He had lived through all the religious and political changes of the Reformation, the hangings of Henry, the confiscation's of Edward, the burnings of Mary, the Puritan reactions and the licence of the Restoration.

It seems these things mattered little to him, so long as he could fish!

CHAPTER EIGHTEEN

The Ghost of Brook Drive, London

An interesting article from the London Evening News – February 27th, 1954:

"The Ghost of Brook Drive has had its way. One by one the interlopers have left the first floor flat of the old house in Brook Drive, Southwark. Now, from tonight it is free to roam above in the big gloomy rooms.

"First to go was 19-year old Mrs Marion Read and her two-year-old son Stephen. Mrs Read went to stay with her mother, 36yr old Mrs Rose Geary and her stepfather just before Christmas. After several weeks of being awakened in the night by strange noises she went back to her own home in Mardyke Street, Southwark.

"Then, a week ago, Mrs Geary left the flat to stay with her daughter, while her husband stayed on there. By yesterday, he too had decided to go, and Mrs Read told the story of ghostly happenings today.

'I slept in the back room when I stayed with mother,' she said. 'I would put brooches and earrings on the mantelpiece and every morning they would be thrown off on to the floor. 'Every night always at 11.45 there would be a raking sound in the fireplace. My baby son would wake up crying and say, "A pussy cat keeps tickling my face" and "what is that big shadow over in the corner?"'

"There was no cat in the flat.

"Mr John Geary, a 37 year old driver, slept in the flat until last night. But, he said, he would feel himself going ice cold as he stood shaving in the bedroom. From tonight he will join his wife in Mardyke Street."

The Ferry Boat Inn, Holywell

On March 18th, 1954, at the Ferry Boat Inn, Holywell, hunters were assembled for what must have been the biggest ghost hunt in the history of psychic research. Over 300 people crowded in and around the 903-year-old inn.

The object was to wait and watch for 19-year-old Juliet Tousley, who committed suicide there in 1050. She made her first appearance in 1953 – her first appearance in recent times, that is, for she is reputed to have haunted the Ferry Boat Inn for nine centuries.

In anticipation on March 18th, extra police were called out to cope with a stream of coaches, cars and motorcycles. The village of Holywell, population 578, had never seen a sight quite like it. Members of the Society for Psychic Research filled the Ferry Boat with electric cables, an infrared image converter and other equipment. An hour's extension had been granted the Inn so that drinks could be obtained up to 11pm.

Juliet was due at midnight.

Landlord Jack Rodd waited and watched with the rest after 11 o'clock, though up until then he had been too busy serving drinks to discuss the ghost. However, nothing happened. It never does when they are expected - for ghosts do not appear to order.

The Brown Lady, Kent

The ghost of the Brown Lady is said to haunt the 14th Century rectory in the village of Southfleet, Kent. The peculiarity of this particular ghost is that it only appears inside the rectory. The Brown Lady, in her long flowing brown cloak, has never been seen out-of-doors. A former vicar, the Reverend Marcus Falloon, when he lived in the rectory he would say he had seen the Brown Lady and that she appeared regularly. He also said that she appeared to walk through a door that is no longer there.

The explanation here is that the rectory was once part of a monastery and that the door in question may have bricked up at a subsequent time. The late Reverend Marcus Falloon was a very sincere man whose word may be relied upon. He was a man of great integrity.

Even some of the villagers are scared of seeing the ghost at night, in spite of assurances that the Brown Lady has never been seen out-of-doors. Few of the local people will go near the rectory after dark. People who have been along the lane past the rectory after dark have complained of an uncanny atmosphere and of feeling icy cold.

It is said that late in the 16th Century, when the rectory was part of a monastery, one of the village girls crept secretly into the monastery and seduced one of the monks. The tale goes that she was discovered before she could leave the monastery and as a punishment the girl and the monk were buried alive and ever since she has haunted the inside of the building.

The Lockkeeper's House on the Thames

Hauntings have been reported from many and various places but a lockkeeper's house on the Thames and not far from London is surely the most unlikely of all. The house is in a rather remote spot near the lock but not actually on it. It is on the riverbank, and at present is used as the assistant lockkeeper's house. It is a primitive building with stone floors downstairs. In the gable is carved the date, 1812, and the name of the lockkeeper of that period. The date is probably that of a restoration or re-building as the style of construction of the main building is of a somewhat earlier period than 1812.

About 45 years ago a man and his grown up family occupied the house. They complained they were restless there and never felt settled, furthermore all the doors in the house were constantly found open no matter how securely they had been closed. Also footsteps were heard in various parts of the house. After a few years the man retired and a younger man took his place, a man who had been the assistant lockkeeper and had much experience of the other locks on the Thames.

The newcomer had a wife and an 8-year-old son. These people experienced the same restlessness as the former tenants, the doors would not stay closed and the footsteps were heard in addition. The little boy complained that while in bed at night, "a man in a funny hat" would sometimes sit on the side of the bed and smile at him. This in itself did not seem to frighten the boy so much as it alarmed his parents. The "funny hat" the boy described may of course be of an earlier period, say a tall hat of the 1800's. The extraordinary thing is the father could never at any time hear the footsteps or see anything in the boys bedroom. He did, however, testify that the doors were always found open after being closed.

The little boy is now grown up and is a family man himself, but the present writer has heard him declare he would not sleep in that house again for a thousand pounds.

Dr Jessop's Visitor, Norfolk

From Mannington Hall near Blickling in Norfolk comes one of the best-authenticated ghost stories of modern times. A well-known and learned chronicler, the late Doctor Jessop, at one time chaplain to King Edward VIII, gives the report. Dr Jessop related his strange experience during his visit to Mannington Hall in October 1879. The house contained a good library of books, some of which were of deep interest to Dr Jessop and one night he sat up late making notes from some of these rare books. The family had retired to rest and Dr Jessop was writing in a room adjoining the library.

'It was after one o'clock," Dr Jessop says. "I was just beginning to think that my work was drawing to a close, when, as I was actually writing, I saw a large white hand within a foot of my elbow. Turning my head there sat a figure of a somewhat large man with his back to the fire, bending slightly over the table and apparently examining the pile of books that I had been at work upon. The man's face was turned away from me, but I saw his closely-cut, reddish brown hair, his ear and shaved cheek, the eyebrow, the corner of his right eye, the side of the forehead and the large high cheekbone.

"He was dressed in what I can only describe as a kind of ecclesiastical habit of thick corded silk, or some such material. It was close up to the throat and a narrow rim or edging about an inch broad of satin or velvet served as a stand-up collar, and fitted close to the chin. The right hand, which first attracted my attention, was clasping without any great pressure, the left hand. Both hands were in perfect repose, and the large blue veins of the right hand were conspicuous. I remember thinking that the hand was like the hand of a Velasquez's magnificent "Dead Knight" in the National Gallery.

"I looked at my visitor for some seconds, and was perfectly sure that he was a reality. A thousand thoughts came crowding upon me, but not the least feeling of alarm or even of uneasiness. Curiosity and a strong interest were uppermost. For an instant I felt eager to make a sketch of my friend, and I looked at a tray on my right for a pencil, then thought of my sketchbook upstairs and wondered if I should fetch it. There he sat and I was fascinated, afraid not of staying but lest he should go. Stopping in my writing I lifted my hand from the paper, stretched it out to a pile of books and moved the top one.

"I cannot explain why I did this. My arm passed in front of the figure and it vanished. Much astonished, I went on with my writing perhaps for another five minutes, and had actually got to the last few words of the extract when the figure appeared again, exactly in the same place and attitude as before.

"I saw the hand close to my own: I turned my head again to examine him more closely, and was framing a sentence to address to him when I discovered that I did not dare to speak. I was afraid of the sound of my own voice! There he sat, and there sat I. I turned my head again to my work and finished the two or three words still remaining to be written. The paper and my notes are at this moment before me, and exhibit not the slightest tremor or nervousness. I could point out the words I was writing when the phantom came, and when he disappeared. Having finished my task I shut the book and threw it on the table. It made some slight noise as it fell – and the figure vanished. Not until then did I feel nervous, but it was only for a second.

"I replaced the books in the adjoining room, blew out the candles on the table and retired to my rooms marvelling at my calmness under such strange circumstances."

Beckington Castle, Somerset

Beckington Castle in Somerset, a fine many-gabled house dating from the time of James I was empty for many years thus it became neglected and deserted. The reason was that it had the reputation of being haunted by not one, but several various ghosts. There were tales of mysterious subterranean passages and no one could be persuaded to stay there. It was at one time offered for sale for 100 pounds, and still no buyer could be found. It is even said that James II slept here the night before the battle of Sedgemoor.

In Somerset generally, the remote parts abound in superstitions, or at least they did until recent times. It is, or was, considered a sure cure for ague if the sufferer would capture a spider or starve it to death. Consumptives can be eased if not cured by being carried through a flock of sheep in the morning when the animals are first let out. It is said to be lucky if a fly should drop into a mug or glass of beer at the time the beer is being consumed. There is also a belief in second sight and of people being bewitched. To be overlooked means certain misfortune.

Mr Allen Fea in his excellent book "Nooks and Corners of Old England" mentions a case of the wife of an innkeeper at Combe St Nicholas, near Ilminster. The inn, "The Green Dragon" was burned down some years ago.

"The old landlady we remember had a firm belief that the death of one of her sons was foretold by a death's-head moth flying in and the window and settling on his forehead when he was asleep in his cradle. The child, a beautiful boy, then in perfect health, was doomed, and her eldest son immediately set forth with his gun to shoot the first bird he chanced to see, in order to break the spell. However, that night the child died, and upon the wall in a glass case was the stuffed bird as well as the moth, a melancholy memento of the tragedy of thirty years ago."

This was written in 1907.

CHAPTER NINETEEN

Unlucky Houses

There have been many accounts of reputed unlucky houses; at one time they were termed "houses with a curse on them", or "houses that were possessed by the evil one".

However, not all unlucky houses are old, in fact some are quite modern. Further, it would seem that both small and large houses are likely to be affected and of course not only dwelling houses but also other buildings can also be "cursed, or possessed by the evil one". Mills, theatres, schools, etc., have at various times been thought to be harbingers of ill luck to those who conduct them or use them. Superstitions or not there certainly do seem to be houses and other buildings which bring nothing but misfortune to tenants or owners.

The present writer knows several such houses; for eighteen years I lived next door to a house in a SE London suburb. If ever a house merited the term "cursed" this one surely did. Not one of its tenants – and it had twelve in the eighteen years I knew it – was known to prosper or to be free of the direst misfortune while they lived there.

During the period 1890 – 1914, there was one case of wife-murder, three cases of wife desertion, 3 children died, 5 cases of serious accidents to children, such as broken limbs or other serious illness. Upon two occasions a whole family moved out into the workhouse. In every case the families were in robust health when they first took up residence and were all reasonably prosperous.

In connection with these houses or other buildings of evil reputation there are a number of cases where the removal of an article from the house, or in some cases the garden, is thought to bring misfortune to the individual that removed it. So much misfortune in fact that he or she is glad to return the article or substance in order to nullify the evil or curse that seems to follow all those that possess it or even handle it.

Disturbing the Dead

There are numerous cases in various parts of the United Kingdom of curses and spells of ill luck that have been known to follow the removal or disturbance of a dead body or part of it, particularly the skull, and especially if the person had died a violent death or had been the victim of murder.

Many people hold strong views against disturbing the dead even apart from the fear of a curse. Such sacrilege is held to be un-Christian to say the least. There are well known cases of screaming skull phenomena, of which there are several up and down England.

Bettiscombe Farm near Bridport, Dorset; A manor farm at Chilton Cantelo, Somerset; a large farm at Tunstead, near Chapel-en-le-Frith; a manor house in Sussex and another at Burton Agnes Hall, near Bridlington and a manor house in the Lake District.

In every case the houses are very old and have had but little restoration architecturally for a long period. Perhaps the most pathetic story is that concerning the Ambleside screaming skull, or rather in this case two skulls. The account is very ancient and no dates are available. It seems that a farm at Ambleside was coveted by a wealthy and consequently influential magistrate, who at various times had made the farmer substantial offers for the property. The offers were always refused for the simple reason that the farm was indispensable.

Eventually the magistrate, one Myles Phillipson, accused the farmer and his wife of the theft of a silver cup, the property of the magistrate and which he himself had caused to be placed in the farmer's pocket. Theft was at this period a capital offence and the couple were arrested and brought before the magistrate. The farmer and his wife, Kraster and Dorothy Cook were sentenced to death. At once the wife pronounced a curse on the magistrate and "all his breed", declaring that the time would surely come when Phillipson should not own an inch of land. She also threatened to haunt the house night and day. "Never will ye be rid of us."

According to the local account all these things duly came to pass. The farmer and his wife were hanged for a crime they never committed. Some months after, two ghastly grinning human skulls were one night discovered on a ledge at the top of a staircase in the magistrate's house. The skulls were at once taken out and buried at some distance from the house. That same night screams and groans were heard throughout the house, much of course to the dismay of the entire household who experienced a still further shock in the morning when the two skulls were discovered back in their place at the head of the staircase.

The same thing happened on many subsequent occasions and over a considerable period. The skulls were even smashed and burned but always recovered and were back again on the staircase the next morning.

Eventually the curse went the full circle. Nothing that Phillipson did would prosper and at length he did actually lose all his land and house property.

Borley Rectory, Suffolk

A somewhat similar case, of the evil following the removal of an article from a haunted house, comes from Borley Rectory near Sudbury, Suffolk. This is of a much more recent date. Borley Rectory was built in 1863. It was a typical mid-Victorian red brick villa residence of 25 rooms. It was without mains water or electricity, and was burned to the ground in 1939.

The house at one time had the reputation of being the most haunted house in England although the haunting did not actually come to public notice until 1929. The site of the rectory is haunted to this day. It would seem the rectory had been erected on the site of a nunnery. The haunting takes various forms. A nun has been seen also strange lights, luminous patches on the walls, footsteps are heard, formerly the footsteps were heard in the house but now that the house is no longer there the footsteps are heard in the courtyard and on the lawn. Not only human footsteps but the padding of an invisible dog. Also seen in the yard is a phantom coach.

These sensational manifestations are reported over a period of 50 years. The accounts are well founded; there are dozens of signed statements of observers or ghost hunters who at various times have spent a night or several nights at Borley. There are no less than 2,000 poltergeist manifestations between 1930 and 1935.

At present a poultry farmer occupies the coach house, the only part of the rectory that escaped the fire, and the adjacent land. During the summer months the farmer takes boarders, and it is known that when a pebble is taken from the farm by any of the visitors as a souvenir, the pebble is said to bring such bad luck to the holder that in many cases they are glad to return it to the farm.

The poultry farmer, a Mr Williams, is a retired engineer and has been at Borley for three and a half years. He reports having seen a glow, a mysterious light in his bedroom at night-time and one heard footsteps following him in the yard at the back, he turned around but could see no one, and ran to the corner of the coach-house but no one was in sight. Mr Williams thinks he has seen the ghost of the nun on one occasion. He was in one of the chicken-houses and in broad daylight he saw a figure pass the window, "just a vague outline," he says.

In recent months according to the Rev A.C. Henning the present rector of Borley, mysterious footsteps have been heard and more remarkable still, organ notes have been heard from Borley Church when the church was known to be empty and locked. The church stands opposite the site of the rectory, across the road. In 1945 part of a female skull was unearthed under the cellar of the former rectory. The Rev. A.C. Henning had this put in a casket and he buried it in consecrated ground on May 29, 1945.

The first time a spectre was actually seen at the rectory was on July 28, 1900. Ghostly footsteps had been heard previously on various occasions but on this particular night the three daughter of the rector, Rev H.D.E. Bull, who had built the rectory in 1863, had returned from a garden party when they saw the figure of a nun dressed in black. They watched as the figure crossed the lawn in front of the rectory. One of those sisters is still living at Sudbury and still maintains that she and he sisters saw the apparition of the nun on the eventful evening in 1900. Furthermore, she saw the nun again in November of the same year. Servants of the Bull family, Edward Cooper and his wife have stated they too had seen the nun.

There are recorded statements of 16 people that saw the nun during the next twenty years. The Coopers lived in a cottage near the rectory, they reported frequent disturbances at night during the three years they occupied the cottage from 1916 to 1919. They saw the black shape of a man in their bedroom and hear a dog trotting about. Edward Cooper saw from his bedroom window a coach drive silently through the rectory farmyard. This coach was seen twice subsequently, and it proceeded through hedges and even buildings.

By 1929 Borley Rectory had become famous as a haunted place, not only the rectory but the lawns and gardens. Eventually its fame spread to a well-known ghost hunter, Mr Harry price. He wrote various books and articles on ghosts and spirit manifestations, and he also broadcast on these subjects. He was the means of exposing a number of fraudulent spirit mediums.

Borley seems to have fascinated Harry price when he visited it in 1929 and when the rectory was up to let in 1937 he decided to take it on as lease. Having taken it he started one of the biggest and best-organised ghost hunts of modern times. Price advertised in The Times for responsible persons of leisure and intelligence, intrepid, critical and unbiased, "to join a rota of observers in a year's 'night and day' investigation of alleged haunted house in the home counties."

Price received a large number of replies and in due course he had an organised party of 48 observers, among them an army colonel, a doctor, an engineer and an official from the Bank of England. These men kept watch in the eerie unfurnished rectory and took it in turns to sleep in the Blue Room. This was said to be the centre of the ghost walking activities, the room in which the nun had been most often seen. Harry Price had insisted upon them signing an agreement not to divulge anything seen or heard during their vigil.

In due course the party made out reports to Harry Price of muffled footsteps, dragging noises, the smell of incense and a number of poltergeist activities such as the movement of books and other objects, also those were mysterious pencil masks that appeared on the walls and flashes of light. Alas, after all the elaborate preparations and watching the nun was never seen by these ghost hunters and eventually Price left the rectory and the place was taken by Captain W.H. Gregson but the house was burned to the ground on February 17th, 1939.

There are reports from the villagers and others that even as the house was burning figures were seen moving in the flames neat the window of the Blue Room. These were figures in cloaks, one a girl, another a formless figure seen leaving the blazing house.

Eventually, Harry Price wrote, "The Most Haunted House in England", published in 1940. It contains an account of all the phenomena in detail. These accounts are certainly very convincing and it does not seem possible that all the observers could have been tricked in any way. Besides similar happenings had been reported to very many people some years previously. It would indeed be difficult to contradict or doubt so many signed statements made over a long period. However, there were doubters and they criticised the records of Price, much to his discomfit.

When Price died in 1948, the Society for Psychical Research made an independent investigation of the whole subject of the hauntings. This eventually included a systematic checking of the papers and reports of Harry Price regarding the haunting of Borley.

Wardley Hall, Lancashire

Another well-known case of a screaming skull concerns Wardley Hall, Lancashire. Briefly it is this: one of the courtiers of Charles II, Roger Downes by name while out one night with some of his companions one night was rash enough to insult a girl, a tailor who came to the girls rescue was immediately killed by Downes. He was of course arrested and brought before a magistrate and charged with murder. The social status of Downes was such that he was acquitted and discharged. This had a very bad effect on Downes. Instead of reforming he drifted into a life of debauchery and crime.

Friends of his victim the tailor however were determined to avenge his death and one evening some months after the trial when the sister of Downes and their cousin were entertaining their friends at Wardley Hall a servant brought in a box which had just been delivered from London. It was addressed to the sister. Upon opening the box Roger's sister was horrified to discover the head of her brother inside.

A note was enclosed which read. "Thy brother has at last paid the penalty for his crimes. The wages of sin are death. Last night passing over London Bridge he engaged in another drunken brawl with the watchmen, one of whom sliced off his head and threw it into the river, from whence it was rescued by an eye-witness and sent to thee as a memento."

Greatly shocked, the sister gave orders that the ghostly skull should be buried. This was done but the next day it was back again in the house. When it was again removed terrible screams were heard every night in the Hall that so alarmed the household that eventually they decided to let the skull remain in the house in order to ensure peace and quiet.

After many years, actually in the 1890 period, the skull was moved from its usual place to another part of the house. That night a great storm arose that did such dreadful damage that it was thought to have been brought about through the removal of the skull. It was forthwith restored to its original site – a recess made especially for it near the top of the staircase, and where it still rests to this day.

These accounts are of course traditions although well known ones and of great age. It is not possible now to say how much truth is in them, however, in every case the persons named did actually exist and much of the account as regards the cause of the hauntings are recorded historical fact. To believe that the skulls returned again and again to the houses, and that evil follows their removal savours of witchcraft, therefore to believe such things is to believe in witchcraft.

It is remarkable that some hauntings, even apart from those of the screaming skulls, have persisted at regular intervals for a considerable period – well over 200 years in some instances.

Chester-le-Street, County Durham

A case in point is that of the White Lady that is said to haunt Lumley Castle, near Chester-le-Street, in County Durham. Reliable witnesses have seen this apparition over a period of 200 years and as recently as July 1954. The present steward of the castle, Mr Fred Mitchell, relates that he has seen the ghost of the White Lady quite distinctly literally dozens of times, and not always at night-time. She wanders in all parts of the castle; even into the servants old quarters, but is seen mostly coming down the main staircase.

This ghost is said to walk and not glide as most of them do. Mr Mitchell says the White Lady completely ignores him if he is standing at a window on the staircase. The cause or object of these wanderings or even the exact identity of the lady is now lost in antiquity. Lumley Castle was the seat of the Earl of Scarborough, John Lumley-Savile.

A remarkable case of poltergeist haunting – that is, a ghost that is heard and can make its presence felt but is not seen – comes from a hotel at Chester-le-Street, County Durham. The building is mainly modern but it m be built on the site of an ancient monastery. This poltergeist actually plays an invisible organ, and he or she has never been seen by anyone. The music is always heard at night and at various times between 1230am and 2am. As regards the music, there is not an actual melody but only chords. One chord will be repeated or at times only played once, and this is usually followed by two chords in harmony repeated several times. As a finale all the keys of the organ are played at once as if the organist is impatient or in a bad temper. It is significant that the same performance is never repeated, for at each performance – at long intervals – different chords are struck.

There can be no question of wind in the chimneys or tricks of water gurgling in spouts or pipes. The music has been heard when there is no wind at all – on a very still night and all the indoor water pipes and waste pipes have been put to strict tests.

In connection with Chester-le-Street there is another strange tale. Surtees in his "History of Durham" first published this. A girl named Anne Walker who was housekeeper for a kinsman, also named Walker, was about to have a child by him. He took her to the house of Dame Care in Chester-le-Street late one night in November 1630. Mark Sharp, who lived six miles away at Lumley, accompanied him on the journey.

Fourteen days afterwards a man named Graime, a miller who also lived at Lumley saw a young woman, dishevelled, bloodstained and with wounds in her head – he said there were five wounds – standing in a room in his mill. He said she spoke and said her name was Anne Walker and that she had been murdered by Mark Sharp with a colliers pick, he had thrown her body in a coal-pit and had hid the pick under a bank.

According to Graime this apparition appeared upon several occasions subsequently and at last Graime went to a magistrate and told of his adventure. At once a search was made and the body and pick were discovered. Walker and Sharp were arrested and faced their trial at Durham. This was in August 1631. Sharps bloodstained boots were found where the spirit of Anne Walker said he had hidden them – in a stream. There was no direct evidence against Walker, but the judge summed up against Walker and Sharp and they were both found guilty and hanged. They protested their innocence to the last.

It was said afterwards that Graime was himself the murderer, and the chief suspicion against him was that he knew so much about the event. However, Walker and Sharp were last seen with the girl and while Walker may have had a motive, there was certainly no motive so far as can be judged at this distance of time, in the case of Graime. If his tale of the apparition of Anne Walker was untrue then how did he know where the body lay?

A Miss Morton, who was at one time Chief Observer for the Society for Psychical Research reports a case that came to her notice. A lady of far from temperate habits had died in 1878. She was a widow. In April 1882 the house where the lady had died was taken over by Miss Morton's family. Nothing unusual happened until June, then one night Miss Morton saw the apparition of the lady, though no one else saw it.

The ghost was of a tall old lady in widows' weeds holding a handkerchief to her face as she walked downstairs. From 1882 to 1884 Miss Morton saw the ghost six times but did not mention this to the rest of the family. A sister of Miss Morton's had seen the ghost of the old lady in 1882, a maid saw it in 1883 and two boys saw it in the same year. On several occasions

Miss Morton followed the spectre from the stairs and spoke to it, but it merely uttered a faint gasp as if unable to speak.

As a test Miss Morton stretched threads across the stairs at night, but the ghost always descended without disturbing them, yet her footsteps could be heard on the stairs. This ghost could not, or did not, make any noise at all beyond light pushes at doors and very light footsteps, and it was material enough to make a slight noise as it walked but not material enough to brush away a thread.

There have been many similar instances.

CHAPTER TWENTY

The Curse of the Pharaohs

Not a new story by any means, but a notable case of such manifestation is of course the mummy of reputed ill fame in the British Museum. Whenever the mummy has been moved all the people who have in any way helped in its removal – even those who did not actually handle it – have been speedily overtaken by ill luck and in some cases even death. This is recorded fact. Even a sign-writer in the Museum, who happened to have been employed in the Mummy Room and died of natural causes, was thought to have been a victim of the curse.

In 1923, Lord Caernarfon financed the excavations in the Valley of the Kings in Egypt. This was to lead to the discovery of the fabulous golden shrine in which, covered in jewels, Tutankhamun, the boy King of Egypt who had been buried 30 centuries before. 1335 BC. A curse was thought to follow all those who in any way assisted to open and disturb the tomb - the Curse of the Pharaohs. Even those people who had only examined the relics some months later were thought to be victims of the curse.

The Valley of the Kings, on the banks of the Nile 450 miles from Cairo, was the burial ground of many of the greatest kings of ancient Egypt. Here were laid to rest the mummified corpses of at least 40 Pharaohs. In connection with the opening of the tomb of Tutankhamun, which was without doubt the greatest archaeological discovery of modern times 20 people in all are said to have died mysterious or violent deaths, these are thought to have been victims of the curse. In the tomb Lord Caernarfon found a delicate alabaster vase, which was semi-transparent. Round the neck of the vase were the words, "Death shall come to him who toucheth the tomb of a Pharaoh."

Lord Caernarfon looked into the vase in the light of a match and remarked to one of the party present that he could detect some kind of aroma. He dipped his hand into the opening of the vase and quickly withdrew it with a little exclamation. On the tip of his finger was a tiny drop of blood. He put his finger to his mouth and took no more notice of it. One of the party then put his hand into the vase and at the bottom found an incrustation as sharp as needles.

These little incidents were re-called when Lord Caernarfon died in a Cairo hospital on April the 5th 1923. The medical reasons given were septic pneumonia following erysipelas. In a few weeks an American Jay Gould died of pneumonia following a cold, which in turn was brought on while visiting the tomb. In the following July, Prince Ali Fahmy Bey who had inspected the discoveries at Luxor, met a violent death – shot by his wife in their bedroom.

A famous Egyptologist, Dr J.C. Mardrus, said in 1926: "The Egyptians during a period of 7,000 years, knew how to condense around their mummies a dynamism by means of magic ritual and amulets charged with unknown fluids of which we have only the vaguest idea to-day."

It is only fair to add that the idea of a curse is scorned by many Egyptologists who also deny that any such inscription was found on the vase in the tomb. They say that in any case the actual wording is impossible. However there are still a large number of superstitious people who still believe in the Curse of the Pharaohs. In addition to this there are many people who consider it sacrilegious to disturb the tombs or to remove the contents or the mummies. Such people of course like to believe in the Curse.

It was recalled that Arthur Weigall, Inspector General of Antiquities to the Egyptian Government had remarked at the light-hearted way in which Lord Caernarfon treated the opening of the tomb, which was in itself generally considered a serious undertaking. Seeing Lord Caernarfon laughing and joking with his friends on the morning of the actual opening of the tomb, Arthur Weigall remarked, "If he goes down in that spirit I give him six weeks to live."

The tomb was opened on Friday February 17th, 1923, and Lord Caernarfon died as stated above on April 5th in a Cairo hospital.

After this any sudden or violent death of a member of the party or in fact anyone that had even handled or examined the relics was ascribed to the Curse. Sir Lee Stack, a visitor to the tomb was assassinated in Cairo in 1924. Dr Jonathon Carver, a geologist who had assisted in the excavations was killed in a car accident in 1929. Two French Egyptologists, M. Benedite and M. Pasanova, both died suddenly. Both had taken part in research at Luxor three years before.

The death of another Egyptologist, Mr H.E. Evelyn White was attributed to the Curse. He committed suicide and it is reported that he had said, "I knew there was a curse on me". An American society woman, Mrs E. Waddington Greely also committed suicide. Both had visited the tomb of Tutankhamun.

In 1930 Lord Westbury, who had some of the relics from the tomb, committed suicide by jumping from a 70ft window. A child of 8 years of age, who was accidentally killed by the hearse on its way to Lord Westbury's funeral, was thought to be a further victim of the curse, although it must be admitted on somewhat slender grounds. Further, an American playwright, A. Liggins, who had written a play on the subject, dropped dead in the street in Detroit.

Arthur Weigall, above mentioned, was one of the Egyptologists who believed in the Curse. He died at the age of 53 in 1934 in poverty. He died of an unknown fever according to the newspapers and he was described as the 21st victim of the Curse of Tutankhamun.

When Sir Percy Loraine was appointed High Commissioner in Egypt in 1929 he was invited to visit the tomb of Tutankhamun. One of his bodyguards in the 12th Royal Lancers was a Mr A. George on this occasion. Upon reaching the Valley of the Kings the whole party were met by Mr Howard Carter and conducted to the various tombs. While in the tomb of the Boy King, Mr George obtained as a souvenir of the visit a small piece of stone chipped from the sarcophagus in the inner chamber; he etched his name and the date and place on the stone. Three days later in Alexandria, a train knocked down Mr George: his left leg was severed and he had other serious injuries that nearly caused his death.

CHAPTER TWENTY-ONE

The Massacre of Mountain Meadow

The doings of Brigham Young have been the subject of much ink and breath. In his early years he had been a carpenter and house painter but he seemed to be of a restless spirit and in 1832 he went to Meridian, NY, and was converted to Mormonism. Joining Joseph Smith at Kirtland, Ohio, he was sent on a missionary tour to Canada. In 1847 Young founded Salt Lake City and in due course he was appointed Governor of Utah.

Things continued to prosper and Brigham Young became a powerful man, and in fact became a law unto himself, as the saying goes. So arrogant was he that ten years later President Buchanan appointed Alfred Commings Governor of Utah, and dispatched a force of 2500 troops under General J.P. Johnston to bring Young to terms of submission and order. The followers of Young wanted to fight but he knew he was in the wrong so he wisely gave in and laid down his arms and received the governor's pardon.

Not all of the follower's of Brigham Young were Americans; for he sent missionaries to all parts of the world to recruit fresh disciples and many converts were thus obtained. There was a big outcry in England in 1864, and at later dates, against these recruiting missions but it made very little difference to the results. Numbers of English people joined the Mormons and settled in Salt Lake City.

Brigham Young died in 1877, aged 76 years. He left seventeen widows and forty-two children. He also left between two or three million dollars, a vast fortune in those days.

In 1857 a party of 170 emigrants, well-to-do people, set out from Arkansas and Missouri for California far across the mountains. The means of transport in these days was ox-wagons. These were quite respectable people; men, women and children. They were anxious to better their condition. The way was long, hot and dusty, with overpowering heat by day, danger from Indians and wolves by night, and of course the fatigue and hunger incidental to such a journey. Supplies of food ran short and were difficult to obtain. When the emigrants reached Utah they attempted to get food; they wanted no charity for they had the money to pay for their needs but they were denied any assistance. The only explanation given for this refusal was that Brigham Young had instructed his Mormon followers that he would sentence them to death – he actually had this power at that time – if they gave food, clothing, medicine or any help whatever to these emigrants.

The reason for this cruel order was that just previously a furious husband in Arkansas had killed a member of the Mormon Church – one Elder Pratt – who had stolen his wife, taken her to Utah and Mormonised her. The emigrants were thus forced to push on a little further to the Mountain Meadow. Here Indians savagely attacked them. However, they fought their attackers and managed to barricade themselves in. They were safe for a time but soon afterwards the Mormon militia attacked them, and these in turn were repelled but the emigrants were now self-made prisoners.

They needed water from a spring just outside their stockade so two little girls were dressed in white and sent for the water, as it was thought the children would be safe from attack. However, they had not gone many yards when there was a roar and a flash from the Mormon militia and the little girls fell dead. After this cold-blooded double murder the emigrants were desperate. They made the sign of distress and sent a petition to the Mormons signed by the Odd Fellows and the Masons to brother Mormon members of their particular lodge.

One of the emigrants, a Methodist, raised his voice and hands in prayer in blessing over the heads of three men who bravely volunteered to go out and present the petition for relief, but these too were shot down like dogs. Days passed and then some Mormon wagons approached the stockade waving a white flag of truce, declaring that if the emigrants would surrender and lay down their arms they might walk out unharmed and be at perfect liberty.

This was eagerly agreed to. First came the men, then the women and children. They gladly marched out from the barricade. At a given signal the Mormon militia with guns and knives murdered the old, the young, the men and the women, the parents and the children. All were killed except only a few children thought to be too young to tell the awful story. The women that were too old or too weak to walk were dragged out to where their dead lay and were then stripped naked and shot dead, their bodies being piled up in heaps. After this the Mormons took their victims jewellery, clothing, stock and wagons to the amount of $300,000,

All this is recorded history. Fifteen years later when John D. Lee the Mormon Bishop was on trial in court, he testified that in the massacre of the emigrants he was only acting on orders and that Brigham Young had given orders how the property of the murdered emigrants was to be distributed. It is said that in later years, Brigham Young visited the scene of the murder. He learned that the U.S. Government officers had gathered up the bones of the murdered emigrants buried there, and placed a head board over the large grave with the inscription, "Vengeance is mine, I will repay saith the Lord." Young gave orders to have it torn down.

From that day it is said that Brigham Young knew no peace. He was set by various diseases and was continually wracked by pain. His Mormons were never accepted by the American public, and continuously persecuted by the U.S. Government. Present day Mormons deny that the killings ever took place, and say it was all a plot on the part of the Government to shame them for all time.

The place of this hideous massacre, the Mountain Meadow, is said to be haunted. There are many accounts from travellers, and people unknowingly camping in the area, of dying screams from men and women and the heart-rending cries of children. It is said that the Mormons must enjoy their life on earth, for surely they will know no peace in the hereafter, for their religion is tainted by the terrible crimes committed by their sect in the year 1857.

CHAPTER TWENTY-TWO

The Ill-Fated Great Eastern

Towards the end of the year 1854 the building was commenced at Millwall of the largest steamship in the world, at that time. The vessel was designed by Isambard K. Brunel and was much more than a 9-day wonder. It was talked about throughout the length and breadth of this country and in fact the world. The engineer Brunel was of course a famous designer of bridges, many of them are still standing and this giant boat was his pet design. It had five funnels, was 692 feet long and weighed 19,000 tons, which made it five times larger than anything afloat at that time. Furthermore, this record held good until the "Lusitania" was launched in 1906.

The cost of constructing the Great Eastern was over one million pounds and the fitting out cost a further two hundred and fifty thousand pounds.

But the ship was cursed. Nothing but bad luck attended the Great Eastern from the time construction was begun alongside the Thames until she was taken to the ship breakers in 1890. In modern times we should term this ship a Hoodoo ship. It really is a remarkable instance of a curse or evil influence attending a ship. There was trouble from the start. While the frames were being constructed at Millwall, two men fell to their death and yet another man was killed by a falling riveter, who himself was not killed. There was also a visitor to the shipyard killed by a steam hammer.

There was talk at this time of a riveter being, by accident or design, walled up between the plates. The remarkable thing is that there seems to have been no attempt to prove or disprove the facts, the idea was accepted from the first without the slightest effort being made to ascertain if it was true or not.

Of course the boat had to be launched broadside into the Thames. Brunel began this on November 3rd 1857. There was more trouble. The huge hull dragged a windlass with it into the Thames with the result that the wheel of the windless spun round at terrific speed. The men in charge of it were whipped off their feet and flung among the onlookers, with one of the men later dying of his injuries.

Brunel himself with the aid of one of the shipwrights managed to scotch the windlass and the hull settled on the slips and refused to budge. It took 3 months to get her into the water. This extra work cost nearly 100,000 pounds in addition to the original bill. This meant ruin to the owners and the shareholders lost 600,000 pounds. The net result of this was that the ship was taken over by a new company for 160,000 pounds.

It was proposed that the vessel when finished should be put on the Atlantic run. In due course the vessel was finished so far as the work at Millwall was concerned and it was intended to take her to Holyhead, which would be her first voyage - her maiden voyage. Brunel himself was on board for this great event – the fulfilment of his desire.

This was on September 5th 1859, however, the excitement proved too much for him and he was seized with a paralytic stroke. He was carried off the ship and died ten days later. He was only 53 years old.

On September 7th 1859 the ship proceeded at 12 knots down the Thames, but more trouble was in store for this already ill-fated ship. She was to be on show at Holyhead for some time. The first incident occurred off the Kent coast where a water jacket exploded and six of the firemen died. Next began mutiny. Certain members of the crew for some reason refused to holystone the decks, with the ringleaders later being proceeded against and sentenced. However, Holyhead was reached at last and among the first of the sightseers was the Prince Consort.

This was considered to be the event that was to change the luck of the vessel, but in spite of this the owners applied to the Government for assistance. This however was not forthcoming. Troubles followed in quick succession. The first master, Captain Harrison, and a boy were drowned while going ashore. Soon after this the directors resigned and now the locomotive superintendent of the Great Western Railway took charge. This was Daniel Gooch and he seems to have got busy and in a short time, in June 1860 in fact, he sent the ship to New York.

She carried only 35 passengers and a little cargo. There was accommodation for 2000 passengers. There were great rejoicings in New York when the Great Eastern arrived, for nothing so big had ever been seen before and excitement ran high. At Portland, Maine, a 25,000 pounds pier had been built to accommodate the huge ship. In more modern times the owners of such a notorious vessel would have sent competent advance agents to boost its merits and the whole exhibition would have been conducted on business lines.

This was not done, and thus the incompetence of the owners resulted in the Americans becoming less and less enthusiastic. At last they complained at the high cost of tickets to view this unique ship, and of the treatment by the Britishers to American sightseers when they – the Americans – were the worse for drink. The resentment of the Americans was brought to a climax when 2,000 trippers booked a two-day cruise only to find that no sleeping accommodation and no food had been provided, and also the passengers had no protection from the soot and smoke from the 5 funnels.

All of this was of course brought about by lack of competence on the part of the organisers. Even the New York newspapers advised their readers against cruising in the Great Eastern. All this had in due course had a very bad effect on the crew and trouble continued to follow the ship. A quartermaster drank himself to death in his bunk. Two members of the crew were drowned in the North River. Another died in a fight in the boiler-room and a fireman murdered yet another. On the voyage back to Milford Haven, the Great Eastern broke a propeller shaft and after reaching home, two visitors were drowned when their boat was swamped. Then came a claim for 350 pounds damages to the figurehead of HMS Blenheim, when the Great Eastern was swung by the tide against her.

Later it seemed as though the boat was in for a change of luck for she was chartered by the Government to transport 2,000 troops and families to Canada. The crossing took 8 days 6 hours to Cape pine, and was a record, but the charter for some reason or other was not repeated. On the next voyage 27 fare-paying passengers were injured during a storm and this resulted in a passengers committee taking over the engine-room alleging incompetence on the part of the crew.

This of course is further evidence of bad management. Following this was a bill for further repairs for 60,000 pounds. Another ray of hope for prosperity for the Great Eastern sprang up in 1862 when the practical Captain Walter Paton took over command and this man really did try to make a success of it. He restored the popularity of the ship on both sides of the Atlantic.

On his first voyage there were 1500 passengers. The second voyage however was not quite so successful, for the ship hit an uncharted rock off Long Island. The bill for repairs in America was 70,000 pounds and during these repairs occurred the first report or suspicion of the ship being haunted.

Up until now the Great Eastern had been regarded merely as a very unlucky or ill-fated ship – but now one of the divers employed on this repair surfaced hurriedly one day and declared he had heard a ghost. It was now remembered that there had been a story of a riveter who during the construction of the ship at Millwall had been trapped alive between the inner and outer plates. This legend had never really died down since 1854 and had been repeated many times but without any attempt being made to investigate the rumour properly. Now, however, the gossips began to get busy again.

To account for the noise the diver heard, Captain Paton proved that the noise had been caused by and unshackled chain but the gossips would have none of it, and so the original tale of the trapped riveter gained both notoriety and credence. There were some who maintained that the hammering and frantic screams of the imprisoned riveter had been heard above the sounds of the storms or when the ship was thought to be in danger. Still there was no actual investigation.

The popularity of the Great Eastern as a passenger ship dwindled and eventually she was sold for 20,000 pounds and was used as a cable-layer. She was ideally fitted for the job as things transpired. The steadiness of such a huge vessel was a great advantage when laying out thousands of miles of cable.

The first Atlantic cable from Ireland was laid by the Great Eastern as was the cable from France to the US and after that a cable across the Indian Ocean. The cable laying ended, so far as the Great Eastern was concerned, in 1874. After that she became, in turn, a floating theatre and a sort of sideshow with dancing girls in the Mersey, and then later an advertisement hoarding at Liverpool in 1886.

This unkind treatment of such a notorious ship greatly disturbed Mr James Paton, the son of Captain Walter Paton. He declared he would rather blow up the ship than see her so low as to be an advertisement hoarding. James Paton was a chip off the old block, as he had served a marine apprenticeship and then went into business ashore. He was later knighted.

At last, in 1890 the Great Eastern was taken to the ship breakers and there broken up. Now at long last was to be settled the rumour that the ship had carried a murdered riveter between her plates.

In the lower parts of the shell and between the plates, one workman uncovered the skeleton of the riveter, and near him lay another skeleton. This was the riveter's mate, a mere boy. They had been entombed together at the Millwall shipyard nearly 40 years before.

The gossips maintained that this had been the cause of all the misfortunes and calamities that befell the ship and furthermore there were ugly rumours that these two people, the riveter and his boy, had been foully murdered and walled up. Indeed, there appears to have been some evidence to support this, but nothing came of it. James Paton declared that the cause of the failure of the Great eastern to make good was the actual design of the ship. This may very well have been but there can be no doubt that there was mismanagement from the start. The design may have been too advanced for the materials available at that period but the loss of time and cost of repairs was a heavy burden for the owners.

Nevertheless, had there been more showmanship in exhibiting such a remarkable ship, one feels the result would have been an astounding success.

An account of the ill-fated Great Eastern was published in the London Evening News in November 1954. A few days later a reader wrote to the editor as follows:

"I read with interest your account of the Great Eastern and of the riveter and his mate, whose remains were discovered in the bowels of the ship, when after 40 years she was broken up.

Members of my family have always believed that these two were murdered; that the riveter, James White, was killed while at work by a jealous mate whose wife had received White's attentions.

The boy, twelve-year-old Arnold Croly, was a member of my family and my namesake. He was, we believe, a witness to the crime, and was therefore also murdered by the jealous husband, who then walled the bodies up in the ship before they could be discovered."

Were the troubled spirits of the riveter and his young mate the real cause for the unfortunate history of a fine vessel, or was it just bad management, bad design, and sheer bad luck?

Who can say?

CHAPTER TWENTY-THREE

The Strange Burial of Hofrath Von SCHILLER, Austria

When Mozart died at Salzburg in 1791, so little was he appreciated as a musician that his body was thrown on a refuse heap. In a few years even the exact site of the refuse heap was forgotten, so that it was not possible to erect a memorial to the great man at the spot. One cannot help speculating as to what would have happened to some of the modern composers had they lived and died at the period.

It would seem that no form of culture was appreciated in Austria and Germany at that period, for when Schiller died in 1805 he was buried in a plain deal coffin that cost 10/. At the time of his death Schiller left his widow and children almost penniless, and almost friendless, too. Goethe lay ill, and even Schiller's brother-in-law, Wolzogen, was away from home. *Frau* von Wolzogen was with her sister, but seems to have been equally ill fitted to bear her share of the load that had fallen so heavily upon them. Heinrich Voss was the only friend admitted to the sickroom, and when all was over it was he who went to the joiners and knowing the need for economy ordered a plain deal coffin.

In the early part of the year 1805 one Carl Leberecht Schwabe, an enthusiastic admirer of Schiller, left Weimar on business. Returning on Saturday the 11th May, between three and four in the afternoon, his first errand was to visit his betrothed, who lived in the house adjoining that of the Schiller's. She met him in the passage and told him that Schiller was two days dead, and that very night he was to be buried. On putting further questions, Schwabe stood aghast at what he learned. The funeral was to be private and to take place immediately after midnight, and without any religious rite. Bearers had been hired to carry the remains to the churchyard, and no one else was to attend.

Friend Schwabe felt that all this could not go on; but to prevent it was difficult. There were but eight hours left and the arrangements, such as they were, had already been made. However, he went straight to the house of death and requested an interview with *Frau* von Schiller. She replied through the servant that she was too greatly overwhelmed by her loss to be able to speak to anyone." As for the funeral of her blessed husband, Mr Schwabe must apply to the Reverend *Oberconsistoriabrath* Gunther, who had kindly undertaken to see done what was necessary. Whatever he might direct she would approve of it.

With this message Schwabe hastened to Gunther and told him that his blood boiled at the thought that Schiller should be borne to the grave by hirelings. At first Gunther shook his head and said it was too late: everything was arranged, and the bearers were already ordered. Schwabe offered to be responsible for the payment of the bearers if they were dismissed. At length the *Oberconsistoriabrath* inquired whom the gentlemen were who had agreed to bear the coffin. Schwabe was obliged to acknowledge that he could not at that moment mention a single name: but he was ready to guarantee his *Hochwurde* that in an hour or two he would bring him the list. On this his *Hochwurde* consented to countermand the bearers.

Schwabe now rushed from house to house, obtaining ready consent from all whom he found at home. But as some were out he sent round a circular, begging those who would come to place a mark against their names. He requested them to meet at his lodgings at half past twelve o'clock that night. A light would be placed in the window to guide those who were not acquainted with the house. They would be kind enough to be dressed in black, but mourning-hats, capes and mantles he had already provided.

Late in the evening he placed the list in Gunther's hands. Several names appeared whom he had not applied to, and in all he had about twenty. Between midnight and one in the morning the little band proceeded to Schiller's house. The coffin was carried downstairs and placed on the shoulders of the friends in waiting. No one else was to be seen before the house or in the streets.

It was a moonlight night in May, but clouds were up. The procession moved through the sleeping city to the churchyard of St James. Having arrived there they placed their burden on the ground at the door of the so-called *Kassengewolbe*, where the gravedigger and his assistants took it up. In this vault, which belonged to the province of Weimar, it was usual to inter persons of the higher classes who possessed no burial ground of their own, and upon payment of a *Louis d'or*.

As Schiller had died without securing a resting place for himself and his family there could have been no more natural arrangement than to carry his remains to this vault. It was a grim old building, standing against the wall of the churchyard, with a steep narrow roof, and no opening of any kind but the doorway, which was filled up with a grating. The interior was a gloomy space of about fourteen feet either way. In the centre was a trap door, which gave access to a hollow space beneath.

As the gravediggers raised the coffin, the clouds suddenly parted and the moon shed her light on all that was still earthly of Schiller. They carried him in, opened the trapdoor and let him down into the darkness and then closed the vault. Nothing was spoken or sung. The mourners were dispersing when their attention was attracted by a tall figure in a mantle at some distance in the graveyard, sobbing loudly.

No one knew who it was, and for many years the occurrence remained wrapped in mystery, giving rise to strange conjectures. But eventually it turned out to have been Schiller's brother-in-law, Wolzogen, who having hurried home on hearing of his death, had arrived after the procession was already on its way to the churchyard.

In the year 1826 Schwabe was *Burgermeister,* or Mayor, of Weimar. Now it was the custom of the *Landschaftscollegium,* or provincial board under whose jurisdiction this institution was placed, to clear out the *Kassengewolbe* from time to time. Whenever it was found to be inconveniently crowded, and by this means to make way for other deceased persons, and of course, more *Louis d'or.*

On such occasions, when the *Landschaftscollegium* gave the order, *"aufzuranmen"* it was the usage to dig a hole in a corner of the churchyard - then to bring up *en masse* the contents of the *Kassengewolbe* – coffins, whether entire or in fragments, bones, skulls and tattered grave-clothes, and finally to shovel the whole heap into the aforesaid pit.

In the month of March, Schwabe was dismayed at hearing that the *Landschaftscollegium* had decreed a speedy "clearing out" of the *Gewolbe.*

His old prompt way of acting had not left him, and he went at once to his friend Weyland, the president of the Collegium.

"Friend Weyland," he said, "let not the dust of Schiller be tossed up in the face of Heaven and flung into that hideous hole. Let me at least have a permit to search the vault, and if we find Schiller's coffin it shall be reinterred in a fitting manner in the New Cemetery."

The president made no difficulty. Schwabe invited several persons who had known the poet, and amongst others was Rudolph who had been Schiller's servant at the time of his death. On March 13 at four o'clock in the afternoon the party met in the churchyard, the sexton and his assistants having received orders to be present with keys, ladders, etc.

The vault was opened, but before anyone entered it, Rudolph and another stated that the coffin of the deceased Hofrath von Schiller must be one of the longest in the place. After this the secretary of the *Landschaftscollegium* was requested to read aloud from the records of the said board the names of such persons as had been interred shortly before and after the year 1805.

This being done, the gravedigger Bielke remarked that the coffins no longer lay in the order in which they had originally been placed, but had been displaced at recent burials. The ladder was then adjusted and Schwabe, Coudray the architect, and the gravedigger were the first to descend. Some of the others were asked to draw near, that they might assist in recognising the coffin. The first glance brought the hopes very low. The tenants of the vault were found "over, under and alongside of each other."

One coffin of unusual length having been descried underneath the rest, an attempt was made to reach it by lifting out of the way those that were above it; but the processes of the tomb were found to have made greater advances than met the eye. Hardly anything would bear removal, but fell to pieces at the first touch. Searches were made for plates with inscriptions, but even the metal plates crumbled away on being fingered, and their inscriptions where utterly effaced.

Two plates only were found with legible characters and these were foreign to the purpose. Probably everyone but the Burgermeister looked on the matter as hopeless. They reascended the ladder and closed the vault.

Meanwhile, these strange proceedings in the *Kassengewolbe* began to be noised abroad. The churchyard was a thoroughfare and many passengers had observed that something unusual was going on. There were persons living in Weimar whose near relatives lay in the *Gewolbe*, and though neither they nor the public at large had any objection to offer to the general "clearing out," they did raise very strong objectives to this mode of anticipating it. So many pungent things began to be said about violating the tomb, disturbing the repose of the departed, etc, that the Burgermeister perceived the necessity of going more warily to work in future.

He resolved to time his next visit at an hour when few persons would be likely to cross the churchyard at that season. Accordingly, two days later he returned the *Kassengewolbe* at seven in the morning, accompanied only by Coudray and the churchyard officials. Their first task was to raise out of the vault altogether six coffins, which it was found would bear removal.

By various tokens it was proved that none of these could be that of which they were in search. There were several others which could not be removed but which held together so long as they were left where they lay. All the rest were in the direst confusion. Two hours and a half were spent in subjecting the ghastly heap to a thorough but fruitless search, and not a trace of any kind rewarded their trouble.

Only one conclusion stared Schwabe and Coudray in the face – their quest was in vain, and the body of Schiller must be left to oblivion. Once more the *Gewolbe* was closed, and those who had disturbed its quiet returned disappointed to their homes.

Yet, that very afternoon, Schwabe went back once more in company with the joiner who had twenty years before made the coffin. There was just a chance that he might recognise one of those that they had not ventured to raise. But this glimmer of hope faded like all the rest. The man remembered very well what sort of coffin he had made for the Hofrath von Schiller, and he certainly saw nothing like it there.

The coffin had been of the plainest sort, and he believed it was even without a plate, so in such damp as this it could have lasted but a few years. The fame of this "second expedition" got abroad like that of the first and the comments of the public were louder than before. Invectives of no measured sort fell on the mayor in torrents. Not only society in general took offence, but also a variety of persons in authority, particularly ecclesiastical dignitaries, and began to talk of interfering.

Schwabe was haunted by the idea of the "clearing out" which was closer at hand. That dismal hole in the corner of the churchyard once closed and the turf laid down, the dust of Schiller would be lost forever. So he determined to proceed. His position of *Burgermeister* put the means in his power, and this time he was resolved to keep his secret. To find the skull was now his utmost hope, and for that he would make a final struggle. The keys were still in the hands of Bielke the sexton, who of course was under his control. He sent for him, bound him again to silence and ordered him to be at the churchyard at midnight on the 19th March.

He also summoned three labourers whom he also pledged to secrecy, and engaged to meet him at the same place and at the same hour, but singly and without lanterns. Attention should not be attracted if he could help it.

When night came he himself, with a trusty servant, proceeded to the entrance of the *Kassengewolbe*. The four men were already there. In the darkness they all entered, raised the trap door, adjusted the ladder and descended to the abode of the dead. Not until then were the lanterns lighted. It was just possible that some late wanderer might, even at that hour, cross the churchyard.

Schwabe seated himself on a step of the ladder and directed the workmen. Fragments of broken coffins they piled in one corner, and the bones in another. As skulls were found, they were placed in a heap by themselves, and this work went on from about twelve o'clock until about three. This was continued for three successive nights, at the end of which time twenty-three skulls had been found. The *Burgermeister* caused these to be put into a sack and carried into his house, where he himself took them out and placed them in rows on the table. Hardly had he done so ere he exclaimed, "That must be Schiller's".

There was one skull that differed enormously from all the rest, both in size and in shape. It was found to be remarkable too in another way. Alone of those on the table it retained an entire set of the finest teeth, and Schiller's teeth had always been noted for their beauty.

But there were other means of identification at hand. Schwabe possessed the cast of Schiller's head, taken after death by Klauer, and with this he undertook to make a careful comparison and measurement. The two seemed to him to correspond, and of the twenty-two others, not one would bear juxtaposition with the cast. Unfortunately the lower jaw was wanting, to obtain which a fourth nocturnal expedition had to be undertaken.

The skull was carried back to the *Gewolbe,* and many jaws were tried ere one was found which fitted and for beauty of teeth corresponded with the upper jaw. When brought home, on the other hand, it refused to fit and other cranium. One tooth alone was wanting, and this was said by an old servant of Schiller's to have been extracted at Jena in his presence.

Having got this far, Schwabe invited three of the chief medical authorities to inspect his discovery. After careful measurements they declared that among the twenty-three skulls there was but one from which the cast could have been taken. Schwabe then invited every person in Weimar and its neighbourhood, who had been on terms of intimacy with Schiller, and admitted them to the room one by one.

The result was surprising. Without exception they pointed to the same skull as that which must have been the poets. The only remaining chance of mistake seemed to be the possibility of other skulls having eluded the search, and remaining yet in the vault. To put this at rest, Schwabe applied to the *Landschaftscollegium,* in whose records was kept a list of all persons buried in the *Kassengewolbe.*

It was also ascertained that since the last "clearing out" there had been exactly twenty-three interments. At this stage the *Burgermeister* saw himself in a position to inform the Grand Duke and Goethe of his search and its success. From both he received grateful acknowledgements. Goethe unhesitatingly recognised the head, and laid stress on the peculiar beauty and evenness of the teeth.

The new cemetery lay on a gently rising ground on the south side of the town. Schwabe's favourite plan was to deposit what he had found – all that he now ever dreamed of finding – of his beloved poet on the highest point of the slope. He planned to mark the spot by a simple monument, so those travellers at their first approach might know where the head of Schiller lay.

One forenoon in early spring he had led Frau von Wolzogen and the Chancellor von Muller to the spot. They approved his plan and the remaining members of Schiller's family – all of who had left Weimar – signified their assent. They "did not desire" as one of them expressed it, "to strive against Nature's appointment that man's earthly remains should be united with herself". They would prefer that their father's dust should rest in the ground rather than anywhere else.

But the Grand Duke and Goethe decided otherwise.

Dannecker's colossal bust of Schiller had recently been acquired for the Grand Ducal library, where it had been placed on a lofty pedestal opposite the bust of Goethe; and in this pedestal, which was hollow, it was resolved to deposit the skull. The consent of the family having been obtained, the solemnity was delayed until the arrival of Ernst von Schiller, who could not reach Weimar until the autumn.

On September the 17th the ceremony took place. A few persons had been invited amongst whom of course was the *Burgermeister.* Goethe, more so dreaded the agitation and remained at home, but sent his son to represent him as chief librarian. A cantata having been sung, Ernst von Schiller, in a short speech, thanked all persons present, but especially the *Burgermeister,* for the love they had shown to the memory of his father. He then formally delivered his father's head into the hand of the younger Goethe, who, reverently receiving it, thanked his friend in Goethe's name, and having dwelt in the affection that had subsisted between their fathers, vowed that the precious relic should thenceforward be guarded with anxious care.

Up to this moment the skull had been wrapped in a cloth and sealed: the younger Goethe now made it over to the librarian, Professor Riemer, to be unpacked and placed in its receptacle. All present subscribed their names, the pedestal was locked and the key carried home to Goethe. None doubted that Schiller's head was now at rest for many years.

But it had already occurred to Goethe, who had more osteological knowledge than the excellent *Burgermeister,* that the skull being in their possession, it would be possible to find the skeleton. Thus, a very few days after the ceremony in the library, he sent to Jena, begging the Professor of Anatomy, Dr Schroter, to have the kindness to spend a day or two at Weimar. He also asked the Professor to bring with him, if possible, a functionary of the Jena Museum, Farber by name, who had at one time been Schiller's servant.

As soon as they arrived Goethe placed the matter in Schroter's hands. Again the head was raised from its pillow and carried back to the dismal *Kassengewolbe,* where the bones still lay in a heap. The chief difficulty now was to find the first vertebra: after that all was easy enough. With some exceptions, comparatively trifling in nature, Schroter succeeded in reproducing the skeleton, which was then laid in a new coffin "lined with blue merino" and would seem to have been deposited in the library.

Professor Schroter's register of bones recovered and bones missing has been both preserved and printed. The skull was restored to its place in the pedestal. There was another shriek from the public at these repeated violations of the tomb, and the odd position chosen for Schiller's head apart from his body called forth, though not without reason, abundant criticism

Schwabe's idea of a monument in the new cemetery was, after a while, revived by the Grand Duke Carl August, but with an important alteration. This was that on the spot indicated at the head of the rising ground there should be erected a common sepulchre for Goethe and Schiller. The latter's remains should at once be deposited, and the mausoleum to be finally closed only when in the course of nature, Goethe should have been laid there too.

The idea was doubtless very noble and found great favour with Goethe himself, who entering into it with enthusiasm, commissioned Coudray, the architect, to sketch the plan of a simple mausoleum, in which the sarcophagi were to be visible from without. There was some delay in clearing the ground – a nursery of young trees had to be removed – so that at midsummer, 1827, nothing had been done.

It is said that the intrigues of certain persons, who made a point of opposing Goethe at all times, prevailed so far with the Grand Duke that he became indifferent about the whole scheme. Meanwhile it was necessary to provide for the remains of Schiller. The public voice was loud in condemning their present locations, and in August 1827, Louis of Bavaria again appeared as a *Deus ex machina* to hasten the last act. He expressed surprise that the bones of Germany's best loved should be kept like rare coins, or other curiosities, in a public museum.

In these circumstances, the Grand Duke wrote Goethe a note proposing for his approval that the skull and skeleton of Schiller should be reunited and "provisionally" deposited in the vault that the Grand Duke had built for himself and his house, "until Schiller's family should otherwise determine". No better plan seeming feasible Goethe himself gave orders for the construction of a sarcophagus.

On November 17th, 1827, in the presence of the younger Goethe, Condray and Riemar, the head was finally removed from the pedestal and Professor Schroter reconstructed the entire skeleton in this new and more sumptuous abode. We are told that it was seven feet in length and bore on its upper end the name

SCHILLER

in letters of cast-iron. That same afternoon Goethe went himself to the library and expressed his satisfaction with all that had been done.

At last, on December 16th, 1827, at half past five in the morning, a few people again met at the same place. The Grand Duke had desired – for what reason we know not – to avoid observation. It was Schiller's fate that his remains should be carried hither and hither by stealth and in the night. Some tapers burned around the bier and the recesses of the hall were in darkness. Not a word was spoken, but those present bent for an instant in silent prayer, upon which the bearers raised the coffin and carried it away.

They walked along through the park, the night cold and cloudy, though some of the party had lanterns. When they reached the avenue that led up to the cemetery, the moon shone out as she had done twenty years before. At the vault itself some other friends had assembled, amongst whom was the *Burgermeister*. Ere the lid was finally secured, Schwabe placed himself at the head of the coffin and recognised the skull to be that which he had rescued from the *Kassengewolbe*.

The sarcophagus having been closed, and a laurel wreath laid on it, formal possession, in the name of the Grand Duke, was taken by the Marshal, Freiherr von Spiegel. The key was removed to be kept in the possession of his Excellency, the *Geheimrath* von Goethe, as head of the Institutions for Art and Science. This key, in an envelope addressed by Goethe, is said to be preserved in the Grand Ducal Library, where however we no recollection of having seen it.

The "provisional" deposition has proved more permanent than any other. Whoever would see the resting-place of Goethe and Schiller must descend into the Grand Ducal vault, where through a grating, in the twilight beyond he will catch a glimpse of their sarcophagi.

The above account of a very extraordinary case of exhumation is abridged from an article by Mr Andrew Hamilton, published in Macmillan's in May 1863, and possibly lost to the general reading public since that time, as the present author chanced upon it in a rare copy of the magazine.

Through the years not all exhumations have been performed with such a perfectly legitimate object – to give the remains a more honourable sepulchre.

CHAPTER TWENTY-FOUR

Other Famous Exhumations

When Katherine Parr died in childbirth at Sudely Castle she was given a most magnificent funeral of almost royal splendour. Lady Jane Grey, who had been there with her all the time, was chief mourner. The interment was originally on the north side of the altar in the chapel at Sudely. A mural tablet of alabaster was afterwards erected above the grave.

In the course of time both the castle and the chapel fell into ruins except only a small part of the domestic quarters, which was made habitable. This part was used for many years as an inn and farmhouse. We read in Rudd's History of Gloucestershire that in the year 1782 a party of ladies was staying at the inn. They noticed in the ruined roofless chapel a block of alabaster on the north wall and suspecting it to be the back of a vanished monument, had the ground opened below it.

There near the surface was discovered a leaden coffin, which they had opened in two places and found a human body, wrapped in cerecloth. In lifting this from the face they found the features, particularly the eyes, to be in a perfect state of preservation. The ladies now became so scared at the sight, and at the smell of spices that came from the cerecloth. So much so that after a hasty examination of the inscription of the breast plate on the coffin, which proclaimed it to be that of Queen Katherine, they ordered the earth to be again thrown into the grave.

A few weeks later the tenant of the property again removed the earth from the grave and coffin, which was now two feet below the surface. This time the body was removed from the coffin and subject to examination.

There were six or seven linen cerecloth's wrapped round the body and so well had they preserved it that it was uncorrupted and in an almost perfect state, though it had lain in the grave for a hundred and fifty two years. The flesh was white and moist.

It has been stated that these investigations were carried out quite decently and in order: this seems hard to understand and these are of course likely to be more than one opinion on the subject. At base the object of such vandalism could only have been to gratify a morbid curiosity and even to settle a question of disputed identity. But the body of Queen Katherine was not to be left long without further disturbances. Two years later the body was again dragged from the grave, this time it is thought by some treasure-hunting ghoul.

The body was thrown on a rubbish heap where it lay exposed to public gaze. It was obviously done in a drunken frenzy by some local men, and it is said that they all came to an untimely end. One is appalled at the apathy of the local inhabitants in tolerating such vandalism. It was stated by a credible witness who was present at the time, that there were remains of costly clothing, not a shroud, still on the body. There were also shoes on the tiny feet. At first there were traces of beauty on the features, but of course decay rapidly set in so far so the face was concerned when exposed to the air. The vicar interfered and ordered that the body be reinterred. However, by now local curiosity was aroused and the unfortunate Queen was not even now allowed to rest in peace.

In volume nine of "Archaeologia", is an account of an investigation authorised by the Reverend Treadway, a famous archaeologist and historian in Worcestershire. This was in 1786 and it is reported that by this time the face of the Queen had decayed but the body was in perfect preservation, the hands and nails being entire and of a brownish colour.

Miss A. Strickland in her book, "Queens of England", mentions that she had seen a lock of Katherine's hair that had been clipped off on one of these occasions. It is of a very fine texture like threads of burnished gold, with an inclination to curl naturally.

At long last in 1817 the then rector in order to prevent further desecration had the remains once more reburied in a small lean-to building adjoining the ruins of the chapel. The Elizabethan portion of the castle has now been restored, as taken from designs by the late Sir G.G. Scott RA. The body of Queen Katherine now lies beneath a canopied tomb with a recumbent figure in white marble of exquisite workmanship by J.B. Philip. This was erected when Mr Dent-Brocklehurst restored the castle.

This is not of course the only case of the exhumation of an exalted personage. In 1812 it was decided to exhume the body of Charles I at Windsor and to reinter it in Westminster Abbey. There then arose the question of the whereabouts of the King's coffin at Windsor. Lord Clarendon had declared that a search for it had proved fruitless. A mausoleum had just been built in the Tomb House at Windsor Castle, which was not finished until March 1813. It was then decided to open a passage of communication with St George's Chapel. During the course of construction an opening was accidentally made in one of the walls of the vault of Henry VIII, through which the workmen could see three coffins, one of which was covered with a black velvet pall.

Henry VIII and Queen Jane Seymour were buried in this vault and it was assumed the third coffin must be that of Charles I. Upon conveying this news to the Prince Regent his Royal Highness realised that a doubtful point in history might've cleared up by opening this vault. He at once gave orders accordingly.

On the first of April 1813, the day after the funeral of the Duchess of Brunswick the search was commenced in the presence of his R.H. himself. Present also were his R.H. the Duke of Cumberland, Count Munster, the Dean of Windsor, Benjamin Charles Stevenson, Esq., and Sir Henry Halford. The vault was now further opened and explored. It was found that the palled coffin was of lead, and bore the inscription "King Charles 1648".

The coffin was opened at the head. By his presence the Prince Regent had guaranteed the most respectful care and attention to the remains of the dead during his enquiry and subsequent examination. The lead coffin was found to contain one of wood. When the wood coffin was opened the body was discovered carefully wrapped in cerecloth, into the folds of which a quantity of unctuous or greasy matter, mixed with resin or other gum as it seemed, had been melted so as to exclude, as effectively as possible, the external air. This completely filled the coffin and from the tenacity of the cerecloth, great difficulty was experienced in detaching it successfully from the parts that it enveloped. Wherever the unctuous matter had insinuated itself the separation of the cerecloth was easy: and when it came off, a correct impression of the features to which it had been applied was observed in the unctuous substance.

At length the whole face was disengaged from its covering. The completion of the skin was dark and discoloured. The forehead and temples had lost little or nothing of their muscular substance. The cartilage of the nose was gone, but the left eye in the first moment of exposure was open and full, though of course it vanished almost immediately, and the pointed beard so characteristic of the reign of Charles, was perfect. The shape of the face was long and oval. Many of the teeth had remained, and the left ear, in consequence of the interposition of the unctuous matter between it and the cerecloth was found entire.

The head was found to be loose and was at once held up to view. After a careful examination of it had been made and a sketch taken, and the identity fully established, it was immediately replaced in the coffin, which was forthwith soldered up and restored to the vault. Of the other two coffins; the larger one was found to have been battered in about the middle and the skeleton of Henry VIII, exhibiting some beard upon the chin, was exposed to view. The other coffin was left as it was found; intact and undisturbed. Neither of the coffins bore any inscription.

The above account is abridged from an essay by Sir Henry Halford, which he wrote in 1831 describing the opening of the tomb.

CHAPTER TWENTY-FIVE

The Extraordinary Daniel Dunglas Home

Daniel Dunglas Home was certainly one of the most remarkable men that ever lived. He became famous the world over as a spiritualist medium. From a spiritualist point of view no one has to this day excelled Home in the cult of mediumship. He began his spiritualist activities early in life. As a boy he was studious and particularly fond of long walks in the woods and studying nature.

Home was born near Edinburgh, March 20th 1833. Through his mother, whose maiden name was McNeill, he was descended from a Highland family in which the traditionally Scottish gift of "second-sight" had been preserved. His mother was gifted that way and while the son was still an infant she had a vision concerning him that found fulfilment 20 years later.

At the age of nine he emigrated to America with his aunt and uncle. Here his habits and tastes had the effect of separating him from most of the children of his own age and eventually he made friends with an older boy of similar tastes. The boy's name was Edwin, and they became very firm friends. However, they were parted when Home and his relatives moved to Troy in the State of New York, some 300 miles from Norwich, where they had first settled.

A few weeks before this separation, when Home was 13, they were on one of their usual jaunts through the woods. Both boys were great readers and Home was further gifted with a prodigious memory. At the time of this particular walk Edwin was eager to discuss a ghost story he had just read. The subject of this ghost story furnished Scott with the theme or the groundwork for one of his ballads. It was of a lady and her lover who mutually agreed that if there was a life hereafter, the one who died first should appear to the survivor.

Accordingly it came to pass that within a few days of his death he presented himself to his lady friend. He stretched forth his hand and laid it in hers, leaving there a mark that was ineffaceable. Many years later Home was to meet in England a member of the family to which this episode – which was said to be true – related and was assured that the family possessed a portrait of the lady known in the family as "the Lady with the black ribbon". From a covering she wore to conceal the mark.

After the reading of the story in the woods the boys naturally wanted to bind themselves to a similar promise and agreement, which they did. A few weeks later Home left the district. In the following June, Home spent an evening at a friend's house. He returned to his aunts rather later than usual, to find that his aunt had already retired so he too went to bed.

After saying his prayers he was getting into bed when the room was suddenly darkened. Outside it was actually a moonlight night. He looked up and saw a vision, which he later described in his book, "Incidents of my Life, published in 1863:

"I was about to draw the sheet over me, when a sudden darkness seemed to pervade the room, which surprised me, inasmuch as I had not seen a cloud in the sky. Looking up I saw the moon still shining but it was on the other side of the darkness, which still grew denser until through the darkness there seemed to be a gleam of light. I cannot describe it but it was similar to those that many others and I have since seen when the room has been illuminated by spiritual presence.

This light increased and my attention was drawn to the foot of my bed, where stood my friend Edwin. He appeared as in a cloud of brightness, illuminating his face with distinctness more than mortal. He looked on me with a smile of ineffable sweetness, and then slowly raising the right arm, the hand began slowly to disappear. Then the arm, and finally the whole body, simply melted away. The natural light of the room was then again apparent.

I was speechless, and could not move, though I retained all my reasoning faculties. As soon as the power of movement was restored I rang the bell and the family, thinking I was ill came to my room, when my first words were, "I have seen Edwin – he died three days ago."

A few days later a letter was received, announcing the death of Edwin after a very short illness. Thus we learn that Home very early in life received indications that he was a spiritualist medium.

Home had a second vision in 1850 upon the death of his mother. After this event he devoted more time to the study of a life hereafter. He had various interruptions; his health began to give way. He was never of a robust nature and he now developed chest trouble. His aunt was a member of the Kirk of Scotland. Home at first joined the Wesleyans but this displeased his aunt and he afterwards joined the Congregationalists.

It seemed that he was as yet too young to take an active part in spiritualism. However, one night while in bed he heard three loud knocks at the head of the bedstead, and he searched the room but found nothing. Then soon after the knocks were repeated and in the same place, and then after a brief pause they occurred a third time; Home spent a sleepless night in his anxiety.

His aunt the next morning noted he was pale and asked if he was unwell. There were then a series of raps on the table which startled not only herself but even more so her nephew. So soon as she could speak she accused him of having the devil in him, in other words she decided he was "possessed". It took her some hours to get over the shock but when she did she at once set about ridding her house of the evil presence – as she thought it to be. She accordingly invited three pastors (a Baptist, a Wesleyan and a Congregationalist) and they proceeded to question Home. At this stage in his spiritualistic developments Home could furnish no explanation but he was desired to join them in prayer to rid him of the Evil One. In his book Home says:

"Whilst we were thus engaged in prayer there came gentle taps on his chair and in different parts of the room, while at every expression of a wish for Gods loving mercy to be shown to us and our fellow creatures, there were loud rapping's as if joining in our heartfelt prayers.

I was so struck and so impressed by this, that there and then, upon my knees, I resolved to place myself entirely at God's disposal. I promised myself to follow the leadings of that which I then felt must be only good and true, else why should it have signified its joy at those special portions of the prayer? This was in fact the turning point of my life, and I have never had cause to regret for one instant my determination, though I have been called on for many years to suffer deeply in carrying it out."

The result of this meeting seemed to appease no one.

The Congregationalist could offer no opinion as to the cause or the meaning of the raps. He may have thought that Home himself was up to some trickery. However openly he was unwilling to blame Home or to persecute him for what, as he said, he was unable to prevent or cause. The Baptist was of the opinion that their prayers had in fact called forth the raps instead of silencing them. The Methodist only remained firm in his first belief – that these manifestations were the work of Satan. Declaring at the same time to the aunt that her nephew was indeed a lost sheep.

From these criticisms we can deduce, with our more modern and enlightened knowledge, that none of these people had the faintest idea what they were talking about. At this period the cult of spiritualism was little understood. Today all this seeming phenomena would be taken as a positive indication that a medium was present.

Henceforth rapping's were frequently heard in the presence of Home, which naturally increased the terror of his aunt. However worse terrors were in store for her; for in due course it came about that the furniture in her house began to be moved about the room without visible agency. In distraction she once placed a heavy family Bible on a table that was moving across the room with no one near it.

Said the aunt, "There! That will drive the devils away." The only effect this had been to cause the table to move even faster.

Another relative of Home, a widow, lived near the aunt. One evening when Home was visiting the widow, raps were heard. The alphabet was called over. The letters indicated by the raps were written down, thus communications were received and replies given to questions. This appears to be the first attempt of Home to obtain such messages. By this time many local people had become aware of the powers of Home. He had many and frequent visitors much to the annoyance of the aunt. One of the visitors was a Mrs Force. In her presence the raps spelled out the name of her mother. A message was received from the mother reminding Mrs Force of neglecting to write to a sister, almost forgotten, who had gone to live at a great distance with her husband some thirty years before. To the message was added the name of the town in which the sister lived. When subsequently Mrs Force wrote to the address she was agreeably surprised to receive a letter in reply.

All these happenings distressed Home's aunt almost beyond endurance. She feared all these communications to be unholy. The increasing number of visitors to her house decided her that if she could not get rid of the spirits she could, and would, get rid of her nephew. She therefore turned him out. Home took refuge in the house of a friend in the nearby town of Willimantic. Here again, visitors, who came in increasing numbers, besieged Home. He was offered money, which he refused. He could not bring himself to trade in his mysterious gift. He thereupon laid down a rule to which he adhered all his life, that he would never accept cash payment for a séance.

The story of his rare powers got into the local newspapers. This seems to have been the last straw, for Home left his friends and left for Lebanon in 1851. It was in Lebanon that the first of many remarkable cures was brought about through the agency of Home. At this time however the health of Home began to cause him some anxiety, for he had frequent fainting spells. However in time he rallied somewhat. Whilst at Lebanon his powers increased and he had frequent visions and trances. It was becoming plain now that his health suffered chiefly as a result of too frequent séances and strangely enough his powers diminished as his health became undermined.

He stayed at Lebanon until 1852, and then went to Springfield, Massachusetts, where he became the guest of a Mr Regis Elmer. In a short time the Elmers threw open their house to all enquirers and Home sat quite frequently morning noon and night, up to six or seven times a day. This proved very exhausting. It was at Springfield that the powers of Home increased so also naturally his fame.

He was now still only 19 years old.

People came from great distances having read accounts of the remarkable powers of Home in newspapers. One such visitor was a Mr S.B. Brittan of New York. This started in the nature of a friendly chat with no thought of a séance. Suddenly the conversation was interrupted by a startling incident. Home quite unexpectedly went into a trance: all conversation at once ceased.

Then Home said, "Hanna Brittan is here."

Mr Brittan afterwards wrote an account to a friend of what then transpired.

He says, "I was surprised at the announcement: for I had not even thought of the person indicated for many days perhaps months, and we had parted for all time when I was but a little child. I remained silent, but eventually inquired how I might be assured of her actual presence.

"Immediately Mr Home began to exhibit signs of the deepest anguish. Rising from his seat, he walked to and fro in the apartment, wringing his hands and exhibiting a wild and frantic manner and expression. He groaned audibly and often smote his forehead and uttered incoherent words of prayer. Ever and anon he gave utterance to expressions like the following:

"Oh, how dark! What dismal clouds! What a frightful chasm. Deep down –far, far down, I see the fiery flood. Save them from the pit. I see no way out. There's no light. The clouds roll in upon me, the darkness deepens. My head is whirling."

"During this exciting scene, which lasted perhaps half an hour, I remained a silent spectator. Mr Home was unconscious and the whole was inexplicable to Mr and Mrs Elmer. The circumstances occurred some twelve years before Mr Home was born. No person in that entire region knew aught of the history of Hannah Brittan, or that such a person ever existed.

"But to me the scene was one of peculiar and painful significance. She was highly gifted by nature and endowed with the tenderest sensibilities. She became insane from believing in the doctrine of endless punishment, and when I last saw her the terrible reality, so graphically depicted in the scene I have attempted to describe, was present in all its mournful details before me.

"Thirty years have scarcely dimmed the recollection of the scene which was thus re-enacted to assure me of the actual presence of the spirit. That spirit has since informed me that he present life is calm, peaceful and beautiful, and that the burning gulf with all its horrible imagery, existed only in the traditions of men, and in the fitful wanderings of her distracted brain."

About this time Home was again urged by his friends to turn his natural ability to pecuniary account. Home since he had left his aunt's had been the guest of various friends, and although he was without means he firmly refused to accept cash for any of his sittings. However, after he had wrought some astonishing cures as a result of his powers as a medium, his mind turned towards the medical profession. He proposed training himself for that profession by the usual course of study.

This much he mentioned to the Elmers, with whom he was staying. They in turn were favourable to the suggestion and went further, they offered to adopt home and make him their heir. They were wealthy and childless and would look upon him as a son on condition that he change his name to Elmer.

This was indeed a tempting offer, and after due consideration Home wrote for advice to his friends the Ely family. They advised against changing his name since he had already become famous in his own name. After much thought Home therefore graciously declined the offer. This of course did not in any way affect the friendship existing between Home and the Elmers.

Shortly thereafter home left Springfield and went to New York. Here he met many distinguished and influential people, among them: Judge Edmonds of the US Supreme Court, Professor Mapes and Professor Hare, the chemist and electrician, who had invented the oxyhydrogen blow-pipe. All these men satisfied themselves that the phenomena that occurred in Homes presence were perfectly genuine and also that they had a spiritual origin. Judge Edmonds, who devoted three years to the study of Spiritualism, wrote in 1853:

"I went into the investigation originally thinking it a deception, and intending to make public my exposure of it. Having from my researches come to a different conclusion, I feel that the obligation to make known the results is just as strong."

While in New York Home also met Doctor John Gray, a physician who subsequently encouraged him to enter on a course of medical study in accordance with his expressed wish. However, events unforeseen prevented the studies being taken up for some considerable time afterwards.

Home was next invited to visit Doctor Hull at Newburgh on the Hudson. Here he was offered considerable cash payment but the offer was politely refused. At the house of Dr Hall, Home met many more influential friends and between them they proposed that as his education had been somewhat retarded, Home should go through a course of study in general knowledge before entering the medical training he had set his mind upon.

This offer was accepted and in the following year he accordingly began his studies. Here again his health broke down and he was ill for some considerable time. This was in 1852. When he could get about again home visited Mr Ward Cheney of South Manchester, Hartford, Connecticut. Here began a life long friendship and Ward Cheney visited Home in England in 1869 where remarkable manifestations occurred. These were even commented on by Lord Dunraven.

However, as Home entered the hall of the house of the Cheneys in South Manchester he heard the sound of silk rustling; as if someone had passed wearing a silk dress. No one was in sight. A little later in the presence of Mr Cheney in one of the sitting rooms Home again heard the rustle as of a ladies silk dress and again looked around to find the cause.

Mr Cheney, who asked what the matter was, noted his startled look. Home merely said he had been ill and his nerves were a little out of order, then upon looking through the open door into the hall he saw what he took to be a small elderly lady and she was wearing a heavy grey silk dress. Here then was the explanation of the rustling. The dress again rustled and this time Mr Cheney also heard the sound. However, this elderly lady was not noticed by Home about the house, neither was she seen at dinner that evening. But as Home was leaving the dining room with the others the sound of rustling was again heard and this time Home heard a voice say, "I am annoyed that a coffin should be placed upon mine."

Home immediately informed his host of what he had seen and heard. For a moment they were dumbfounded, but they afterwards told Home that they knew to whom the dress had belonged but the story of the coffin was unexplainable. Home at this stage was still under the impression that the lady in the silk dress was actually present in the flesh; he now became aware that it was an apparition.

Later in the evening the same words were repeated in his ear, only with this addition: "What is more Seth had no right to cut that tree down."

Home repeated the full message to his host who in turn was greatly perplexed. Mr Cheney said, "My brother Seth did cut down a tree that rather obstructed the view from the old homestead, and we all said at the time that the one who now claims to speak to you would not have consented to his felling it had she been on earth. The rest of the message is sheer nonsense."

Home relates this strange incident in his book, "Lights and Shadows of Spiritualism", published in 1877. Just before the party separated for the night the message was again given and again met by a point blank contradiction. Home says, "I went to my room feeling greatly depressed. It was the first time an untrue message had been received through me, and even were it correct, it astonished me that a liberated spirit should occupy itself with such a matter. I could not sleep for thinking of the occurrence."

Next morning Mr Cheney took Home to the cemetery to show him the family vault in order as he said to show how "impossible it would be to place another coffin above hers."

The man who had the keys of the vault was sent for and he was desired to open it. As the man drew the door of the vault open, he seemed to remember something. He said, "By the way, Mr Cheney, as there was just a little room above the coffin of Mrs...(the lady in grey silk), I have placed the coffin of Mrs L's baby there. I suppose it is all right but perhaps I ought to have asked you first about it. I only did it yesterday."

Mr Cheney turned on his companion a look that Home could never forget, saying, "It's all true then – it's all true."

The same evening the spirit once more made known her presence. "Think not," ran the message, "that I would care were a pyramid of coffins to be piled on mine. I was anxious to convince you of my identity once and for ever."

Mr Ward Cheney died in 1876.

It was while staying at the Cheney's house in 1852 that Home gave his first demonstration of levitation. In this he was lifted in mid-air without visible support of any kind. He was to do this many times in after life not only in America but also in England, and in the presence of reliable witnesses.

Home declared on more than one occasion, "I feel no hands supporting me and since the first time I have never felt fear, though should I have fallen from the ceiling of some rooms in which I have been raised, I could not have escaped serious injury. I am generally lifted up perpendicularly: my arms frequently become rigid and are drawn above my head, as if I was grasping the unseen power, which slowly raises me from the floor."

Home returned to Newburgh in 1853, where he now commenced the course of study proposed by Dr Hull. Afterwards he entered the Theological Institute, where he was a boarder but he did not attend lectures. He did, however, start to learn French and German. Later in the same year he went to New York, where it was his intention to begin a course of medical studies. Yet Home seemed fated never to achieve his ambition. Various hindrances cropped up and for various reasons he was unable to get started.

Eventually it occurred to him that he was destined by fate for another career. Very reluctantly he had for the time to abandon his pet ambition. Home spent most of the year 1854 in Boston where he gave séances, some of, which were very remarkable. The latter part of the year he spent at Roxbury. Here his health gradually improved so much so indeed that he again and in spite of many obstacles and disappointments commenced to study for a medical diploma.

He spent the next winter in New York, and here he again continued his medical studies and again had to give up because of bad health. His condition grew worse and gave him cause for much anxiety. Home had been told in 1853 that his left lung was much affected, and hereafter his studies had to be once more abandoned.

He now consulted Dr Gray and other of his medical friends and they all concurred his condition to be grave. They held out one hope, however, and that was a trip to Europe. So it came to pass that Home arrived in England in April 1855. This proved to be a wise action in more ways than one. Home's presence in London soon became known, for his fame had gone before him. To many people of course he was known by repute long before he visited England. In a short time Home was to meet more influential people in England than he had in America. Also his powers seemed to increase as he became older, and in particular the case of levitation where he floated in mid-air.

In England the critics were more forthright than they had been in the States. Most of the people that Home met were of the influential class, many were titled people and these came to investigate. A certain percentage that attended the séances came to scoff, for they at first suspected some form of trickery, but in due course they became convinced there was no trickery and that the phenomena they had witnessed was brought about by the cult of Spiritualism; via the agency of this remarkable medium.

One of his most ardent disciples was Elizabeth Barrett Browning. Her husband, Robert Browning, did not share his wife's beliefs in Spiritualism, for he pilloried Home in his poem, "Mr Sludge the Medium".

Throughout his life Home was never detected in any form of trickery. He relates that he was from the very first always suspected, particularly by those with little knowledge of Spiritualism, of being a pretender. Of course this was not altogether surprising because at that period many bogus mediums were exposed, and of course we still have bogus mediums to the present day.

Home found his greatest difficulty, here as in America, was that the more reliable and influential, witnesses were at times reluctant to admit in public that they were convinced or converted to the belief in Spiritualism. They were willing to admit they had witnessed some remarkable happenings and at the same time to be convinced that there was no form of trickery or humbug but were unwilling to agree that they were believers in a supernatural agency.

Within a few days of his arrival Home received so many requests for séances that it was quite impossible to satisfy all. The first séance was held at Coxes hotel in Jermyn Street W. This was held in daylight, and the meeting was called at the request of Lord Brougham, who was most anxious to investigate the remarkable phenomena. Present also were Sir David Brewster and the proprietor of the hotel Mr W. Cox. So impressed

157

were these people with what they witnessed that Mr Cox wrote to the Morning Advertiser, October 15th, 1855: "I assert that both Sir David and Lord Brougham were astonished at what they heard and saw and felt. I assert that Sir David in the fullness of his astonishment, made use of the expression, 'This upsets the philosophy of fifty years'. I assert that Lord Brougham was so much interested that he begged me to arrange for him another sitting and said he would put off every engagement for the purpose of further investigation."

In Mrs D. Home's book, "D.D. Home – His Life and Mission", published by Kegan Paul, 1888, she said that later Home wrote to a friend in the States describing his experiences in England. He mentioned that Lord Brougham and Sir David Brewster had brought their whole force of their keen discernment to bear upon the phenomena with a view to accounting for them by natural means and had been unable to do so. This letter was published and commented upon in America, and the statements in the American press presently found their way into English journals. Long before they did so Home had left Jermyn Street on a visit to Mr Rymer of Ealing, a London solicitor in large practice, and at Ealing Sir D. Brewster was present at a second séance.

Here a dining table 12ft long was lifted. Sir David ventured the opinion that the feet of Mr Home might have lifted the table. It is recorded that after this séance Sir David Brewster, Mr T.A. Trollope and Mr Rymer experimented with this table to discover if it were possible to move it or raise it with their feet. They admitted they could not move the table even by the combined efforts of the feet of all three.

When Home was in good form not only did tables rise from the ground with the hands of all the sitters present on them, but at times tables, chairs and other objects have moved about the room and rose in the air. This when neither Home nor anyone else was touching them. And this was all done in good light.

On one occasion in 1868 at the home of Mr J.H. Simpson in Camden Grove, Kensington, Mr Simpson, who was a disbeliever in Spiritualism, placed rollers on a table. On the rollers was rested a large flat music book. Home's fingers, and the fingers of the sitters present, rested lightly on the book. While disbelievers above watched the rollers and the book, Mr Simpson lay on the floor under the table to see that no foot touched the table below.

The table moved violently and Mr Simpson was quite satisfied that the movement of the table was not caused by any person present.

Nearly always when Home was present at a séance and a table was tilted or lifted the various articles on the table, pens, lamps, candlesticks etc, would remain in their place and not roll off the table. This has happened upon many occasions in strong light. Furthermore at the command of any of the sitters the retaining force has been relaxed and the articles slide to the ground. This request was always complied with.

Regarding this phenomena Mr Robert Bell wrote an article in the Cornhill Magazine in 1860, called "Stranger than Fiction":

"Of a somewhat similar character is another movement, in some respects more curious, and certainly opening a stranger field for speculation. The table rears itself up on one side, until the surface forms an inclined plane, at an angle of about 45%. In this attitude it stops. According to ordinary experience everything on the table must slide off or topple over, but nothing stirs. The vase of flowers, the books, the little ornaments are as motionless as if they were fixed in their places.

"We agree to take away our hands to throw up the ends of the cover, so as to leave the entire round pillar and claws exposed. And we remove our chairs to a little distance that we may have a complete command of a phenomenon, which, in its marvellous development at least, is, I believe, new to us all. Our withdrawal makes no difference whatever: and now we see distinctly on all sides the precise pose of the table, which looks like the Tower of Pisa, as if it must inevitably tumble over.

"With a view to urge the investigation as far as it can be carried a wish is whispered for a still more conclusive display of the power by which this most extraordinary result has been accomplished. The desire is at once complied with. The table leans more and more towards the perpendicular, two of the three claws are high above the ground, and finally the whole structure stands on the extreme tip of a single claw. It is fearfully overbalanced, but maintaining itself as if it were all one solid mass, instead of being freighted with a number of loose articles. It was as if the position had been planned in strict accordance with the laws of equilibrium and attraction, instead of involving an inexplicable violation of both."

Thackeray was editor of the Cornhill at this time and subsequently he was present at a séance. In publishing the above article, Thackeray added this note: "As editor of the magazine, we can vouch for the good faith and honourable character of our correspondent, a friend of twenty-five years standing."

In the autumn of 1855 Home, accompanied by the son of Mr Rymer of Ealing before mentioned, visited Florence. Home had been invited by Mrs Trollope and her son, Mr A. Trollope, who were then living in Florence and had attended the séances at Ealing that summer, having come from Florence for that purpose. Mrs Trollope and her son were believers in the séances held by home and in the spiritual agency of the manifestations.

Home was even more popular in Florence than he had been in London, being well known by repute. He received many applications and requests to hold séances. There were however a certain element at this period that were ardent disbelievers that Home's skills came not from divine origins, holding that the phenomena that occurred in the presence of Home were, instead, of demoniac origin. It is thought that the Church fostered and even encouraged this belief.

It was said openly that Home was a necromancer and they were convinced, or pretended to be convinced, that Home was in the habit of administering the sacraments to toads in order to form spells to raise the dead. However, Home continued to hold séances and they were very popular among the intelligent classes but eventually he received a warning from the Minister of the Interior to the Grand Duke of Tuscany.

It was said that in consequence of reports of his séances and the excitement they had created among the peasantry, his life was in danger in Florence. Home ignored this warning but he was beset one night on the doorstep of his lodgings. He was beaten up and left for dead, but after hospital treatment he recovered. The assassin was never arrested.

Concerning the séances held in Florence, Mr Hiram Powers a sculptor of the period wrote:

"I recollect we had many séances at my house and others, when Home was there. I certainly saw, under circumstances where fraud, or collusion or pre-arrangement of machinery was impossible – in my own house and among friends incapable of lending themselves to imposture – very curious things. That hand floating in the air, of which the entire world has heard, I have seen. There was nothing but moonlight in the room, it is true, and there is every presumption against such phenomena, under such circumstances. But what you see – you see. And must believe, however difficult to account for. I recollect that Mr Home sat on my right hand: and besides him there were six others of us round one half of a circular table, the empty half towards the window and the moonlight.

"All our fourteen hands were on the table, when a hand delicate and shadowy, yet defined, appeared dancing slowly just to the other side of the table

and gradually creeping up higher, until above the elbow it terminated in a mist. The hand slowly came nearer to Mrs… at the right side of the table, and seemed to pat her face.

"Could it take a fan?" cried her husband. Three raps responded "yes", and the lady put her fan near it, which it seemed trying to take. "Give it the handle," said her husband. The wife obeyed, and it commenced fanning her with much grace. "Could it fan the rest of the company?" Someone exclaimed. Three raps signified assent, and the hand, passing round, fanned each of the company, and then slowly was lost to view.

"I felt on another occasion, a little hand – it was pronounced that of a lost child – patting my cheek and arm. I took hold of it: it was warm and evidently a child's hand. I did not loosen my hold, but it seemed to melt out of my clutch."

The health of Home suffered greatly as a result of the attempt on his life in Florence and also from the very trying winter ("D.D. Home – His Life and Mission"). Early in 1856 he made the acquaintance of a Polish nobleman, Count Branicka and of his mother, the niece of the famous Potemkin. The count with his family was about to visit Naples and Rome and invited Home to accompany him. Hardly had the invitation been given and accepted when Home" power left him. His conduct under the unexpected circumstances was characteristic of the self-respect and delicacy of his nature, and met with a worthy response from Count Branicka.

"The spirits", writes Home in "The Incidents", "told me that my power would leave me for a year. This was on the evening of February 10th, 1856. Feeling that the Count and his family must have felt an interest in me arising from the singular phenomena which they had witnessed in my presence, and that this cause being removed, their interest in me would have diminished, I wrote the following morning to inform them of what I was told and to say that I could no longer entertain the idea of joining them. They at once told me that it was for myself, even more than for the strange gift I possessed that they had become interested in me. I went to them, and in a day or two we left for Naples."

Here in due course Home met many influenced people and received some very valuable presents. From Naples the party went to Rome and eventually to Paris. But his health again laid him low, and he fell ill and was for a time confined to his bed. He writes,

"On the night of February 10th 1857, as the clock struck twelve, I was in bed, when there came loud rapping's in my room, a hand was placed gently on my brow and a voice said, "Be of good cheer, Daniel, you will soon be well."

But a few minutes had elapsed before I sank into a quiet sleep and I awakened in the morning feeling more refreshed than I had done for a long time."

"D.D. Home – His Life and Mission" states that the predicted return of Home's power on February 10th 1857 was known on the French Coast, and he was sent for by the Marquis de Belmont, chamberlain of the Emperor, Napoleon III.

A séance was held the same evening. No account of this séance was published but the gossips got busy and there were many fabulous tales told openly in Paris. The result of the gossip was that Home gained the reputation, as he had previously in Florence, of being a necromancer with a host of familiar spirits at his command. It was in vain for him to make known again and again in the most emphatic terms, the fact that he was nothing but the instrument of the phenomena and had never pretended to evoke spirits or to exercise any influence over them. Home declared he was neither angel demon nor charlatan and wished it to be distinctly understood that apart from his extraordinary gift, he was a man like other men.

On the first visit to the Tuileries preparations had been made to have present the entire suite, Home had sometimes sat with as many as fourteen people present but always preferred a smaller number, seven or eight being an ideal number. It was thought the manifestations were of more frequent occurrence with only a few people present.

Upon this first visit Home informed their French Majesties that he could allow eight persons at the most to the séance. This decision did not please the Empress who at once refused to be present unless her whole suite sat at the table with her. Home had to persist however in only a few sitters. He gave his reason that with too many people present the séance would probably be spoilt. The Empress would not give way and withdrew, whilst the Emperor remained.

Home informed the party that they could select any table in the room at which to sit. A large table was selected, and five personages of the Court with the Emperor and Home took their places. Almost at once the table began to vibrate and tremble under the hands placed upon it. Presently the table was lifted from the ground, and then came raps upon it. The alphabet was called over and answers were received to spoken questions of the Emperor. But what is more remarkable is that replies were given to queries that the Emperor had put mentally.

In other words replies were received through Home to unspoken thoughts. This miraculous exhibition of the power of Home so impressed the Emperor that he began there and then to take a deeper interest in the proceedings and to follow every manifestation with keen attention in order to satisfy himself by the closest scrutiny that neither deception nor delusion was possible. After a short time the Emperor asked Home if the Empress might be allowed to witness some of these marvellous happenings.

The Empress was duly brought in and took her place at the table. Almost immediately raps were heard and then the Empress received through the rapping's a reply to an unspoken thought, and there was at that time a gentle pull on her dress. At this the Empress started and uttered a cry. Home then suggested that the Empress might prefer to place her hand below the table, with his own hands, meanwhile, resting on the top of the table. Soon the Empress began to smile and then the smiles gave way to tears and she became agitated. When asked the reason for all this by the Emperor she replied, "I felt the hand of my father in mine."

The Emperor asked how she could distinguish it, and the Empress said, "I would distinguish it among a thousand, from a defect in one of the fingers, just as it was in life. As it lay in mine, I satisfied myself of this defect." The séance ended soon after this and Home was assured by the Empress that at any subsequent sittings he should decide the number of persons that were to be present, and that they should always be the same individuals.

At the second séance held at the Tuileries, a massive table rose in the air several feet and a bell placed on the table was lifted and rang. A handkerchief was taken from the hands of the Empress and was seen to float in mid-air.

In a third séance at the Tuileries in the Salon Quinze the hand of a man appeared above the table. This was in a good light as were all the other séances at the Tuileries. A sheet of paper and a pencil had already been placed on the table so that any communications might be written down. The hand that was seen by all present to be beautifully formed then wrote the word, "Napoleon."

At a subsequent séance an empty chair was seen to move across the room and to come to rest in front of the Empress. After a few moments the chair moved back a little way and began to sway backward and forward. The Empress remembered that her father had been in the habit of rocking himself thus in his chair. The Empress then asked Home if he could see anyone in the chair. Home replied that he could see a soldier seated in the chair. At this the Empress asked for a description of the soldier and Home described exactly her Majesty's father. Home had not known the man and there was only one portrait of him. This portrait was in the possession of the Empress and she was sure that Home had never seen it.

Home left Paris for America in March 1857. The day before he sailed he received a letter from a stranger, Madame A. de Cardomme, requesting an interview regarding her young son. The boy had been deaf for four years from the effects of typhoid fever. An appointment was made for the next day, the day of sailing, being March 20th. Home received the lady in the morning, and she had brought her son with her. Present also were the Princess de Beauvean and Miss Ellice.

This was Home's first attempt at healing deafness and he did not feel quite sure of the success however he decided to do his best to cure the deafness of the boy. The uncertainty was due to the fact that the boy had previously undergone various operations by eminent surgeons in Paris who had said that it was impossible he should ever be restored to hearing. The boy was 15 years of age, tall and of a delicate complexion.

The mother was seated on a chair and Homes and the boy sat on a sofa nearby. During the description by the mother of the boy's illness, Home felt great sympathy for the boy and drew the lad towards him so that his head rested upon Home's shoulder. The mother was telling of some of the most painful particulars of the various operations and Homes passed his hand caressingly over the boy's head and face. The boy, lifting his head suddenly said in an emotional voice, *"Maman, je tentends"* ("Mother I can hear you.").

The effect of this on the mother was of course startling. She was astounded and said, "Emile," (the boy's name). He at once replied, *"Quoi?"* "What?" The mother, then seeing that her boy had heard her question, fainted. When she had been revived there was a touching scene, the mother asking many questions for the mere pleasure of hearing her boy speak, all the time pressing him to her. The cure was permanent and the boy was able to resume his studies. The news of this remarkable case of healing quickly spread far and wide.

Home only stayed a short time in America and was back in Paris again in July 1857. He was, in a short time, again summoned to the Court, which was then at Fontainebleau. Here a particularly striking séance took place after demonstrations of similar manifestations to those of a few months before. A servant of the Court was sent to purchase an accordion at a shop in Fontainebleau. The accordion was quite new and no one present had ever seen it before. It was handed to Home who held it in one hand.

The instrument at once began to play. Notes were moved down and up again without the aid of the fingers of Home. Afterwards, Home placed the accordion on a table and at once stood back away from the table, it played a pretty tune without anyone touching it. The listeners present were all spellbound. Presently voices were added to accompany the music. In a short time both the music and the voices seemed to recede to a distance and gradually became more faint until at last the music died away altogether.

It should be mentioned here that all the above manifestations that occurred through the mediumship of Home were afterwards reproduced by the then famous illusionists the Davenport Brothers at public entertainments. Needless to state, all these reproductions were merely theatrical tricks, and in fact they never pretended to be anything else. But the Davenports and J.N. Maskelyne introduced such tricks in an attempt to dethrone Home and all other spiritualist mediums, whom these men declared to be bogus.

Indeed, they pretended to believe all mediumship to be trickery, though they must have known in their hearts that some at least of the mediums, and Home in particular, were genuine. There had been many bogus mediums and in the case of Mr J.N. Maskelyne his mind had been poisoned against mediums whilst he was working as a watchmaker at Cheltenham.

Maskelyne had been present at a spiritualist séance in the town at which the medium had performed seeming wonders. A few days later the medium brought to the shop where Maskelyne was employed a rather complicated small mechanical instrument. He enquired if it could be repaired. The job was duly handed to Maskelyne, who recognised it at once as part of the apparatus used by the bogus medium at the séance. When he had repaired the instrument Maskelyne made out the bill, "To repairs to spiritualist's mechanism." The bogus medium, realising he was discovered, paid for the repair and at once left the town. Henceforth Maskelyne set himself to dethrone all mediums by reproducing by trickery all the manifestations that take place at a séance.

Unfortunately the Davenports and J.N. Maskelyne refused to recognise any medium as genuine as I have stated above. However, all this controversy brought grist to the theatrical mill and the professed conjurers and illusionists continued to give public exhibitions over a very long period – long after the death of Home in fact.

Some of the illusions performed by the famous Davenport Brothers were at the time considered little short of miraculous. The brothers seem to have been the originators of these cabinet tricks, in this country at any rate, and their performance caused a great sensation in Victorian times. They declared they could emulate any of the spirit manifestations that Home was responsible for, and further they would produce more marvellous tricks than he.

One of their illusions, or cabinet tricks, was to have a cabinet brought onto a stage, for the tricks could only be performed on a specially prepared stage. This cabinet was really a sort of square tent raised from the ground so the audience could see all around and underneath it. One of the brothers would then be securely tied in a chair, and members of the audience were invited to tie him. He was then lifted into the cabinet, which was open to the front. A small table was brought on the stage and on it were a cornet, a concertina, a hand bell, a revolver and an umbrella.

Thus loaded the table was lifted into the cabinet and placed in front of the bound man but out of his reach should he have escaped his bonds. The curtain was now drawn across the front of the cabinet. The top was open. The front curtain was not long enough to entirely hide from view the man. His feet could be seen quite plainly.

Immediately the curtain was drawn the concertina would be heard to play, also the cornet, the revolver was fired, the bell would ring and occasionally the umbrella, now open would be thrust over the top of the curtain. In a short time all would be quiet again, the curtain would be drawn back and the man was discovered still tied to the chair.

There were several variations of this cabinet trick. The curtain would be drawn and almost immediately drawn back again. The man would be seen still tied to the chair but in his shirtsleeves now, with the coat he had been wearing a moment ago being now neatly folded and placed across his knees. Or when the curtain was drawn back it was discovered that a woman was sitting in the chair instead of the man.

For some years these and similar tricks were very popular with the public. All efforts to find out "how it was done" were defied. The Davenport Brothers were proud to announce they claimed no spirit association or psychic manifestations, and their whole performance was trickery and nothing else. Good showmanship no doubt and they prospered for a time. In later years they had imitators who did these same tricks, and various ways and methods were discovered of performing them.

In fact, the Davenport's methods were actually improved upon and at first these performances must have done immense harm to spiritualism. Yet eventually the Davenport Brothers overstepped the credulity of the public, for they had brought about the feeling among certain people that they were in fact actual spirit mediums, although they themselves declared otherwise. Certainly their performances had the effect of provoking bad feeling in the minds of the opponents of spiritualism and equally in the minds of its supporters.

Some spiritualists had been invited to enter the cabinet in which the phenomena was produced and had declared afterwards that they had seen spirit hands emerging from the darkness. The reign of the Davenports came to an abrupt end in a serious riot during a performance at Liverpool in 1865. This was the end of their career, in England at any rate. Harold Scott thinks they were in part the scapegoats of a larger controversy that that provided by their rather innocuous mystery show.

In 1859 Home paid his second visit to England. He stayed 7 months, but re-visited England at the end of 1960 and remained until the end of 1961. Home had married while on a visit to Russia on August 1st, 1859. He married mademoiselle Alexandrina de Kroll, sister of the Countess Koncheleff.

During the year 1860 Home gave a larger number of séances that ever before. At this particular period his power was very strong and some very remarkable séances was the result. Between 1860 and 1868 Home gave sensational exhibitions of his talents, which included levitation, healing and the power to elongate himself. As before stated his first attempt at healing was in 1857 but he was still further extended his remarkable gift and cured a number of people in London and elsewhere. A well-known barrister, Mr H.D. Jencken, in an article in the "London Spiritual Magazine" of January 1868, described the sensational incident of elongation:

"Lord Adare was seated next to Mr Home, who had passed into a trance-like state, in which after uttering a most beautiful and solemn prayer, he alluded to the protecting spirits whose mission is to act as guardian angels to men.

"'The one who is to protect you," he said, addressing Lord Adare, "is as tall as this." Upon so saying Mr Home grew taller and taller. As I stood next to him, my height being 6 foot, I hardly reached to his shoulder, and in the glass opposite he appeared a full head taller than myself.

"The extension appeared to take place from the waist and the clothing separation eight to ten inches. Walking to and fro Mr Home specially called our attention to the fact of his feet being firmly planted on the ground. He then grew shorter and shorter, until he only reached my shoulder, his waistcoat overlapping to the hip."

During this visit to England Home was again troubled with the usual scoffers and disbelievers that he had encountered in all the countries he had visited. On one occasion in London a scientist had been persuaded to attend a séance. His first request upon arrival was to be handed a programme of events!

The man insisted, and finally declared that unless he knew beforehand what he was to investigate he would refuse to remain. He was as good as his word and left the meeting before the séance began.

It was considered by many people that the most remarkable phenomena brought about by the mediumship of Home was that known as levitation or floating in mid-air. Remarkable also were the attempted explanations of this seeming miracle. The most wild and grotesque statements were made and in a short time the professional conjurers were producing by means of trickery the levitation not only of humans but also of animals. Some of these illusionists made fortunes.

At Easter 1866, Home gave a demonstration at Camden Hill for a small group of his friends consisting of Lady Dunsany, Mrs Henry Senior and Mr and Mrs Samuel Carter Hall. The latter were the respective editors of "The London Art Journal" and "The St James' Magazine", from which I have this account of the meeting:

"In a very few moments his hands became perfectly rigid and it was evident that they were not moved by his own volition. Very loud and heavy knocks were heard…Mr Home was then raised up to the ceiling, which he touched."

It is perhaps natural for people in general to scoff at what they do not understand. Clairvoyance or ghosts, spiritism or the suspension of the law of gravitation, are subjects so widely contradictory of general experience and of ascertained laws, that they are flatly pronounced to be impossible.

Few people who witnessed these levitations of Home were bold enough to brave the ban of ridicule and admit their belief in the spiritual agency that alone could and did bring about such happenings. The favourite explanation was thought to be mesmeric or hypnotic influence, perhaps for want of a better solution. Eyewitnesses were for the most part loath to have their names mentioned as having become converts to the spiritualists' cult or belief.

To a certain section of the community, both in England and abroad, there can be no doubt the séances were regarded as good entertainment at which it was fashionable to attend, particularly was this so in London. Only a few years previously their grandparents would consider it fashionable to visit the Bedlam Asylum on certain evenings where they were permitted to watch some of the worst cases in the padded cells. However a large proportion of Homes audiences were genuinely interested in spiritualism.

Andrew Lang wrote:

"Even people of open minds can at present say no more that that there is a great deal of smoke, a puzzling quantity, if there be no fire. And that either human nature is very easily deluded by simple conjuring tricks, or that, in all stages of culture, minds are subject to identical hallucinations. The whole hocus-pocus of spirit-writing on slates, etc, has been exposed and explained, as a rather simple kind of leger-de-main."

This was written in 1894 before the cult of spiritualism had advanced very far, before it was understood and thus accepted.

Some theorists declared that when the Earl of Crawford saw Home in full light rise from the ground that he, the Earl, was hypnotised. It was even suggested that Home carried with him a magic lantern! Magic indeed would that lantern have been. Still another theory was that Home bribed the servants at the house in which the séance was held to hide the apparatus needed for the levitation!

Home wrote in 1883, "If such statements are circulated during my lifetime I often wonder what will be said of me when I shall have passed into the spirit life."

In London Home became acquainted with some distinguished people including the above mentioned Earl of Crawford, Sir E.B. Lytton, Dr Ashburner, Dr Elliotson, the Duchess of Sutherland, Lady Shelley, Lady Gourm, Dr Robert Chambers, Lady Otway, Sir Daniel Cooper, Lady Dunsany (afore-mentioned), Sir Charles Nicholson, Lord Dufferin and Sir Edward Arnold.

Regular séances were held over a long period at the house of Mrs Gibson in Hyde Park Place, near the residence of Dr Ashburner. As I have written above, in due course it became the vogue for many of the best-known people in society to attend these séances. There were, of course, the half-convinced, and those that would express no opinion. Science naturally did not recognise clairvoyance as an actuality, and still less the spiritual practices even of well-known mediums. Gradually, however, the men of science began to take notice. A number of tests were made; although these far from satisfactory from the scientific point of view, in that they, the scientists, could offer no explanation of such seemingly impossible occurrences.

All this took some years to bring about, and things are somewhat different today. Sir Arthur Conan Doyle wrote in 1921, "Home is a man to whom the human race and especially the British public, owes a deep apology. He was most shamefully used by them."

Regarding the floating in mid-air or levitation, "The Quarterly Journal of Science", for January 1874, had this to say:

"There are at least a hundred recorded instances of Mr Home's rising from the ground, in the presence of as many separate persons. I have heard from the lips of three witnesses to the most striking occurrence of this kind, the Earl of Dunraven, Lord Lindsay and Captain W. Wynne, their most minute accounts of what took place.

"To reject the recorded evidence on this subject is to reject all human testimony whatever, for no fact in sacred or profane history is supported by a stronger array of proofs.

"The accumulated testimony establishing Mr Home's levitation's is overwhelming. It is greatly to be desired that some person whose evidence would be accepted as conclusive by the scientific world, if indeed there lives a person whose testimony in favour of such phenomena would be taken, would seriously and patiently examine these alleged facts."

Lord Lindsay related one instance of Home's levitation to the Dialectical Society:

"Home floated around the room, pushing the pictures out of their place as he passed along the walls. They were far beyond the reach of a person standing on the ground. The light was sufficient to enable me to see clearly."

Describing the levitation to the Dialectical Society, the Earl of Crawford was questioned as to the possibility of explaining the phenomena by contrivance. Said the Earl:

"The more I studied them the more satisfied was I that they could not be explained by mere mechanical tricks. I have had the fullest opportunity for investigation. I once saw Home in full light standing in the air seventeen inches from the ground."

At a séance in November 1868 Lord Adare and Lord Lindsay witnessed levitation. Home on this occasion rose four or five feet in the air. At another séance on December 20th, 1868 Home again rose from the ground, this time in the presence of Lord Adare, Captain C. Wynne, Lord Lindsay and Mr Arthur Smith Barry. At an open air séance in the ruined abbey of Adare in daylight, Home was seen by Lord Dunraven, Captain Wynne and Lord Adare to float in the air over a distance of ten to twelve yards. It was high enough to carry him over a broken wall that was two feet high.

The most striking of the levitations of Home occurred on December 16th, 1868. This would appear to be the most marvellous manifestation of any spirit medium at any time either before or since. This occurred during a séance at Ashley House, Ashley Place, London, SW. This is not far from Victoria Station. The house is still standing. The séance took place at night in an upper room on the third floor, some 70 feet from the ground. The moon was shining brightly. Present were Lord Adare, Captain C. Wynne and Lord Lindsay. Home walked about the room in a trance, and after a while he went into an adjoining room. He was heard to raise the window.

At this Lord Lindsay said, "I know what he is going to do, Oh, Good Heavens, it is too fearful."

"Lord Adare said, "What is it?"

Lord Lindsay replied, "Oh, it is too horrible. Home is going out of the window in the other room and coming in at this window."

As they spoke, the party was astounded to see Home floating horizontally outside the window in mid-air. He remained thus for a few moments then raised the window and glided easily into the room. He then sat down beside the astounded company. In describing this remarkable incident afterwards Lord Adare wrote:

"Home said, 'Adare shut the window in the next room.' I got up; shut the window, and coming back remarked that the window was not raised a foot and that I could not think how he had managed to squeeze through. He arose and said, "Come and see."

"I went with him and he told me to open the window as it was before. I did so, and he then told me to stand at a little distance off. Then Home leaned backward and with a quick movement he glided out of the window in the horizontal position head first, his body rigid.

"In a few moments he returned in the same way. We then returned to the other room."

Of all the remarkable manifestations brought about by the mediumship of Home, this was undoubtedly the most marvellous and certainly the most talked of for many years to follow. In due course the accounts of this levitation were discussed far and wide and many influential people closely questioned the witnesses. Lord Lindsay was invited to give a full and detailed account of the event before the Dialectical Society.

In addition to this Lord Lindsay published a second and even more minute description of the levitation. He declared that he himself received a spirit-intimation of what was about to take place on this memorable occasion. This he had communicated to his friends present, Lord Adare and Captain Wynne. Lord Lindsay said that at the moment Home walked into the adjoining room, "I heard a voice whisper in my ear that he would go out of one window and in another. I was alarmed and shocked at the thought of so dangerous an experiment."

Lord Adare also wrote an account of the occurrence as follows:

"There was no light in the room, but the light from the window was sufficient to enable us to distinguish each other. Home went into a trance, and Lindsay cried, "Oh, good heavens. I know what he is going to do. It is too fearful. A spirit says I must tell you."

"I asked Lindsay how the spirit had spoken to him. He could scarcely explain, but said it did not sound like an audible voice, but rather as if the tones were whispered or impressed inside the ear.

"When Home awoke from the trance he was much agitated, and said he felt as if he had gone through some fearful peril and that he had a most horrible desire to throw himself out of the window. He remained in a very nervous condition for a short time, then gradually became quiet.

"I make no attempt to offer any explanation of the phenomena, or to build up any theory upon them. I only say that these things have occurred as I have stated them. Lord Lindsay has told the Dialectical Society, "I have no theory to explain these things."

As I have before stated many were the explanations offered as possible solutions of these levitation's; Biologised, Hallucination, Hypnotism and so on. It is to be regretted that not all the criticisms were honest. According to the account of Mme. Dunglas Home, in "D.D. Home his Life and Mission", Dr W.B. Carpenter, VPRS, imagined, indeed, another theory, and communicated his imaginations to the public under circumstances more daring than honest.

The narrative of Lord Lindsay informed him that here had been a third sitter present when the levitation occurred – Captain Wynne, the cousin of Lord Adare. In the absence of any detailed testimony from this gentleman, Dr Carpenter chose to assume that his evidence, if made public, would have contradicted that of Lords Lindsay and Adare. A little inquiry would have informed Dr Carpenter that Captain Wynne had narrated to Mr Crookes, Mr S.T. Hall and others what he saw, and that his evidence corresponded with that of Lord Adare and Lord Lindsay.

This trained man of science, this exact investigator made no inquiry however. The temper in which he conducted his assaults was not that of a philosopher desirous to arrive at the truth and nothing but the truth, but of a theorist who thought no sacrifice of the truth too great in the interests of his favourite doctrine of unconscious cerebration. To throw doubt on the phenomena of the levitation of Mr Home, he ventured on one of the boldest of these sacrifices. Knowing all the while that his assumption concerning Captain Wynne was sheer supposition; he deliberately stated that his statements would not bear it.

It was sufficient for him to tell the public, in an article published in the "Contemporary Review" of January, 1877"

"The most diverse accounts of the facts of a séance will be given by a believer and a sceptic….a whole party of believers will affirm that they saw Mr Home float out of one window and in at another, whilst a single honest sceptic declares that Mr Home was sitting in his chair all the time.

"And in this last case we have an example of a fact, of which there is ample illustration, that during the prevalence of an epidemic delusion, the honest testimony of any number of individuals on one side, if given under a prepossession, is of no more weight than that of a single adverse witness – if so much."

Mme Home continues:

'It seems to me that written under the circumstances I have just detailed, nothing could well be more discreditable to Dr Carpenter than this passage. Published in a widely circulated organ of opinion, it could not but leave, and was evidently intended to leave, upon the minds of all who read it the impression that Dr Carpenter's "honest sceptic" had actually been present with Lords Adare and Lindsay. This on the only occasion when Home ever floated out of one window and in at another and he had, to the knowledge of Dr Carpenter, declared "that Mr Home was quietly sitting in his chair all the while."

'If so, this single adverse witness could be no other than Captain Wynne. Only once had Mr Home been seen to float out of a window and in at another – in Ashley Place on the 16th December, 1868. Three persons in all had observed the phenomenon; two of them, Lords Lindsay and Adare, had printed their testimony to the occurrence.

"They were therefore Dr Carpenter's "party of believers". The third and last sitter present when Mr Home was carried out of one window of Ashley House and in at another was Captain Charles Wynne. To him, therefore, Dr Carpenter's statements concerning the "honest sceptic" referred. Everyone understood them so to refer, Captain Wynne included."

So far as can be traced home did not communicate with Dr Carpenter in this matter but he did however write to Captain Wynne asking him to confirm what he saw at Ashley place:

"My Dear Wynne,

I have been reading a book – intensely stupid and absurd – called 'Spiritualism and Nervous Derangement", by W.A. Hammond MD.

On page 81 of his book I found the following question regarding the very extraordinary manifestation you witnessed in Ashley Place. When I was brought in at the window eighty feet from the ground, in the presence of your cousin, Viscount Adare (now the Earl of Dunraven), Lord Lindsay and yourself.

"There were three gentlemen present in the room besides Mr Home. Lord Adare, we may admit, accepts the account given by Lord Lindsay. Indeed, he may be said to be the father of it. But why have we no word from the "cousin of his" who formed one of the company? There cannot be too much evidence on so important a point as this."

I would have paid no attention to this question, but on the same page I found the following reply, which perfectly suited this Dr Hammond. He has either arranged it so as to be a reply to the above question, or it may be that it is an arrangement of Dr Carpenter's. I am sorry to say that Dr Carpenter is not innocent, as regards these little arrangements to suit his own convenience.

Hammond says: "But as these lines are being written, the true (save the mark) explanation comes to hand, showing that both Lord Lindsay and Lord Adare suffered from an hallucination."

In an interesting paper, Dr Carpenter, evidently referring to the account of Lord Lindsay, says; "A whole party of believers will affirm that they saw Mr Home float out of a window and in at another, while a single honest sceptic declares that Mr Home was sitting in his chair all the time. This "honest sceptic" is probably the cousin incidentally mentioned by Lord Lindsay. It is scarcely necessary to pursue the inquiry further."

Under ordinary circumstances, I would have paid no attention even to this, but in December 1876, Dr Carpenter, at the London Institution, made a statement so utterly at variance with the truth that it is just as well to remind him that, whatever his peculiar prejudices may be, he does wrong in stooping to falsehoods. I give you his words, as reported in the public prints: "Mr Crookes admitted that…Mr Home's having exhibited marvels, Mr Crookes afterwards devised scientific tests, but the marvels were no longer shown."

That was Mr Crookes statement.

Mr Crookes never made such a statement, and it is a most audacious and wilful falsehood on the part of Dr Carpenter to have said so.

You will fully understand why I wish a reply to this. You have read the statement as given to the world by Lord Lindsay and Lord Adare. Is it, or is it not, a simple and precise statement of the facts just as they took place? I am well pleased that this question should have been asked while you were here to give your testimony. Else these would-be great men who condescend to untruthful statements might have found those capable of giving credence to their inventions,

Ever yours,

D.D. Home.

The reply of Captain Wynne to the above letter is here appended:

Dear Dan,

Your letter has just come before me.

I remember that Dr Carpenter wrote some nonsense about that trip of yours along the side of the house in Ashley Place. I wrote to the medium to say that I was present and a witness. Now, I don't think that anyone who knows me would for one moment say that I was a victim to hallucination or any other humbug of the kind.

The fact of your having gone out of the window and in at the other I can swear to: but what is the use of trying to convince men who won't believe anything, not even if they see it. I don't care a straw whether Dr Carpenter or Mr Hammond believe me or not, for it does not prevent the fact having occurred.

But this I will say, that if you were not to believe the corroborative evidence of three unimpeached witnesses there would be an end to all justice and courts of law...

Ever yours,

C. Wynne

P.S. Honest but not sceptic.

We gather from the above letter and the postscript that Captain Wynne believed the testimony of his eyesight.

All things considered it seems evident that Dr Carpenter was an extreme egoist and was not at all times sincere in the opinions expressed in his writings. As he never was present at a séance with Home he would not be capable of expressing an opinion on the phenomenon or if he did such an opinion would not be of great import.

It transpired subsequently that he not only regarded Home as an honest man – he had said so in as many words – but also he thought it probable that the spirits of the departed influenced the minds of the dwellers on earth.

It remains a fact that Home was never at any time detected in the production of fraudulent phenomena. Furthermore it is extremely unlikely that any Maskelyne or Cooks or Davenport Brothers tricks and illusions would deceive such men as Lord Lindsay and Adare. Which, after all, could only be performed on a specially prepared stage, with expensive apparatus and with the aid of skilled assistants, and nowhere else. The phenomena that occurred via the agency of Home were neither delusions nor deceptions; they were fact. Daniel Dunglas Home was a spirit medium. That is the only real explanation.

Those who were present were men of the world and army officers - altogether difficult men to hoax and deceive.

Lord Adare was a Guards officer and all round sporting type; he had been a big game hunter. As a war correspondent he reported the Abyssinian War for the Daily Telegraph. He had attended in all some 80 of Home's séances and afterwards wrote a book as a result of his experiences.

The book, "Experiences in Spiritualism with D.D. Home", was so strongly criticised that it was withdrawn, but was republished in 1924 when the author wrote in his preface:

"To the best of my ability I scrupulously examined certain strange phenomena which came under my observation and faithfully recorded the facts…"

Early in 1871 Home visited Russia and then in turn Geneva, Florence and Nice. Séances were held at all these places. For health reasons Home spent the winter of 1874 at Nice and nearly all the ten following winters.

At a séance on the 23rd December 1875, the circle was composed of the Countess Potacka, Count de Komar, Mademoiselle de Komar, Mais d'Attainville and a certain Countess de In. This was at Nice, and the salon was brilliantly lit. So soon as all were seated at a table, they felt a distinct vibration, which was communicated to the chairs and even to the floor. Five raps were struck on the table – this was a call for the alphabet.

Several of those present received communications. A small hand caressed Count de Komar and rested a little while in his. Soon after this Home went into a trance and while in this condition walked about the room, with his eyes closed. At last he approached the fireplace in which a large fire was burning. Home knelt down at the fire, and then proceeded to bathe his face and hands in the flames as if it were water. The flames in which it was plunged actually encircled his head.

One of the sitters called to him, "Daniel! Daniel!"

This seemed to startle Home who at once recoiled from his position. No one dared to speak for some moments. Presently Home said in a low clear voice, "You might have caused great harm to Daniel by your want of faith, and now we can do nothing more." In England, several times before this date, Home had bathed his face in the flames and even put red-hot coals in his long hair.

Home, with his wife, passed the winter of 1883 at Nice. He was 50 in the March of that year, by this time his health was too feeble for him to go much into society, however, on March the 20th, his birthday, he received a large crowd of visitors, who had come to fete the invalid. They had brought many presents of flowers and fruit. Home sat in his armchair and received his visitors graciously. Also he recited to them several poems in French and English.

The following winter was passed in Russia.

Towards the end of 1884 Home felt that his illness was approaching a crisis. He was breaking fast but his will stood him in good stead and he lingered on until June 1988. On the 21st of that month Home passed from this earth, and his grave is at St Germain.

It is generally agreed that Daniel Douglas Home was one of the most remarkable men that ever lived. As I have before stated there were many disbelievers and scoffers and Home made enemies in consequence. It is difficult to believe however that all the scoffers were sincere.

Mr J.W. Maskelyne, who made a good living by giving conjuring performances, once said to Mr Andrew Lang:

"The old historical reports of physical phenomena such as those said to accompany D.D. Home do not impress me at all, their antiquity and world-wide diffusion may be accounted for with ease.

Like other myths, equally uniform and widely diffused, they represent the natural play of human fancy. Inanimate objects are stationary; therefore let us say that they move about. Men do not float in the air. Let us say they do."

This of course is not to be considered a good specimen of Victorian logic but merely a man arguing to suit his own purpose. Maskelyne no doubt was a good showman.

It is certain that Daniel Dunglas Home had very many followers who believed implicitly in his power as a spirit medium. As I have stated there were doubters many of whom were jealous of his powers and of the popularity it brought to him. These people, while endeavouring to claim some sort of notoriety for themselves put forward all sorts of theories to account for the phenomena. Hallucination and hypnotism were advanced as possible explanations of the levitations.

The fact remains that Home was never throughout his career detected in the production of fraudulent phenomena; neither did he ever accept payment for any of his séances. Although on the other hand, the doubters claim that is "not a convincing argument in Home's favour, especially when one studies his domestic life history and finds that he was at times not over-scrupulous in some of his dealings."

Spiritualists claim that mediums that have been detected in trickery may still produce genuine phenomena. Spiritualists will always consider manifestations produced by the mediumship of Home as a proof of the supernatural.

Now what of the legal aspect of the practice of mediumship?

In actual fact all mediums practising their craft or gift, that is acting as the receivers of messages stated to come from the spirits of the dead, could until quite recently be convicted and branded as rogues or vagabonds under the obsolete Witchcraft Act of 1753. Under this Act every séance and every spiritual religious service was an illegal activity in England and Scotland. This Act had been more or less winked at for many years but could be and was made use of in cases of flagrant fraud by impostors pretending to be mediums. Then there is a section of the Vagrancy Act Of 1824, which could also be called into use; this Act provides penalties for people pretending to tell fortunes, and the same Act also includes punishment for such rogues as peddlers of obscene pictures.

However, the practise of Spiritualism has now been brought within the law. A Private Members Bill formulated by Mr Tam Brooks MP for Normanton was quietly passed through the House of Commons in June 1951.

Needless to say this Bill does not protect bogus mediums or fortune-tellers.

EPILOGUE

On behalf of the author of this eclectic collection of half-remembered stories from the distant, not too distant, and very recent, past, thanks are extended for your perusal of his work.

Scoff you may, for that is the right of anyone who has completed the reading of a tome on any subject, but hopefully you may also have picked up some doubt as to the authenticity of these tales.

Do the spirits of dead people hang around on Earth after their time here is done? Do they have a singular purpose – a purpose often so appalling that their restless souls are doomed to roam forever, or until that purpose is fulfilled? Is there a link between the spirits of that other world, and is it in the form of a spiritualistic medium? Out of a million so-called séances, are at least a few authentic?

And of the millions of recorded sightings of ghosts down through the ages – has even one been proved real? If you think on the affirmative, then perhaps there are more.

But only - perhaps.

Lightning Source UK Ltd.
Milton Keynes UK
UKOW051039211111

182418UK00001B/2/P